Cary grew up in the UK, but now lives in Sweden. After a varied career that saw her tap-dancing in pantomime and selling towels on shopping channels, she settled down to write contemporary fiction. She swims in the Baltic year round, stands on her head once a day and enjoys Merlot over Shiraz.

For more books and updates visit:

www.caryjhansson.com

A Midlife Holiday

CARY J. HANSSON

Cover design and art direction by Berenice Howard-Smith, Hello Lovely. Illustrations by Amy Williams, Beehive Illustration Ltd.

Typesetting by preparetopublish.com

Part One

1

'*Stevie Nicks is a legend!*'

'What?' Daisy, who sat nearest the door and whose job it should have been to say this coded warning, looked up, eyes blank as buttons.

'*Stevie Nicks*,' Helen hissed again, '*is a legend!*' She already had her coat on, ready to go home, and her arms were filled with a bouquet of M&S Finest Seasonal Blooms, a bottle of Buck's Fizz and a box of Honey Dust Kissable Body Powder. Still she managed to jab her elbow in the direction of the corridor.

The penny dropped. Daisy grabbed her mug, making a show of drinking from it. So did Anne. And Tina. Then, along with Helen, they all turned and beamed at Dr Ross, who was now standing in the doorway having seemingly forgotten why she was there.

'Anything you need?' Helen asked lightly.

'No,' Dr Ross managed. 'Umm…lovely flowers, Helen. Birthday?'

'Yes. Well…tomorrow.'

'She'll be fifty!' Tina offered, mug at her lips.

Dr Ross narrowed her eyes at Tina's mug. 'Really?' she said. 'I…' And abruptly she closed her mouth and turned to go.

'Was there anything else?' Helen called.

'No.' Dr Ross turned. Looking straight at Helen, she smiled and said, 'Nothing at all. Have a lovely birthday.' And this time she did go.

Daisy, having downed a mouthful of tea, spat it back out. 'Ugh! Stone cold.'

'Worth it, though.' Anne grinned. She put her own mug back on her desk. 'No one messes with Helen. Isn't that right?'

Helen smiled. Dr Ross had been with the surgery for approximately three weeks, stalking corridors like an extra in *The West Wing*, on the prowl for improvements that she needed to be seen to make. All to pave her way up to senior partner, Helen supposed. She didn't really care. She'd been here long enough to see more young ambitious doctors than she cared to remember come and go, along with their various improvements. But this latest diktat had been so ridiculous – such an obvious example of change for the sake of change – she'd felt obliged to respond. Reception staff were no longer permitted to bring coffee mugs to their desks. Nine pounds an hour they earned! Primark (Daisy said) paid better! And of course, because Helen was the oldest and the longest-serving, it had been up to her to lead the fightback. Which she had, with relish, inventing this signal phrase to act as a warning system. (It had taken some rehearsing. None of the others seemed to know who Stevie Nicks was. *Is she on Spotify?* Daisy had asked. *Of course not!* Helen had responded, ten seconds before Tina had opened the app and found her. Which had left Helen with an all too familiar feeling nowadays, that sense of arriving at a party, just as everyone else was leaving.) Two days the fightback had been going, and she couldn't, judging by Dr Ross's face just now, imagine it needing to be continued come Monday. So why didn't she feel victorious?

'Have a lovely birthday!'
  'Don't do anything I wouldn't!'
  'Behave now!'
The voices of her colleagues rang out after her as Helen opened the door and stepped into a cold April evening. *Don't do anything I wouldn't?* Either her colleagues lived extraordinarily dull lives or her public persona was a lot more exciting than her private one. Because her first and only stop for the evening was Asda. Then home, *Poirot*, bed. And even Anne, who used Fridays to swap out her foil-wrapped sandwiches for a takeaway Cornish pasty, could probably beat that end-of-week line-up. Sighing, Helen tipped the flowers and the bottle and the Kissable Body Powder onto the passenger seat, fell into the driver's side and turned the rear-view mirror to her face. Fifty. What possible use was Kissable Body Powder ever going to be?

The circuit of Asda didn't take long. She was, after all, pleasing herself. No rainbow of vegetables to pick out for fussy children, no super-lean protein sources for overachieving husbands, and – since she didn't have sex any more – no low-calorie insipidity either. Into her basket went

3

a tub of hummus and a packet of tortilla chips, a giant slab of Cadbury Dairy Milk and a bottle of Chablis. The fizzy stuff could wait for tomorrow. It bloated her out and made her fart, and she needed to be slimmer tomorrow than she was today. Caro would be. Caro would be as slim as a pin.

With dinner sorted, she made a pit stop by the magazines to throw in a copy of *Hello*, then wandered over to the freezer section and found a bag of part-baked pains au chocolat. Perfect. She was almost at the till before she remembered the real reason she'd come in. Milk. There were many things that Jack, her eighteen-year-old son, could not be trusted with, and number one on that very long list was not to have drunk all the milk. And tea without milk, on the morning of her fiftieth birthday, might bring the curtain down on her second act before it had even begun. Suddenly and inexplicably sweating like a racehorse, she yanked her jacket off and hurried back to the chiller section. Lately her body seemed to do this. Transformed itself, with zero warning, into a pizza oven – no temperature control whatsoever. Off it went, a towering inferno against which Marks & Spencer breathable tights had no defence. Damp in all the wrong places and struggling to shed layers, she didn't, as she bumped along, hear from the depths of her handbag the low and ominous thrum of her phone.

Back home, elbows for hands, she wedged the front door open and bludgeoned the hall light on.

'Jack?'

Jack? Her voice echoed back, and the note of hopefulness was unmistakable. If he wasn't home, she didn't have to

4

cook him anything. And if she didn't cook him anything, she wouldn't eat his leftovers, or pick from the pan… The dress she had for lunch tomorrow with Kay and Caro was tight enough anyway. A couple of glasses of wine and an early night (maybe half the Cadbury) were exactly what the zipper needed.

She sighed, the kind of giant-sized sighs her mother used to make, and went into the kitchen where, camouflaged by the semi-gloom, Jack jumped up and shouted:

'Surprise!'

Helen screamed, and the bottle of Buck's Fizz slipped from her hand, shattering on the terracotta tiles.

'Bloody hell, Jack!' she yelled, watching as the patch of sticky orange spread. It looked for all the world like orange juice – which it was, mostly. Thank God it wasn't the Chablis.

'Sorry.' Jack stuck his hands in his pockets. He was taller than her, as lanky as his dad and irresistibly handsome to every eighteen-year-old girl within a five-mile radius. 'It was meant to be a joke,' he mumbled, watching Helen dump her things and bend to pick up the broken glass. 'What's for dinner?'

Over a hunched shoulder, Helen looked at him. 'Haven't a clue.'

'I'm just asking.'

'Well, how about you don't ask?'

'What? I can't even ask what's for dinner nowadays without you getting angry?'

She straightened up. 'No, Jack. At this particular moment you can't ask what's for dinner. Without. Me. Getting. Angry.'

'You don't even like Buck's Fizz,' Jack shrugged.

'That,' she hissed as she slammed her handbag on the table, 'is not the point!'

'And you're always in a mood!'

'I'm not always—'

But he'd gone.

As simply as that. Off and out of the house as only a teenage boy can. Helen stood, hands on hips, staring at the mess. He was right. She didn't like shop-bought Buck's Fizz (who did?) and she was always in a mood.

In the hallway, the home phone began to ring. Thanks to the special jingle tone that Libby, her daughter, had programmed to denote that it would be her ringing, Helen knew who it was before she'd picked it up. Libby. Surprise! *So you won't be worried, Mum,* Libby had explained at the time. Helen hadn't had the heart to say that she never had been – and had now resigned herself to the fact that she never would be – worried. Libby had been born sensible (at 4.30 – half an hour before the five o'clock feed and a good early night). She was currently in her final year at university studying Politics and Modern History. Putting the world to rights, thinking local, not global. Starting with as local as it came: her own mother.

Helen sighed – another mother-sized sigh. Did she have the energy for her daughter? Had she ever had the energy for her daughter? Her finger wavered over the phone. There wouldn't be another chance to speak, though. Libby had an all-day thing on tomorrow. Launching a "plastic attack" outside Tesco, which sounded as much fun as shopping *in* Tesco. The idea of setting an alarm to go and stand outside a supermarket on a Saturday morning befuddled

Helen. (When she was a student, Saturday mornings hadn't actually existed.) And then, of course, tomorrow was also her birthday lunch, which hopefully would turn into an all-day thing as well. She answered the call.

'Hi, Mum. Had a good day?'

Had a good day? 'Well, I didn't die,' she said.

'Right.'

Helen smiled. Libby's tragedy was that she had yet to find a sense of humour, despite Helen's prolonged attempts to locate it for her. In this Libby took after her father – something that, once she had realised it, had astounded Helen. Not the fact that her daughter should take after one or the other of them, but the fact that Helen had married a man who was also missing such a vital human function. How hadn't she noticed?

'I had a good day,' she lied. A nearly fifty-year-old playing office games with a woman half her age wasn't something she felt proud of now, alone in the gloom of her kitchen. So she wouldn't be telling Libby about that. Or the Kissable Body Powder. She stepped clear of the orange puddle. Or Jack's stormy exit.

'Is Jack home?'

'No. He's just gone out,' she said, and winced. It was the wrong answer.

'He's out!' Libby fumed. 'Where's he gone?' She didn't wait for a response. 'He said he'd stay in tonight! Honestly, Mum, it's not fair! He's supposed to be staying in with you for your birthday. I'll bet he didn't even—'

'Well,' Helen interrupted gently, 'it's not actually until tomorrow—'

'That's not the point! He promised he wouldn't go out. He said he'd…'

Helen put her daughter on speakerphone, laid the phone on the table and opened the shopping bag. Libby had been policing her younger brother since he was born; she wasn't likely to stop within the next two minutes. She pulled out the Chablis and went to the drawer for a corkscrew. 'It really doesn't matter,' she called across the kitchen when her cue finally came. 'I'm fine, Libby.'

'You're all alone, Mum,' Libby opined.

Pop! The cork slipped free. *Thank God*, she didn't say. And as her glass filled with the familiar fairy-tinkle and weighty glugs, she felt as she often did: pouring a glass of wine at the end of the day was a simple and eternal pleasure.

'I knew this would happen! I just knew. What with Dad gone, and you alone.'

'Libby.' Helen looked at her phone. Poor Libby. She took life so seriously. Always trying to make things right for everyone. The missing humour chip she could understand, but where had all this earnestness come from? Lawrence, her father, didn't understand the concept of consideration. That much was clear from this latest trip of his. And no one could ever have accused Helen of taking life too seriously. Not at Libby's age, anyway. Maybe now, though. The thought was disturbing enough to turn her away from the phone, and as she did she caught sight of her reflection in the darkened window. Plump, fifty, unsmiling. Ah, Helen. Once upon a time she would have had that Kissable Body Powder open and half used up already. It was Friday evening, for heaven's sake! Where did they go – Friday evenings?

8

'Mum!' Libby's voice chimed through the phone speaker like a pocket-sized dictator. 'I know you're worried about Dad,' she said, 'but he'll be fine. He texted me yesterday. He says it should be within—'

'He texted me as well.' Helen picked the phone up.

Silence.

'I have a smartphone too,' she added, because she was ever so slightly irritated. One of the things that, as a mother, she hadn't been prepared for was the way her much younger and therefore much less experienced daughter presumed to understand her mind. And, from there, to offer unwanted and unnecessary solutions. Because she wasn't unduly worried. Yes, climbing Everest was dangerous. But statistically Lawrence had a one in a hundred chance of dying, which was less than the chance he had of dying of heart disease. When he'd told them all this, it had surprised Helen. Preoccupied her for weeks. As she yanked fluff out of the tumble dryer, it had caused her to pause and wonder what else in life she'd arbitrarily dismissed as outstandingly dangerous when actually it wasn't.

Libby was silent.

And suddenly Helen didn't have the energy she knew it would require to coax her daughter around. All she wanted to do – the only thing she wanted – was to sit down and watch TV. Anything with a butler and a murder would do. So that was what had happened to Friday evenings. Her Friday evenings, anyway.

'Right. Well, good. So…well, happy birthday for tomorrow,' Libby harrumphed.

'Thank you, darling,' Helen said, pretending not to

notice the sulk in her daughter's voice. She was nearly twenty-two, not two.

So…that was that. She was free to relax. Except, of course, for Sasha, Libby's indestructible rabbit, bought for her twelfth birthday and, at this rate, still probably chewing the cud on her thirtieth. She grabbed a handful of pellets from the sack by the back door, jogged down the garden and threw them through the wire of the compound. She didn't notice how wet her feet had got until she was curled up on the settee, remote in one hand, wine in the other, tortilla chip stuffed whole into her mouth.

But before she'd even gone through the rigmarole of switching on all the various devices everyone else in the house seemed to think were necessary for watching TV nowadays, the home phone rang again. Helen sighed. And now there was no escaping it: she was her mother. There were only three people in the world right now she would answer the phone for. Her husband, because…well, she just had to. Because although he had selfishly chosen to go off on a stupendously expensive trip to climb the world's highest mountain over both her fiftieth birthday and their twenty-fifth wedding anniversary, he might be that unlucky one in a hundred.

And Caro or Kay, of course.

She scrambled for the phone.

'Why aren't you answering your mobile?' It was Caro.

'Don't start,' Helen muttered.

'You sound as knackered as I feel.'

'I am,' Helen said. 'And I don't know where it is.' She sat

up and looked around the living room. Her phone would be in her bag, which would be in the kitchen, which was simply too far away right now. Leaning forward, she put her glass on the coffee table. 'What's wrong?' She hadn't seen Caro in months – which wasn't unusual given Caro's schedule – and suddenly the idea that there might be a problem, that she might be cancelling tomorrow, was unbearable. Kay wouldn't be cancelling. Kay, Helen suspected, viewed this birthday lunch much like she did: a thrusting of the head above water, a foray into a parallel universe. Caro, on the other hand, just back from Shanghai, or was it Chicago (somewhere soft-syllabled anyway), already lived in a parallel universe. 'Please,' she said, interrupting her own thoughts. 'Please don't say you're ringing to cancel. It's been so long since we were all together.'

'Are you kidding?' Caro laughed.

Cool relief flooded through. She felt about eight years old. Caro was coming! And Kay was coming! If she'd had the energy she'd have got up and skipped with happiness.

'I wouldn't miss this for the world,' Caro said. 'I just wanted to confirm the time. Kay said one, I thought it was two.'

Helen sighed. 'Kay can't remember her head right now.'

'I know. Her mother's really gone downhill, hasn't she?'

'She has, yes.'

A moment passed, and neither of them spoke.

'So it's two?' Caro said.

'It's two.'

'Great. See you tomorrow. And cheer up. I've got a little something that should make you smile.'

'I'm smiling now,' Helen said. She was. Looking at her tired and fuzzy reflection in the dark TV screen, she saw that she was. Kay was coming and Caro was coming and there was, therefore, a seed of potential for fun! God knew she needed it, and they'd never had any problems in the past, the three of them, conjuring up a little fun. Although lately "the past" felt distant enough to require separate grammar. She peered at the TV screen and, using her free hand, stretched the skin of her forehead so the furrowed lines disappeared. What was Caro bringing that would make her smile? Hopefully that Botox voucher she'd been teasing Helen about for a while now.

'Any news on Lawrence?' Caro asked.

Helen looked out towards the kitchen. She should get her phone. 'Still climbing,' she answered. 'Not quite there yet.' Yes, her husband was still climbing, as he had been since the day they'd met. Striving and trying, achieving and climbing. Recently she'd come to the conclusion that he'd probably never stop. The problem was that even more recently she'd come to the conclusion that she didn't much care any more.

The call ended and she flicked the TV on. Out of (what seemed like) 7,000 channels, not a single one was showing *Poirot*. Mindlessly she scrolled through, pausing at something called *Hits of Yesteryear*.

Three hours later, when Jack came home, he found her asleep on the settee, her cheeks honey-dust shiny, a splatter of powder on the coffee table, the wine bottle empty and Cindy Lauper belting out 'Girls Just Wanna Have Fun' on the TV.

*

The next morning Helen woke, eyes stuck with mascara, back stuck to the sheets, tongue stuck to mouth. Crawling out of bed, grasping for furniture and generally hobbling over the carpet as if it were hot coals, not cool wool, she made the mistake of glancing sideways at the wardrobe's full-length mirror. The pale, hunched specimen that she was stared back at her.

In fright more than anything else, she turned sideways. Her bottom, once round as a bun, was now a flatbread. Stretching her arms forward, she lowered herself into a squat, and the creaking and cracking from her knees sounded like static from a pre-WW1 radio. She straightened up and stared at herself. What had she become? She was fifty today, not eighty! And in a few short hours she'd have to face Caro, who seemed to be growing younger. A real-life Benjamin Button.

She leaned in, closer to the woman in the mirror. Her jawline had blurred, her mouth turned down (even when she wasn't unhappy), her eyelids drooped…a little. But apart from that she was still – just about – an attractive woman. More so – and, ashamed as she was of the thought, she couldn't help thinking it – than Caro.

'Stop it!' Helen dragged her fingers through her hair. She hated it when she had these thoughts. Not least because if it wasn't clear a decade ago, it certainly was now. Her looks had in some way been a hindrance. Because what had she done exactly? What had she achieved with her life aside from marrying Lawrence and having children? She'd given up her career at the Heritage Society so long ago it was hard to remember she'd ever had one. And she'd been at the health centre eight years now, which was seven more than she'd ever intended. It was supposed to have been an easy stepping stone back after children. The work wasn't taxing – everything she'd needed to know had been learned in the first week. But it had suited her. Her co-workers had been fun. Mornings filled with gossip and silly jokes, afternoons ferrying the kids around. Gardening, school runs, office drinks, Christmas dinners. Easy to take life easy, file away any lingering regrets about her lost career. But the women she'd started with had either retired or left to start families. And the women who had replaced them seemed increasingly young to Helen. The jokes weren't as funny, and lately she had found herself fantasising about what her life might have looked like if she'd taken a different turning here, made another decision there. It wasn't regret so much as a too-easy portal into a wishful way of thinking that only left her feeling empty. It was, anyway, all far too late. She leaned forward to the mirror again. 'Happy fiftieth, Helen,' she muttered. 'You're in snipers' alley now!'

Downstairs in the kitchen, she opened the drawer where she'd hidden Libby's birthday card (the only one that seemed to have arrived in time).

Happy Birthday, Mum! I'm so glad I have you to look out for me, the card read.

She popped it on the dresser and stood looking at it. The sentiment felt odd, coming as it did from her independent, strong-minded daughter. The days when she'd needed to look out for Libby were long gone; still, it was touching that her daughter perhaps felt differently. Vulnerable, almost, which was understandable given that her finals were fast approaching. She poured her tea, profoundly grateful for the milk stop she'd made, and then, nursing her mug, walked over to the window. The rockery was smothered by snow-in-summer, and yellow frothy spikes of forsythia were already tapping above the fence. She'd have to cut it back soon. She turned, leaned back against the sink and glanced at the clock. 8.10am. Hours to kill before lunch. She opened the freezer, slung a couple of pains au chocolat onto a baking tray and turned the oven on.

Out in the hallway the letterbox flapped and, padding through, Helen saw that although there were no birthday cards, there was a brochure from Cruiseworld. Her heart lifted. This was what she'd do! On the first day of her fiftieth year she'd take a long bath and look through the brochure. They could start travelling. Lawrence and her. A ninety-day expedition to Nepal was surely worth a cruise to the Caribbean. He owed her that.

As she settled into the comfort of the bath, the first page she turned to had an image of a grey-haired couple kissing in front of golden sands. But their late middle-aged bodies were as clunky as Lego blocks, and the passion looked unreal and so forced that Helen found herself studying it for a long time. She simply could not imagine kissing anyone like that any more, let alone her husband. It was poppycock, wasn't it? As if a dose of Caribbean sunshine really could reverse the ageing process. Why, she wondered, as she let the brochure fall to the floor, couldn't women – and men – just be allowed to grow older and less libidinous and fatter in peace? Tossing it aside, she slipped back. The water was warm and deeply scented, the house richly quiet. Just as she had submerged herself, hippopotamus like, with only her nostrils clear, a buzzing, like a signal from another world, sounded through the silent house. She pushed herself upright, water dripping down her neck, air cooling her back.

The buzzing got louder. Helen frowned.

Buzz, buzz, buzz, *BUZZ*.

Blotchy-pink, spilling rivers, she clambered out. The buzz, she realised, was her mobile. Still in her handbag, which was still on the kitchen table. It could be the *big* call from Lawrence. Or Kay, cancelling.

Clutching a towel that caught and tripped her, she blotted frantically at her larger surface areas, barrelled down the stairs, tipped her handbag upside down, then, fingers soaking wet, swiped her phone, the pad of her finger leaving a trail of beaded droplets. 'Lawrence?' Because it was Lawrence. And despite herself, she was excited.

She was answered by the sound of wind, unrestrained and raw. Like putting a shell to your ear, only rather than the gentle lap of the ocean you got a tsunami.

'*Lawrence!*' she yelled, and a drop of water fell onto the screen.

'Helen?' Lawrence's voice was tiny, remote, broken by the force of the weather that surrounded him. As it would be.

'Wh—' she started, and was immediately interrupted.

16

'*Where the bloody hell were you?*'

And although his voice was still tiny, his shout as small as a snail, Helen was so shocked she didn't – couldn't – answer.

'I summited yesterday,' Lawrence barked. 'And rang twice! Once at the summit and once from camp four, and you didn't pick up the bloody phone!'

Her mouth made a slack, round shape. 'Yesterday?' she managed. 'What time?'

'I don't know! Six maybe, your time. Where the bloody hell were you?'

Yesterday? She was thinking, scrabbling to put it together. 'It's my birthday,' she said. 'The girls at work gave me a cake…and then I had to pop into Asda for milk.' Abruptly she stopped talking. Everything she said sounded ridiculous.

Lawrence sighed. His winds blew.

And Helen? She looked up, across the kitchen, right into the full-length mirror in the hallway. The wet, naked, plump, sagging woman that she was looked back at her, and the ringing silence of the house gathered itself up to fold around her like a tepee.

'Helly.' Her husband's voice had never sounded more remote. 'I'm *so* disappointed. Didn't I tell you to keep your phone on? *All* the time. We talked about this, about the window of opportunity and all…'

Helen didn't try to fill the gap, the ever-so-tiny gap he left.

'And I know, I know. It's your birthday. You know I'll make it up to you, but it's not like there won't be another

17

one, Helly. I mean, birthday. Whereas Everest! Helly! I did it! The single greatest moment of my life and I wanted to share it with you. Can you imagine what a prick I looked? Everyone got a minute on the satellite phone and you're the only one who doesn't pick up?'

Numb, Helen looked in the mirror again. What she saw this time wasn't herself but an image of Lawrence. The stock image of a high-altitude climber – fluorescent jacket, space-like goggles. And if that was it, if that was what he'd looked like, then yes, what a prick indeed he must have looked, standing there at 29,000 feet, listening to the sound of her phone ringing out.

A bubble formed in her throat – of laughter, of relief, of pure absurdity. She should have that on her headstone.

Here lies the body of a woman who missed the single greatest moment of her husband's life, because she was in Asda, buying milk.

2

Helen, the face that could still launch them! Happy Fiftieth! Thirty
years of friendship, thirty more to come. All my love, Caro x

'Oh God, those days are long gone.' Helen laughed. She took off her reading glasses and put the package back on the table. Five hours and thirty minutes since her husband had rung to shout that she'd missed the single greatest moment of his life, and her anger was showing no sign of abating. All morning it had bubbled away, longer than the pease pudding her mother used to stir on Christmas Eve. It crackled like a live wire – hard little pops that had her biting the inside of her mouth. So alive that she was almost scared of it. This afternoon was about her and Caro and Kay. About keeping intact the thread of a friendship that had extended thirty years. Strengthening it. Because there was no doubt it was fraying. Life, for all of them, pulled from both ends. Elderly parents, children, jobs, husbands. And what used to be oh-so-regular frothy occasions like this, when they were all in

19

the same room, glammed up, with a few hours to spare, could probably be counted now. Were, in fact, finite. So the last thing she wanted to do, the very last thing, was derail the reunion by lifting the lid off the great steaming mess that she was beginning to see her marriage most definitely was. Not in front of Caro, at least. She looked so good. Her skin was as full as a plumped cushion. (*Fillers?*) 'Well,' she said, keeping it as light as she could, 'it certainly doesn't look like a rotary washing line!'

'A what?' Kay laughed.

'Lawrence's Christmas present one year. He even wrapped it.'

Caro smiled. 'How is he? Have you—'

'Can we not talk about it?' Helen stopped her with a raised palm. 'If you don't mind.'

'Of course.' And, exchanging looks with Kay, Caro fell silent.

'Seriously, it does look gorgeous, Caro,' she said, concentrating on the gift. She knew what they were thinking. That she was too worried about her husband to be able to bear any discussion of him. She wasn't. Right now she couldn't care less if he was wedged down a Himalayan crevasse slimmer than Caro's waist. And although a part of her felt like a fraud for not coming clean, it was a relatively small part. The giant inside was still anger, and it felt easier to live with Little Miss Fraud than unleash the colossus of her anger. Plus it was actually easy to concentrate on Caro's present. Because the package did look lovely. A mysterious rectangle of fuchsia foil, held together by plush scarlet ribbon. Gorgeous and expensive, and wrapped, no doubt, by Caro's secretary, Mel.

20

Which didn't matter a jot! Fingers tracing the plush velvet bow, she murmured, 'Whatever did happen to Helen?'

'Of Troy?' Kay asked.

'Did she make fifty?'

'She got old and fat. Like we all do.' Kay picked up her glass. 'Cheers!'

'Speak for yourself,' Caro said. 'I don't intend to get fat.'

'And I never intended to get old.'

Ignoring Kay, Caro turned to Helen. 'Well? Are you going to open it?'

'Of course.' She pulled the package closer. 'It's funny,' she mused, 'how we're never told what her fate was.' She was studying the shape of the package. What could it be that had Caro so excited? It didn't look like a Botox voucher. A voucher would come in an envelope.

'Not really.' Kay shrugged. 'Women past a certain age get forgotten about. *But*—' She tipped her glass at Helen. 'I always thought Helen of Troy sounded interesting. I mean, she started a war, survived it, had three husbands, then buggered off and retired in the sun. *And*—' Kay winked. 'I also always thought *you* were very suitably named.'

'I never started a war!'

'A duel, though.' Caro laughed.

Helen turned to her. 'Those two idiots? At university?'

'Two more than I ever had fighting over me.'

'And of course,' Kay added, 'you've only had the one husband.'

'So far,' Helen murmured. She turned back to the fuchsia package.

'Go on,' Caro nudged. 'Go ahead and open it.'

'Right.' But Helen didn't move. She didn't want to open the present. If she did, the excitement would be over. Which was silly, but she hadn't felt so excited in a long time and she didn't want it to end. Which was even sillier. Like a child. Or, in fact, Lawrence. The way he always was when he came back from surfing or skiing or climbing. *It's the rush, Helen! You never want it to end!* An image popped into her mind from years ago. Lawrence and the kids at Newquay, smiles as wide as the bay. Herself parked on the beach with the egg sandwiches. Why – her nose crinkled as she frowned – hadn't *she* ever tried surfing? And, more to the point, why hadn't she even noticed that she wasn't trying these things, especially when she was married to someone who never stopped?

'Come on, then!' With a lopsided smile, Kay raised her glass to the package. 'The excitement is killing me.'

Helen smiled. Kay's own gift had been a (very nice) bottle of champagne, folded into a Tesco bottle carrier, the type that hung at the end of the white wine aisle. Which also didn't matter. Not in the slightest. Kay, dear Kay, barely had time to brush her hair these days. At least she'd gone for the foil, rather than the cardboard carrier.

'Okay.' As she looked at the gift, she exhaled, and her lungs felt tight and she realised she'd been holding her breath. So silly! To be fifty and this excited by the sight of an expensively wrapped gift...

'Start with the ribbon,' Caro whispered. 'It's holding everything together.'

Of course (Caro was far too classy for Sellotape).

22

'Okay. Here goes nothing!' Helen breathed in and pulled the ribbon, and the wrapping fell away as easily as she'd sometimes hoped her dress might. 'Oh.' Leaning forward, she squinted. '*Oh.*' Leaning back, she frowned. She needed a moment to double-check that what she was seeing really *was* what she was seeing.

It was.

'A cheese grater,' she managed, and bit down so hard on her lip she drew blood. A cheese grater! At least she didn't cry.

'It's not a grater, silly!' Caro turned the gift so the packaging was better displayed.

'A...' Helen faltered. 'A melter?' she read. 'A cheese melter?' And her voice collapsed...like melted cheese. 'Sorry,' she gasped in a hiccup of sobs. 'S...sorry.'

Caro opened her mouth but Kay was quicker, shaking her head in furious tiny movements that had Caro easing back, both of them watching as Helen grabbed a nearby napkin and pressed it to her eyes.

Blinking furiously, she looked up and made a last-ditch attempt to laugh the moment off; but she wasn't fooling herself, let alone Kay or Caro, her two oldest friends. Caro? Of all people! Caro had just bought her a cheese melter? For a fiftieth birthday present? So that was that, then! She was fat and she was fifty, destined (just like her namesake) to be forgotten, left behind, eating melted cheese and shopping in Asda, while her husband forged ahead, conquering mountains. She blew her nose, trying to shake away a question that had formed. An important, urgent question to which she had no answer. *Why* had she wasted all that time making egg sandwiches when she could have been surfing? Struggling to regain composure, she screwed the napkin into a tight ball and said, 'It's lovely, Caro. Thank you.'

'You hate it,' Caro said flatly.

'I don't. I…' Helen turned the cheese melter round. 'What do you do with it?'

'Melt cheese?' Kay offered, fangs of red wine curling up from each side of her mouth.

'Very helpful.' Scowling, Caro turned to Helen. She picked up the cheese melter, and her fuchsia nails matched the discarded wrapping so perfectly that Helen wondered if it was deliberate – if Caro's secretary hadn't used the same colour for that extra touch. She was, from what Caro said, that organised.

'It's from Lakeland.' Caro stretched the package away to read the label.

'Just put your glasses on,' Kay muttered.

Caro read on. '*Now you can enjoy endless amounts of gooey cheesy loveliness whenever the fancy takes you*—ouch!' Bending to rub her shin, she glared across the table. 'What was that for?'

But Kay was making furious *eyes left* signals, and they both turned to look.

Helen's head had dropped like a shorn poppy; elbows on the table, she'd covered her face with the napkin, her shoulders moving up and down as she sobbed.

Caro put the package down, folded her hands in her lap and looked across at Kay. No one spoke, and throughout the large and beautiful dining room musical notes of crockery and cutlery played across the sound of Helen's heart breaking.

And they knew, Caro and Kay, not to breach the moment. That these pauses were the knots in the bracelet of their friendship. Sacred memories that bound them. Like the day a weary Kay had told them of her husband's affair, or the evening Caro had discovered her ex had become a father, or the afternoon Helen had spoken quietly of her mother's diagnosis. Times in their lives when a marriage had ended, a parent had died, a lover had cheated. When they had grieved for children who were never born, men who had left or dreams that had perished, that they buried together and toasted the passing of with a glass or a mug. And if, in the beginning, what they had found in each other was not much more than a sympathetic mirror for the naive indignation of life not meeting expectations, it had in these later years transformed into a granite-like awareness that being present was enough. All that was required. So they sat and they waited, and eventually Helen looked up.

Her eyes were wrinkly black raisins, hairy with mascara. Her nose was red. Today she was fifty years old. She'd missed the single greatest moment of her husband's life and her best friend had bought her a cheese melter.

'Helen?' Kay whispered.

'It's hormones,' Caro said, and slid another napkin across the table. 'My gynaecologist—'

'It's not bloody hormones,' Helen hissed. Hormones? She could have laughed. If she hadn't actually been dead inside, she might have laughed. 'It is *not*,' she repeated, 'my hormones. Could you please pass me the wine?' She blew her nose and poured the wine, the bewilderment that had engulfed her when she understood that Caro *really had* bought her this thing morphing into a frustration, which meant that the pan lid was hopping and jumping and almost ready to blow. Caro? Of all people. *Glug, glug, glug* went the wine, Helen's knuckles white at the neck of the bottle. How long had they known each other? Thirty-two years? Thirty-two years since the day they had found themselves seated together at that first Modern Philosophy lecture, which was about the only lecture they'd shared. Their areas of study had, like their lives, been profoundly different. Economics was Caro's area of expertise and…what? What exactly was Helen's area? Once upon a time it had been history. Not modern like her daughter, because nothing really changed, did it? No, medieval history. Two years of a PhD… So what was it now? Homemaking? She tipped a mouthful of wine back and sat staring across the table, seeing nothing at all. Homemaking! Was that it? Was that all that defined her? The house that she lived in? Because if Caro didn't know her any more, who did? Kay didn't have time, and Lawrence couldn't see beyond the end of his nose. So who did know who Helen was? Not Helen – that much she was sure of.

Her mouth pushed down in a hard curve. She'd wanted a Botox voucher. Was that so bad? She *never* got what she wanted. Years and years of microwave food covers for Mother's Day, family calendars – so she didn't mess up everyone else's life – for Christmas. Even on her fiftieth, Jack was still in bed and Libby had bought her a book, *Everyday Feminism* (she'd have to stamp on the spine to make it look like she'd at least opened it). And Lawrence? The usual roses from the usual florist – which, as they didn't have a branch in Nepal, had obviously been orchestrated by Libby. But Caro? Helen stared down at her glass. This was the same Caro who, having no husband or children to rely upon for crap presents, therefore bought her own and was, therefore, never disappointed. Caro, who was more finely preserved than the gourmet pickled onions in her fridge, who would be forging on, reinventing herself year after year. While for Helen it was all over?

She reached out and picked the cheese thing up, turned it over. Frustration fuelled the anger; wine lit the flame. Plus: today she was fifty! And if she couldn't say what she thought now, when could she? No one, she reasoned, can hear you when you're six feet under. Feeling tremendously bold, she held the cheese melter up and said, 'You looked at this, Caro, and you thought, I know just the person who has nothing else to do in their life apart from melt cheese… at the table!'

Caro's mouth fell slack.

Kay sucked in air.

And Helen's hand, holding up the cheese melter, was as steady as a surgeon's.

No one spoke.

Shifting her weight, Caro inched her fingers across the table, gathering in the discarded ribbon. She did not look up.

'Right then,' Kay breathed.

'Right then,' Helen echoed. She put the cheese melter down and picked up the wine bottle.

'Helen.'

'What?'

'Go easy.' Kay nodded at the bottle.

Go easy? The first time in her life she'd actually responded honestly? If it had been anyone else but Kay saying that… She put the bottle back down, a little too hard.

Behind them a waiter passed, and again Helen picked the bottle up, twisting in her chair. 'Another one, please,' she called, and turned back to the table, feeling reckless, brave, a little devil-may-care. And from nowhere she had a memory of her mother calling her that. A happy memory that made her smile, because she really had been a devil-may-care kind of child. A devil-may-care woman…young woman, anyway. As if the memory stood on the table before her, she tilted her head and studied it. Maybe that was what fifty meant? Maybe, when you turned the corner, you found that part of yourself you'd lost. Didn't Einstein say that time can curve, bend back upon itself? Smiling, she picked up the bottle and emptied it into her glass. Life bending back on itself? Now that would be fun. She'd had a lot of fun when she was younger. BM. BC. Before Marriage. Before Children… And as she looked up, full of the idea and ready to share it, she saw Caro's face. It stopped her newly minted bravado in its tracks and sent the devil inside her packing.

Caro, everyone knew, didn't do emotion – tantrums or tears, sulking or shouting. What she did was this pinched look. A facial battening down of the hatches, which had always hurt Helen to witness, almost as much as the hurt she imagined Caro was controlling. Because it had to have been so long practised, hadn't it? She and Kay had

28

discussed this many times. Caro's restraint had to have been learned almost from infancy. She had a terrible relationship with her mother – her whole family, actually. In fact, over thirty years Helen had met Caro's family precisely once, at graduation. To all intents and purposes, she didn't have one. Thinking this, Helen grabbed a napkin and blew her nose (again), then looked back across at Caro, who was squashing the life out of the ribbon. Her heart squeezed. 'Caro,' she whispered.

Caro didn't speak. Her bottom lip trembled, and that made Helen's lip tremble. Caro, who had sat with her through the worst day of her life. Who'd hidden Helen's debit card the night before finals, forcing her to stay home and study. Who'd covered for her so many times when one or the other of her parents had rung their student flat on a weekend morning. *Helen's still in bed* (she was…somewhere). *She's gone shopping. She's at the library.* How could Helen have been so awful? Her eyes stung with tears. 'I'm *so* sorry,' she whispered. Sweat pricked at her hairline. Uncomfortably warm, she unfolded her napkin and began fanning it across her neck. (If it was a hot flush, it could bugger off.) 'You two,' she whimpered, 'are my best friends. I don't know what came over me. I've been so looking forward to today and now…and now I've… I'm sorry, Caro…' Her voice trailed off and her cheeks coloured redder than a robin on a Christmas card.

'Caro?' It was Kay. It was always Kay. Helen could have hugged her.

'Apology accepted,' Caro said stiffly.

'Thank you,' Helen whispered. 'Thank you.'

There was a moment of heavy silence and then Helen took a deep breath, looked down at the table and said, 'Lawrence summited yesterday.' And for all the excitement in her voice, she might as well have said *Lawrence farted yesterday*.

'Oh,' Kay started. 'That's...well, that's great.' She glanced at Caro. 'Isn't it?'

'I missed his call.'

'His call?'

Wrapping her hands around the stem of her glass, she continued, 'He summited yesterday, and he rang this morning to tell me.'

Caro nodded. 'I'll bet he was ecstatic?'

'He was furious.'

'Fur—'

'He said,' Helen sighed, 'that I'd missed the single greatest moment of his life. That's why he was ringing. To make sure I knew that. Not,' she added, 'to wish me happy birthday.'

'Oh.' Again Kay looked across at Caro, who looked back and said nothing.

'Ninety days,' Helen muttered. 'Ninety bloody days and 70,000 quid and he has the nerve to yell at me because I wasn't there to answer the call.'

'Where were you?' Caro asked quietly. 'Not that it matters. It—'

'In Asda.' Helen looked up. 'Buying milk.'

'Oh.'

'I'm always in Asda buying milk.'

'You're not al—'

'I've spent great swathes of my life in Asda,' Helen said as she stared across the table. 'Just buying milk.' She had. She had spent far too much time buying milk.

'Are you okay?' Kay leaned towards her.

Helen looked up. She could see Kay's face, very close, and see her mouth moving, shaping words which she heard as a soft babble. And it was the strangest, most disorientating out-of-body moment. She felt she was tripping along the edge of a void. In an attempt to moor herself, she reached out and picked up the cheese melter. '*Serve as a super-simple starter*,' she read in a voice thick with detachment. '*Just plonk a rustic loaf on the table and let guests help themselves!*'

Neither Caro nor Kay spoke.

Helen put the cheese melter back on the table. 'I stopped getting the Lakeland catalogue over two years ago,' she said, and stretched out her hands and looked at them. She had absolutely no intention of explaining away the lumpy atmosphere that had risen around the table. Couldn't, actually. The pan lid had blown; the genie was out of the bottle. And what was the point of pretending otherwise, when everyone had seen it leave? Bye-bye, fun fiftieth lunch, then. 'Cheers!' she said grimly, and raised her glass. 'To being fifty!'

Exchanging looks, Kay and Caro raised their glasses.

'Well,' Caro said quietly. She nodded at the offending cheese melter. 'I'll return it, Helen. Get something ridiculously impractical instead. I should have—'

'I haven't even had a dinner party in over a year,' Helen murmured. She drained her glass. 'They always end with Lawrence doing a slide show and me doing the dishwasher.'

Frowning at her empty glass, she picked up the empty bottle and turned again to find someone, *anyone*, who could bring her more wine. 'Which,' she said loudly, 'is actually very boring. Very, *very* boring.'

'Helen.' Kay reached over, as if to pull her back.

But Helen tipped further backwards, thrusting the bottle out to the room like a begging bowl. '*I'm so bored of it!*' she cried. The chair wobbled, held, then crashed to the floor, Helen with it. The bottle rolled across the carpet, the seat flipped up and Helen lay spread like a starfish, staring at the ceiling.

Coffee came quickly after that, and Helen was glad of it. The room had become quite hazy, so no matter which way she spread her weight on the chair she hadn't been able to stabilise her horizon, which was odd considering her weight and considering the chair.

Caro took control. 'Milk?'

Helen nodded.

'Say when.'

'When,' she said bleakly.

The coffee was passed, scalding hot, strong and rich. As she sipped at it, the spin in her head began to slow, the edges of the room straightening out.

'So,' Caro said, sliding a cup across to Kay. 'What's going on? I thought you were in favour of Lawrence doing this trip?'

Helen shrugged.

'He was going to go off and get this out of his system and you were happy getting ready for the anniversary party…' That's what you said…' Caro raised her eyebrows and glanced at Kay, then back at Helen. 'I mean, you and Lawrence. You've always had what most of us dreamed of.'

Helen's smile was tight. She couldn't, despite herself and despite Caro's acceptance of her apology, dismiss the thought that this was a dig. A sly *touché* in response to her cheese melter meltdown. Not to mention that it was common knowledge between the three of them that what Caro had once dreamed of was Lawrence. But that was last century. A lifetime ago. The life that Caro lived now really was the stuff of dreams. She was off to New York tomorrow, for heaven's sake! In fact, Caro went to New York as frequently as Helen went to Asda.

'Nothing,' Kay said quietly, 'is what it seems. Especially dreams.'

Helen smiled. Never bothering with the paraphernalia of appearances herself, Kay easily saw through everyone else's disguises. But God, she looked tired. A lick of lipstick and some highlights would go a long way. She put her cup down. 'How's your dad coping?' she said.

Kay leaned back. 'He's exhausted, to be honest, Helen.' There was a rash at her throat which she scratched as she spoke, and Helen noticed that her nail varnish, probably slapped on a few hours ago, had already chipped.

'I'm sorry to hear that,' she said. And she really was, because it was crystal clear that Kay's mother's dementia wasn't just taking its toll on Kay's father. Even the cat, the last time Helen had been over, had looked as strung out as the rest of them. Like a discarded scarf everyone nudged out of the way. Kay's mother had been getting steadily worse for years. There was, she supposed as she sipped her coffee, some relief to be found in the fact that her own parents had both slipped away so swiftly. Then again, she missed them dreadfully and she always would and…her eyes stung with tears, all the fun she'd been so eagerly anticipating sinking fast now, under the horizon.

'I'm sorry too,' Caro interjected. 'I really am. You know that, Kay, but—' She turned to Helen. 'Can we stop with the delaying tactics? Are you going to tell us what's going on?'

'There's nothing much to say.' Helen stretched her arms out, wrapped her hands around her coffee cup and allowed herself to feel its soothing heat.

'Helen.' Kay leaned forward. 'This is us. Whatever there is to say, you can say it.'

Helen sighed. 'Is there any water?' The fuzziness had cleared but she was terribly thirsty.

Caro slid a tumbler and carafe across the table.

Helen poured herself a glass. She took a long draught, and when she put her glass down she looked first at Kay, her grey roots pushing out, sallow hollows under her eyes. Whatever happened to the spiky-haired, milk-skinned Kay? The Kay who was going to change the world? Next she turned to Caro, in a green silk blouse, her hair gleaming with expensive highlights. Whatever happened to the cardigan-clad, bottle-spectacled Caroline? Her two closest friends. She shook her head. 'I'm so unhappy,' she said. 'So very unhappy.'

She felt a warmth and looked down to see Kay's hand on hers.

'Tell us,' Caro said. 'Tell us everything.'

34

*

Six months earlier.

'The really great thing about this set-up is the way they slap on a limit from the get-go. Twenty. That's it!' Lawrence thumped his fist on the table, the tiny teeth of his steak knife glinting. 'Twenty start! Twenty summit! That way everyone gets the best chance on the best day.'

'Right.' Helen nodded.

'What people don't realise, you see, is that there are plenty of organisations out there who say they limit numbers, but what they mean is they limit numbers on summit day. And everyone has to do that, right?'

She opened her mouth, closed it again. Reached for the salt.

'I mean,' Lawrence barged on, 'what they don't tell you is that they've got enough climbers for five summit days! So obviously there's going to be a chance you'll end up with crappy weather and a cat's chance in hell of making it, while Donald the dentist from Wisconsin, who hasn't paid a cent more, gets to the top with clear skies. And that's not right, is it?'

'Who's Donald the dentist?' Helen looked at her husband's dinner plate. He'd barely touched the stroganoff. His wine glass was still full.

'Donald?' Lawrence took a stick of celery (which he'd insisted on bringing to the table) and tore off a huge chunk. 'I don't know…' He chewed. 'Did you hear what I was saying?' His jaw worked sideways and it got Helen thinking of the plastic toy snakes the kids had had when they were little. How they slithered sideways, which was very clever, just like real snakes. 'There's always a dentist, isn't there?'

'Is there?'

'The point is, Helen…' He stuck his finger in his mouth and

yanked out a celery string. 'These guys know what they're doing! There are so many amateurs in the game. Why the hell the Nepalese don't get a handle on the situation I don't know.' Spearing a massive forkful of green beans, he shook his head. 'Money, I suppose.'

'So…' She paused. 'You've decided?'

'What?' He looked up, surprised. 'Of course. You know that, Helly.'

Did she? Helen frowned, her mind searching for that definitive moment in which they'd had the definitive conversation in which he'd told her that he'd be away for ninety days, climbing the world's tallest mountain, leaving her to celebrate her fiftieth birthday and their twenty-fifth wedding anniversary alone. She couldn't find it.

A slither of green escaped his teeth. 'These beans are great. Any more?'

'No.' She looked at the empty bowl of beans. She'd grown them in the garden last summer. Finding, after so many years of experimentation, the perfect spot, which was a south-facing fence at the back of the summer house. Tethered and sheltered from the wind, they'd flourished, ripening into fat little bullets of energy and goodness. She looked down and speared her own forkful. 'They are tasty, aren't they? I grew—'

'Shame!' Lawrence had stretched his arm out to tilt the empty bowl. 'We need to eat more of this stuff, Helly! More plant food. I watched a great doc the other week Paul told me about.'

'Paul?'

'My chiropractor.' Lawrence grinned. 'Keep up, sweetheart. Honestly, you're such a dreamer.'

Helen watched as her husband shoved the last of his beans into his mouth. Dreamer? She hadn't been the day she'd harvested those beans. Wiping off dirt, laying them out individually on trays to retain

36

their shape, so assiduous in her attempt to capture summer's bounty. That wasn't a dream.

'Game Changers, it was called.' Lawrence leaned back in his chair, folding his arms behind his head, his elbows encompassing the width of the room. 'And it certainly was! Martin's gone the whole hog. Vegan everything. Makes perfect sense actually, I…' He stopped talking, his forehead furrowed as he tilted his head at her. 'What? What is it?'

'Nothing.' Helen shook her head. She looked back down at her plate but she could feel her cheeks flushing.

'Come on now, Helly. Helleee.' He reached across the table and patted her arm, like he might a dog. 'I know it's a big thing but there's no need to worry about me. Tough as old boots, me. You know that. If Mont Blanc didn't get me, Everest won't. It's just a hill! And we're all on this high-flow oxygen now. That's another great thing about The Mountain Madmen. Plus the Sherpa ratio on summit day is one to one, which is incredible…'

'And that,' Helen finished, 'is when he called me a glass half-empty kind of person.' She picked her coffee up. 'Glass half-empty,' she repeated, more to herself than anyone else. Relaying Lawrence's words like this, taking them out of the context of that day, of their marriage, of her role as his wife and his role as her husband, playing them here, where she was just Helen, had revealed them clearly as the falsehood that somewhere she had always known them to be. A lie that had burrowed worm-like into her heart, taking tiny bites every hour of every day since he'd said it.

'Why did he say that?' Kay had the coffee pot.

'I don't know!' Helen sighed. She didn't. Suddenly she

had no idea why her husband would have said what he did. What she could have done, in all the long years of their marriage, for him to have formed this view of her. 'Because I wasn't showing enough interest in the client–Sherpa ratio?' she joked.

'Perhaps he was just trying to ease your worries?' Caro suggested.

Helen looked at her. 'I wasn't worried.'

'No?'

'No.' She shrugged. She was thinking back to that evening, and what she was remembering was the fury that had engulfed her. 'I wasn't worried,' she said. 'I was furious.' It was true. She'd been angry for as long as she'd had the energy to be angry. Because Lawrence hadn't told her, and when she'd tried to point that out he'd done what he always did. What he'd been doing for as long as she'd known him. He'd gaslighted her. Switched it around by attacking her character. 'My husband,' she said through a jaw so stiff it might have been wired, 'is an extremely selfish man.' And the only thing she could think now was: why on earth had it taken so long for her to see this?

Caro and Kay looked at each other.

'And that,' she said, 'doesn't make me a "glass half-empty" person! Whatever the hell that's supposed to mean!'

'Pessimist,' Kay muttered.

'I know what it means!' Helen snapped. 'And I'm not!'

Kay paused. 'I know you're not!' she said, tiny quizzical lines between her brows.

'My God, Helen, you're the last person on earth I'd have called a pessimist,' Caro added.

38

Helen blinked, her eyes wide and warm with fresh tears. 'Really?'

'Really.' Both Kay and Caro spoke at the same time.

'A pessimist,' Kay chuckled, 'doesn't plant watermelons in England.'

Helen smiled. 'They didn't work.'

'Not the point,' Kay said. And stretching forward for a pair of silver tongs, she picked up two cubes of sugar and dropped them into her coffee.

'You don't take sugar.' Helen glanced at Kay's rounded midriff, which was noticeably rounder than last time.

'I do when it's posh sugar,' Kay said, winking as she stirred her coffee.

The *chink-chink* of the teaspoon was gently hypnotic, and they all stared at it.

'Sod it! So do I, then!' Helen too reached for a cube of sugar and put it straight into her mouth. 'Glass half-empty?' She shook her head. 'Twenty-five years I've lain next to that man, listening to his farting and his snoring. I should get a medal just for that, don't you think? For sleep lost!'

'I can't imagine Lawrence farting.' Caro was folding a napkin, ready to blot away a spot of coffee on her cuff.

Helen narrowed her eyes. 'Oh, he does.' She grabbed another sugar cube. 'And you know what? In twenty-five years of marriage, he's never even learned to clean his toothpaste spit from the sink. And he empties his razor clippings everywhere. My bathroom floor is always littered with discarded facial hair. Always!' She leaned back in her chair, crunching the sugar cube in half. 'Half-empty? He has no idea of what it's like to be me – of what I do.'

39

'They never do,' Kay murmured, still caught in the hypnotic swirl her teaspoon was making.

Helen turned to her. 'It's all right for him. He's the hero who gets to sweat the big stuff, the stuff that matters, while I'm stuck with...' She paused. They were both looking at her. 'Filters!'

'Filters?' Caro raised her eyebrows.

'Yes, filters, Caro! He doesn't even know they exist.'

'I'm not sure I do.'

And Helen felt, rather than saw, Kay's small sideways smile. She leaned across the table. 'Well, they do! Washing machine filters, dishwasher filters, vacuum bags...'

'I get the picture,' Caro smiled.

Helen leaned back. 'It's not that I mind,' she said. 'I mean, I accept that was my job. Mattress covers were my job. Toilet ducks – my job. Milk. All of that I don't mind. What I *mind* – what I *really mind* – is that he doesn't even consider that I have a job. That I do all this. That I've done it for twenty-five years and I've never moaned or complained or not shown up. And...' She raised her finger. 'I've never had a holiday either. Because when we go on holiday *I'm* not on holiday. Who buys the milk on holiday? No! What I mind is that he has the nerve to call me a glass half-empty person – when he hasn't got a clue of the sheer optimism it takes to keep turning up in the hope that someday someone will actually be aware that you're actually there and remember to inform you they intend to bugger off for three months! That is what I mind!' Her words, louder with every sentence, landed on the table like bricks. *Thump. Thump! THUMP!*

'Right,' Kay murmured.

'Then...' Helen leaned forward and took another sugar cube. She was remembering something else Lawrence had said – something she hadn't thought about since. Something that was almost shameful to admit, because it was both unkind and untrue.

'What is it?' Kay said.

A moment passed.

'He said...' Helen's hands were at her face, fluttering. She took a deep breath and tried again. 'He said that I took after my mother. That she never looked on the bright side of life.' She put the sugar cube in her mouth, and it stuck out from her cheek like a neatly symmetrical growth. 'My mother,' she said tightly, 'worked two jobs most of her life.'

'I know.' Caro reached across and squeezed her hand.

'She barely got twelve months with her feet up, and when she was dyi—' Helen's voice choked; her hand flew to her chest. 'When she was dying,' she gasped, 'and we were planning... You know I asked her if there was anything special she wanted? And she said to make sure the undertaker...' Her voice broke off. She put her fist to her mouth.

'Didn't forget her wig,' Kay finished.

'That's right,' Caro said.

Helen took a deep, shuddery breath. 'She was the first woman in Whitley Bay to wear a bikini.'

'I remember you saying.' Caro smiled.

'So don't tell me...!' Helen began, and her eyes blazed and her face was red. And suddenly it didn't matter that her husband was over four thousand miles away and it was six months too late. Nothing mattered, nothing at all except that she right what was a terrible wrong. 'Do not tell me,' she hissed, 'that a woman who's worrying about her wig in the afterlife is a glass half-empty type of woman. Don't tell me that!'

Kay shook her head. She reached out and squeezed Helen's other hand. 'She wasn't, Helen.'

'Of course she wasn't,' Caro squeezed. 'And neither are you.'

They sat for a moment, the three of them, holding hands. Then Kay eased back and looked across at the ornate grandfather clock on the far wall. 'Let's get another bottle,' she said, and no one disagreed.

The bottle came, along with fresh glasses.

Caro took charge. 'Say when,' she said, pouring Helen's glass, but Helen said nothing at all.

'They just don't see it,' Kay murmured, watching Caro pour.

Caro grimaced. 'My father went to his grave thinking potatoes came out of the ground ready-peeled.' She filled her own glass. 'Not that that makes my mother any less difficult.'

'Martin,' Kay sighed, 'once rang me from Sainsbury's. This was at least a year after the divorce. He wanted to know if he could use liquid washing powder in his washing machine.' She smiled. 'A man with the power to call twenty thousand workers out on strike can't read instructions on the back of a bottle?'

'Oh, Kay.' Crunching through another sugar cube

and blotting her eyes, Helen laughed. She picked up her glass. 'You know what?' she whispered. 'I'm dreading him coming back.' Her wrist went so limp she had to put the glass down. It was only now that she'd actually said the words out loud that she realised how true they were. She was. She was dreading her husband coming back. 'I don't miss him. I don't miss him at all.'

'No?'

'No, Caro.' Helen looked at her. 'And what's more, I haven't baked a single bloody sausage for the anniversary party.'

Both the coffee and the wine were almost finished. Her birthday was slipping into its final hours of daylight. Dreamily, Helen turned to the huge bay windows at the front of the dining room. The low sunlight was transformational. Outside, the front lawns were now glow-in-the-dark lime and the sycamore shadows had grown improbably long, as if in this last hour they had cast off all pretence of conforming to the shapes of the trees that had created them. Now they bolted. Now they ran free.

The idea amused Helen. She sipped the last of her wine and thought how life looked so different with the sun behind, and as she did a flush started – sweat flooding into the structured seams of her dress was suddenly like sitting in a quagmire. She should have known. In the same way that polo necks had become impossible, fitted bodices were out too. What she needed was the clothing equivalent of a marquee. She took her napkin and fanned her face.

'Flush?' Kay mouthed.

She nodded.

'Why do you think I dress like this?' Kay indicated the loose, sleeveless blouse she was wearing.

But Kay looked like she always looked: supermarket-crumpled. The blouse was either Asda or, if the boat had been pushed out like it had today, Next.

Helen smiled. 'I'm so hot,' she whispered. 'Hot and wet.'

'Just not in the way you used to be,' Caro said, her eyebrows making neat little arches.

'No,' Helen smiled. 'Not at all in the way I used to be.'

There was a beat of silence and then, not for the first time that afternoon, the three of them broke into laughter. So there were still nuggets of fun to be mined. Not as consistent or as easily found as before but, if they were careful with each other, and patient, still there.

Wiping away clumps of mascara, Helen whispered, 'I really am sorry, Caro. About earlier. You know that's not me.'

Caro nodded. 'Whatever you think, Helen, some of it will be hormonal. Hot sweats. Irritability. Aching joints.'

Helen shook her head. She wasn't convinced. Then again... 'Jack,' she said, 'reckons I'm always in a mood.'

Chin resting on her hand, Kay slumped forward. 'Well, I'm permanently pissed off. Have been for years.'

'And I've told you both before.' Caro tipped her glass at them. 'HRT.'

'I believe you,' Kay said. 'And if I had time, I'd make an appointment.'

'So make time.'

'What?' Kay said. '*What?*'

'Well, look at you.' With a wide sweep of her arm, Caro turned from Kay to Helen. 'Both of you! You both need to start making some time for yourselves.'

'Caro.' Kay leaned forward. 'I'd love to trip off to a spa, but I barely have time to fart, let alone fanny about in a whirlpool.'

'Jacuzzi,' Caro said, slapping the word out. 'I'm just saying perhaps you could take a little time—'

'There is no time!'

'None at all?'

Kay shook her head. 'You know my job? And the way my mum is? And Alex...and the dog. I do all the shopping—'

'And the cooking,' Helen added, nodding.

'And the washing. Me, Alex, my parents. Hundreds of socks...pants.'

'Thank God the dog doesn't wear them,' Helen murmured. She meant it.

Kay waved a hand. 'I clear up sick and pee. I finished spoon-feeding Alex, had a break of a few years and now I'm spoon-feeding my mother. I find keys, pick up prescriptions on the way home from work, answer emails in bed...even though I love my bed, and God forbid anyone ever comes anywhere near invading that space again.' She tilted her glass to the ceiling. 'I even send birthday and Christmas cards to in-laws I've been divorced from for fifteen years!'

'Really?' Helen turned to her. 'That doesn't stop?'

'Not for me.'

'I've got it!' Caro smiled and raised a palm. Five beautifully lacquered nails. 'You're tired.'

'No.' Kay looked at her glass, swirling the last inch left. 'I'm not tired, Caro, I'm exhausted. I have become my mother. She always used to say she was busier than a cat trying to hide a turd on a marble staircase. Well, that's me! I'm a cat. Trying to hide a turd on a marble staircase. Which brings me to this point – and I'm sorry to break up such a lovely afternoon but I have to get going. Mum's carer can't make this evening.' She leaned down, picked up her handbag and slapped it on the table.

Helen reached for her own handbag. Kay was right. It really was time to go. The dampness under her armpits and the dryness in her mouth were telling her so. Kay checking her phone now was telling her so. The way the waiters had changed shifts and reset all the tables was telling her so; still, it was the very last thing she wanted. For the sun to go down on her – when there was still light, still time. She looked at Caro. 'Shall we go clubbing?' she said, and she was only half joking.

Caro raised her eyebrows. 'I never went clubbing when I was twenty, Helen. You know that.'

'Never,' Helen smiled, 'say never.' She was feeling light, as if the golden hue of the sunset were an energy drink, fizzing through her veins. She did not want to go home. She did not want to!

'I can't. I have a flight at eight.'

'Of course.' Now she looked to Kay, who was already shaking her head – slow, deliberate, you-really-can't-be-serious movements.

Helen smiled. Of course Kay had to get back. Half of Hertfordshire seemed to depend on her. 'I know.' She slumped over her handbag, chin in her hand. 'I just don't want this to end. Not just my birthday. *Us*. I don't want *us* to end. It's been so long since we spent time like this together. It's been cathartic.' It had. Over the course of the afternoon she had felt the ceiling of her life raise, the walls push out. And – as sobering as it was to think this, because that meant admitting its absence – she had felt something she hadn't felt in the longest time. Something like hope. She wasn't at all sure how she was going to hang onto that, but she did know one thing: it wouldn't be by baking sausages.

Caro twisted in her chair, checked her phone one last time and picked up her bag. She took out her purse and laid it on the table, her palm resting on it, her expression distracted.

'Right,' Kay said. 'Split three ways?'

'Absolutely.' Reluctantly Helen sat up.

'Why don't you both come to Cyprus with me?' Caro said suddenly.

Helen laughed. She couldn't tell if the offer was serious or not. Barely twenty minutes had passed since Caro had been telling them how much she was looking forward to her coming holiday. A week of rest. *On her own*. 'I can't,' she said. It felt like the safest thing to say.

'Why not?'

The abruptness of Caro's response threw her. She looked to Kay for help, but Kay was offering nothing more than a bemused spectator look.

'Well…' Helen faltered. 'First off, you said you're going because you needed some space.'

Caro nodded. 'True.' She turned to Kay. 'When are the school holidays?'

47

'Umm...' Kay looked from one to the other. 'Week after next,' she ventured.

'Perfect!' Caro's palm went up, stopping objections before there was time to voice them. 'I'll cover your flights. An early fiftieth for you, Kay. And...' She turned to Helen. 'It'll make up for that.' Caro nodded at the cheese melter. 'You'll be there and back before Lawrence even gets home.'

'I don't know,' Kay mumbled. 'Alex...' she started, and didn't get any further, dipping her head to the sanctuary of the inner workings of her handbag.

Across the table, Helen and Caro looked at each other. Kay's face was partially hidden, but Helen wasn't fooled. Over the last twenty years, she'd watched helplessly as door after door had slowly closed on what her brilliantly smart friend might have achieved. As Alex's limitations had effectively become Kay's, and her world had shrunk. Martin, Kay's ex-husband, had had an affair and then left, and in the most secret pocket of her heart Helen had understood why. There simply hadn't been enough energy left for him. From the day Alex was born, he'd come first and last. And although in the beginning that had been necessary, years of patient devotion and a commitment to securing the best resources had made Alex, Kay's autistic son, far more independent than Helen suspected Kay had ever dreamed possible. So much so that Helen didn't know any more: did Kay keep Alex so close because she was scared of him being alone in the world? Or because she was scared of being alone herself?

A waiter appeared, silent and serious and clearly far less pliable than the Harry Styles lookalike of earlier who'd left them alone to sit (but who had come over and wished Helen a shy and beetroot-red 'Happy birthday' before he left, adding that he couldn't believe she was fifty…the same age as his mum. Which was sweet, but superfluous). Now his replacement eased the bill further into the centre of the table. 'Everything okay here, ladies?' he said, smiling without smiling.

'Fine, thank you.' Caro pushed the bill away again.

The waiter retreated.

'We don't have to be in each other's pockets, do we?' Caro said, and she leaned forward across the table.

Kay took the bill and unfolded it. 'I'd love to, but I just can't.' She opened her purse and took out a small newspaper cutting. 'But you should, Helen. You need a holiday.'

Glass at her lips, Helen narrowed her eyes. She did bloody need a holiday, but so did Kay. 'I can't,' she said with slow deliberation. 'What about Jack?'

'He's eighteen, for heaven's sake!' Caro said. 'He can wash his own socks, can't he?'

'Yes,' Helen admitted, 'he probably can. And, Kay,' she said carefully, 'I think Alex could too.'

Kay's head wobbled – a movement that couldn't commit to a shake but equally refused to form a nod. 'I don't know,' she managed. 'I don't know about Alex.'

And Helen felt as if she'd just stuck a dagger in her friend's heart.

'Listen.' Caro leaned forward. 'Both of you. The hotel is in the foothills of a vineyard. To the east are mountains, to the west the Mediterranean Sea. It's one week. No laundry. No cooking. No shopping. No cleaning. No nothing. And

Alex?' She turned to Kay. 'You're always telling us that Martin thinks he could cope on his own.'

'I…well…' Kay unfolded the cutting.

'Martin can help, can't he?'

'Of course.' Kay coloured. 'That's not the point.'

'Well, what is?' Caro pushed.

'I don't know if *I'm* ready.' Suddenly Kay screwed the paper she'd been unfolding into a ball. 'That's it,' she whispered. 'If you must know. That's it.'

Helen shrank back. Kay was a swan. Everyone always thought she was gliding when she wasn't – she was paddling frantically, and had been since Alex was born. It was unnerving and upsetting to see the mechanics whirring away like this – to understand how much she kept to herself, spinning plates, coping, always coping. She didn't speak; instead she looked across at Caro, about to mouth *leave it* or *not now* or something similar, when Caro reached across and patted Kay's hand.

'Okay,' Caro murmured, 'okay.' Her fingers, wrapped around Kay's, touched on the paper ball. She rolled it towards her and unfolded it. Her face went white. 'You can't be serious, Kay? A discount voucher?' Glancing around the room, she whispered, 'They won't take that here!'

'Actually,' Kay said sadly, 'they do. I checked.' And she stood up, reaching behind for her jacket, which was a hip-length, diamante-studded, zig-zagged, sparkling wonder.

For a moment neither Helen nor Caro spoke, watching in silent awe as Kay slipped the jacket on.

'Is that the one you bought for Vegas?' Helen asked.

Kay nodded.

'But you never went, did you?' Caro said.

'No.' Kay shook her head. 'I never went to Vegas.'

Helen stared at the jacket. 'I've never been to Cyprus,' she said.

'I'll just pop to the loo.' Kay turned to move away, and in the low-lit room her Las Vegas jacket was a shimmering gleam of light, like a magical fishing boat from a children's lullaby.

It entranced Helen – held her like a siren's song and lured her towards a wonderful, tangible possibility. 'Kay!' she called.

Kay turned.

And then Helen was on her feet. 'Are we,' she said loudly, 'or are we not, glass half-full women?'

'We…' Now Caro stood. She looked at Kay. 'We are!'

'I…' Kay's voice trailed away.

'It's time!' Helen declared. 'It's past time!' She turned to Caro. 'I'll come!' she said, and turned back to Kay. 'You don't have to promise to come, Kay, you don't even have to promise to try and come. But you must promise to think about trying.'

'That,' Kay smiled, 'is something I can do.'

'Good.' Waving Kay back to the table, Helen picked up her glass and waited until Kay and then Caro, with bemused smiles, had raised theirs. 'To Cyprus!' she beamed.

3

'So you said you're having problems with your joints? Stiffness? Aching?'

Karma was a bitch. If she had one breath left to speak, one last thing to pass onto her children, Helen thought, it would be this piece of sage advice. Because what else could explain the fact that Dr Cawley, the senior gynaecologist, had called in sick exactly one day after she'd summoned up the courage to have a blood test done and face the possibility that yes, some of her irritability with life might well be hormonal? Which had left only Dr Ross for the follow-up appointment. Mere days after "coffeegate".

Swallowing down her discomfort, she nodded a yes to the doctor's question. If it wasn't for the fact that they worked under the same roof, she'd get up and run away right now. As it was, she was only here because of Kay. Astonishingly, Kay had committed to Cyprus, which was nothing short of a miracle and should have left Helen walking on air. Only it hadn't. The hope that had spawned on the day of her birthday had turned out to be as fragile as a soap bubble. It wavered and wobbled and floated tenuously out of reach. And with every day her mood and her eyebrows and the ceiling of her life had sunk imperceptibly lower. And now that Cyprus was exactly one week away, she was getting desperate. What if a change of scenery didn't work? What if what she needed was a change of attitude? Where was she supposed to get that from?

'And how does that feel?'

'How does that feel?' Helen repeated, biting down on her lip. Dr Ross seemed *so* young. Young enough to be her daughter, to not have graduated from medical school, to know as much about aching joints as a fish did about trees. How could she possibly explain what it felt like to wake up in a body at odds with its mind? Especially when the relationship had once been so smooth. Once upon a time she'd quite liked her body. Back in the days when everything was where she'd expected to find it. Nowadays they were – what was the term? Estranged? Certainly not on familiar terms. Just last summer, Libby had taken a photo of her in shorts, from behind, and when she'd seen it Helen had said, *Who's that?* And no, she wasn't being funny. Her silhouette had changed beyond recognition. No wonder nothing fitted any more. But here she was, and there was Dr Ross, and they did work under the same roof, so running away wasn't an option. With a forced cheer she smiled and said, 'Well, it's the mornings really. You know, my ankles get a bit stiff and creaky.'

Dr Ross looked up. 'But you've always been active, Helen?'

She nodded. She had. She still walked and cycled and

gardened, even if she spent just as long recovering from the walking and the cycling and the gardening. 'I can still touch my toes,' she heard herself say, and didn't add that nowadays the movement felt different. Nowadays when she leaned forward the fold of her belly felt like a whoopee cushion that didn't have a snowball's chance in hell of deflating.

Dr Ross nodded. 'That's impressive.'

Helen looked at her hands. The sooner this was over the better. She'd escape to her favourite coffee shop – or, better still, the garden centre. A cup of tea and a slice of lemon drizzle. What on earth was she doing twittering on about touching her toes?

'You know that stiffness in the joints is a symptom of menopause?'

Cautiously Helen looked up.

'It's a result of the dropping levels of oestrogen. A bit like keeping a car running without ever adding more oil.'

Her jaw dropped. She looked back at her hands, turned them over, flexed the wrists. A car? Oil? The analogy made perfect sense. That was exactly how she felt, moving through each day heavy as a walrus, creaky as a floorboard. She was an engine…an engine without oil!

'Okay. Shall we get it over and done with, then?'

'Sorry…what?' Helen twisted in her chair.

Dr Ross had stood up and was now at the couch, pulling out a sheet of that horrible paper which always reminded Helen of the ultra-cheap kitchen towel she never bought.

'I'd like to do a quick examination if that's okay?'

First she went cold. Then hot. Then cold again. Why

hadn't she anticipated *this*? She felt as if the bones in her legs had dissolved with mortification. How was she ever going to look the woman in the eye again? This was definitely coffeegate coming home to roost. In fact, this was revenge for coffeegate. She forced a laugh. 'Well, I don't think it's necessary—'

Dr Ross turned to her. 'I know you're embarrassed.' She already had her latex gloves on.

Helen's head dipped.

'If it helps you, Helen, so am I.'

Sweet, but not helpful. Not at all. She preferred a less emphatic touch, more old-school, no-nonsense, *please remove your knickers* approach. Now she was so embarrassed she couldn't speak.

For a moment Dr Ross didn't speak either, and the silence in the room thrummed like a drum in her ear. She couldn't do this…

'I just want to do my job right,' Dr Ross said, and her voice was low and calm. 'As I said earlier, your blood tests indicate that your oestrogen levels are extremely low. A quick internal examination will allow me to confirm that.' She leaned back against her desk. 'And then I can help you.'

Helen didn't move.

'You don't have to feel the way you've been feeling, Helen.'

Still she didn't move.

Dr Ross folded her arms across her chest. When she spoke, she spoke to the floor. 'How old do you think I am?' she said.

The unexpectedness of the question made Helen look

up. She felt ashamed and angry at the same time. She wasn't questioning the woman's competence. 'It's not you,' she murmured.

'I know.' The doctor looked at her. 'I understand that. I'm asking because I'm probably older than you think.'

Colouring more deeply, Helen shook her head. 'I don't know how old you are.'

'I'm thirty-two. I didn't go to university straight away. I took some time out to help my mother look after my aunt.'

Because she didn't know what else to do, Helen nodded. She was lost, with no idea why Dr Ross was telling her all this.

'I'm telling you this, Helen,' the doctor said, 'because when I was eighteen, my aunt attempted suicide.'

'Oh.' Helen paled. 'I'm so sorry. I—'

'It's okay.' Dr Ross gave a low laugh. 'She didn't succeed. And she's still here now and she's doing fine.'

'That's good,' Helen said, more confused than ever.

Dr Ross smiled. 'It's true she was going through a divorce at the time, but her mental health problems – and we've talked a lot about this, my aunt, my mum and me – the conclusion we've come to is that she was also going through a really bad menopause.'

'Oh.' For a long moment Helen looked at Dr Ross. The idea was absurd. Suicidal because of the change of life? On the other hand, wasn't that exactly what drove people to suicide – irreversible changes of life?

'She talked about a feeling of hopelessness.' Dr Ross smiled. 'And my mother said she'd had a bit of the same. And joy. That's what struck me, Helen. I remember my aunt

56

saying that at her lowest point she couldn't find any joy in life, and she really believed she never would again.' Dr Ross tipped her head to the ceiling. 'She was on antidepressants for years, when all it...' Looking back at Helen, she stopped talking, crossed her arms and waited. Finally, very quietly, she said, 'Helen? Are you okay?'

Hand at her mouth, blinking back tears, Helen nodded. She was stuck on that word. *Joy*. It was exactly the right word to describe what was missing. And it had slinked off so quietly, she couldn't for the life of her pinpoint when and for how long it had been gone. The years immediately after losing her first child, Daniel, had been bleak. He had died before he'd even been born and there was no doubt in Helen's mind that the experience of delivering a dead baby had shaved a great wedge from her personality. But then Libby came along, and Jack, and although it was a less exuberant type than her younger days, there had still been joy. But now? Now the children were grown and her ankles creaked like dry parchment and her husband was in line for Most Selfish Man on the Planet Award, she understood exactly what Dr Ross's aunt meant when she feared it was lost forever. Joy. Where had it gone?

'Shall we do this?' Dr Ross smiled a lopsided, kind smile.

'Yes,' Helen murmured. She could do this. If it meant that she might stumble across that three-letter word again, she could do it. Layer by layer – cardigan, skirt, tights – she began distancing herself from her body, then the room, then the situation. And by the time she was naked from the waist down, her consciousness had reduced to one word –

joy – and her focus narrowed to an orange-rimmed stain in the far right-hand corner of the ceiling, as if that was where it was hidden.

Forty minutes later, the packet of Novofem already opened and tucked away in her handbag, Helen found herself pausing in front of the bra department on the first floor of Marks & Spencer, Dr Ross's words ringing in her ears.

What you need to do now is go shopping. Buy yourself the prettiest, silliest, most unsuitable thing you can find and then wear it in Cyprus. Every day.

It might be, she considered as she looked at the mannequin in front of her, a decade since she'd bought herself a new bra. She walked over and reached a hand out to trace the hem of the knickers. She and Dr Ross had parted on very friendly terms, and while getting dressed she'd talked about the trip. How it was the first time she'd been away without family since university days (1992, when she and Caro and Kay had gone to Stonehenge for the summer solstice, had sounded too ridiculous to actually voice, like a period of ancient history). *How exciting* had been Dr Ross's response. Which had surprised Helen. Not the words, but the directness of them. It was a declaration, a statement of something decided, and the effect had been that she'd left the surgery knowing that she was decided too. Cyprus *was* exciting, and she should damn well start to believe it.

She turned and looked across at the rows and rows of lacy white underwear. This was a corner of M&S she rarely visited, being long past the days when the thought of white lace against a suntan was a guaranteed spirit-raiser. And although Dr Ross had said it would be a week or so before she began to notice the effects of HRT, standing now in front of all the pretty silly things Helen began to experience a gentle, unobtrusive idea that there *was* something to look forward to. She smiled. The feeling was akin to those odd moments on a spring afternoon looking at the budding wisteria in her garden, or a sunny minute in her living room with a cup of tea and a book. Moments that were different. Rainbow-coloured, lighter – and ultimately cruel in the way they highlighted what had otherwise become a routinely grey existence. She looked up, straight into the eye of the mannequin, tiny-waisted, peachy-breasted, smooth-skinned. 'Just wait,' she said, slinging her handbag over her shoulder. 'Just wait.'

The mannequin didn't blink.

Helen turned away and walked over to the first display, where all the bras seemed to be the shape and size of orange segments. Tiny white hammocks that wouldn't hold a mouse. She looked at the sign: *Balconette*.

Around the corner she found a row of triangular-shaped lace vests. *Bralettes*.

Behind them *High Apex*, and beyond that shelves of cone-shaped oddities reinforced with steel, the likes of which she'd last seen in a Madonna video, circa 1991.

Then there were shelves of T-shirt bras and sports bras. Hidden away at the back (of course), total support bras, hideous full cups and serious-looking high-impact bras. On it went... *Soft Touch, Swiss Designed, Cami, Multi, Backless, Strapless.*

She ran her hand through her hair. When did bras become so complicated? Her jeans were cutting into her belly, chafing. She turned her back and undid the top button, then untucked her blouse so it would cover the gap and slipped her jacket off. Bewildered and hot, she stood in the middle of the underwear department, as lost and forgotten as a penny down a sofa. All she wanted to do was get home, swallow as many HRT tablets as possible and wake up forty-one again.

'Can I help you, madam?'

The sales assistant who had approached blinked improbably long lashes at her. Her make-up was so heavy and smooth she looked like a wooden puppet…or a highly polished sideboard.

'Umm…' Nervously Helen looked away. Number one: why did they all wear so much make-up? Number two: if she said yes, she might have to get undressed again, and the girl was too young to understand about muffin tops…like Dr Ross had been too young to understand about aching joints… 'I'm…umm, I'm…' She took a deep breath and turned to look across the floor of the lingerie department. 'I'm looking for a bra,' she managed finally.

Which was how she ended up, twenty-five really quite fun-filled minutes later, with the most exquisite white laced item, which her boobs seemed to fit as reluctantly as a fluffy duvet fits a newly starched cover. In she'd stuffed them, this way and that, and still they spilled, overflowed, teemed.

The sales girl had called it a balcony bra as opposed to a balconette. So half the fruit, not just a slice. Either way, she'd thought as she'd looked down at her chest, the name was apt. They'd develop vertigo, hanging over the precipice all day like that...which had made her think of Lawrence.

She still hadn't told him. About Cyprus. The two short phone calls he'd managed since had been walls of sound that Helen had listened to almost at arm's length. *His* feelings, *his* excitement, *his* plans shouted against a backdrop of high-altitude winds. On the last one she'd put him on speakerphone and cleaned the sink. Was that wrong? Here was her husband, her life partner, riding the crest of a massive achievement, and she'd been more concentrated upon the tea stains around the plughole. But he hadn't even asked about her birthday lunch, and the void inside Helen now when she considered their marriage had expanded to a great black hole that she knew she could not afford to fall into.

4

The shriek of the electric saw from two houses down fell silent just as Caro got to the point of what she'd been skirting around for the last five minutes. As a consequence the street fell eerily silent, her voice grew correspondingly louder, and opposite, a head shorter, Kay's face had correspondingly drained. She was always pale; now she was white. 'Anyway,' Caro finished. 'Now you know.' That last sentence had felt so loud it seemed to bounce off the pebble-dash of Kay's garage, and nothing would convince her that the old woman across the road didn't also now know.

Kay pursed her lips. 'Let me get this straight,' she said. 'You haven't told Helen?' She was hugging an orange and white traffic cone, the hard edge cutting into her navy fleece. Her short hair had been even more fiercely cropped than usual, lying as flat as a skullcap. Caro had an urge to reach out and fluff it up, inject some softness.

'No.'

'And you don't intend to?'

She shook her head. (Now, she thought, would

be a good time for that power tool to start up again.)

'And you're only telling me because you're going to need me to cover for you?'

'That's not how I'd put it.'

'No, I guess not.' Dumping the traffic cone on the brick post of her boundary wall, Kay sighed. 'Is that why you've been so insistent I come?' she said. 'Because seriously, Caro, you know how big a deal this is for me. And if I'm just needed—'

'No!' Caro shook her head. 'That's not it at all. I understand this is a big step. For you and Alex.'

'Really?'

'Yes, *really*. And actually it was Helen who insisted we make you come. And I agreed. Out of all of us it's you that needs the break most!'

'Mmm.' Kay narrowed her eyes.

Caro looked down at the car keys in her hand. 'This situation has only arisen because of you coming later.'

'Right.' Brushing dirt from her fleece, Kay turned back to her house. 'You'd better come inside.'

'Okay.' But Caro didn't move. She glanced back at her silver BMW, nestled now in the parking space cleared by the removal of the traffic cone. Why Kay insisted upon staying here, so close to her parents and in the very house she'd grown up, Caro had never understood. She shuddered. It wasn't for her. It reminded her too much of where she'd grown up herself. The house, the family, she hadn't been able to leave fast enough.

'The car will be fine,' Kay called. She was standing by her back door. 'Mrs Newall will keep an eye on it.'

'I wasn't worried about the car,' Caro lied. She looked across to the house opposite. A white-haired, frail woman (the one who now *knew*) had bent over a plastic pot, attacking the soil with a trowel, three bags of compost piled up by her front door.

Kay followed her eye. 'She's a one-woman neighbourhood watch society.'

'Right.'

'And weathervane. We know it's going to be warm if she's out with that trowel or on her stepladder washing windows.'

Head bowed, Caro nodded. Every Tom, Dick and Harry knowing your business? Watching all the comings and goings? It wasn't for her. She took a step towards the driveway and then suddenly leapt sideways. 'Shit! What is that?'

'It's dog shit, Caro,' Kay sighed.

Well, of course it was. She knew that. What she wanted to say was *What is it doing there? Right outside your drive, Kay! And why don't you get rid of that stupid traffic cone and just move house?* Car keys jiggling, arms folded across her thin blouse, she sidestepped the dog shit and walked up the drive.

'Now we'll know when it's autumn as well.'

'What?' Just in front of the back doorstep, Caro stopped short. She was eye to eye with Kay, who had the benefit of the step. She switched a glance back across the road to the neighbour. 'Why?'

'Because,' Kay laughed, 'Mrs Newall has just bought herself an electric leaf blower.' And she turned and disappeared inside the house.

Caro paused. She looked back across the road, and as she did, two things happened at once. Mrs Newall waved at her, and the power tool roared back into life. How did Kay stand it? Caro didn't know the name of a single neighbour in her apartment block. She couldn't say she'd ever even heard them come and go. And that was exactly how she liked it.

In the kitchen Kay was filling the kettle, moving cups around.

Caro dropped her keys on the bench and leaned against it. She hadn't intended to blurt everything out on the pavement, but the knot of anxiety she'd had since Helen rang yesterday with final travel plans had unravelled like a demented snake the moment she'd got out of her car and Kay had said, *What's wrong?*

Why should there be anything wrong? she'd tried, which Kay hadn't even dignified with a response. No, it hadn't been what she'd intended. Not out on the pavement, with Kay holding that ridiculous traffic cone, and all the neighbours downing their power tools as if they'd been tipped off. Kay, who'd always had that extra antenna. Who could snuffle out secrets like a pig with truffles. She crossed her arms and looked at the floor, trying and failing to find a way of restarting a conversation that was proving harder than she'd ever imagined.

'Go through,' Kay said, as if she'd heard Caro's thoughts. 'I think I need to be sitting down to hear this.' She hadn't even turned around.

'Right.' Caro smoothed her skirt. 'Right.' Yes, Kay had

an extra antenna. And eyes in the back of her head. And a unique ability to make her feel like a schoolgirl. A schoolgirl who had got too big for her boots.

Kay's living room was small. But then again, Kay's house was small. One blue sofa and two bulbous armchairs all squashed around a huge TV screen, which would, of course, be for Alex. Because in all the years she'd known Kay, Caro had never seen her sit and while away hours watching TV. At university she'd spent whole days reading, tucked into a corner of the library, or flat on her back in her dorm room. Nowadays, Caro knew, her reading spot was a kitchen chair as she waited for various vegetables to boil.

She sat down in the armchair closest to the window, took out her work phone and put it on the arm. On the top shelf of the bookcase opposite, stood a small plastic penguin, the blue of his fur matching the blue of the sofa. Next to him, plastic ivy draped down from the top shelf. Plastic ivy? Caro snorted. Her own mother kept plastic plants. She could never keep the real things alive. But then, why would her mother have been any better with plants than she was with children? Both required a degree of nurture she was clearly incapable of.

She shook her head as if to rid herself of the thought. Aside from the soft urgent sound of the kettle boiling away in the kitchen, the room was quiet and peaceful. A photo of a blonde-haired child stood centre stage of the mantle, his smile so wide it was hard to find anything else within the image. Impossible, actually. It was just a photo of a smile. Alex. Caro's godson. Uncomfortable, she crossed her legs and switched her attention to the window. She hadn't, she knew, been much of a godmother to Alex. In fact, she hadn't been one at all. She was godmother to Helen's son as well, but there was no discomfort there. Jack didn't have the same needs as Alex, either as child or adult.

She leaned back in the chair, let her hands rest in her lap and sighed. The walls in the room were a pale yellow, with a feature wall in orange. Hideous! And no doubt Kay's last attempt at turning what was always going to be a sow's ear into a silk purse. The house had been bequeathed to Kay by her parents, who had retired to a bungalow around the corner. And yes, Caro knew it had provided Kay with a much-needed and affordable sanctuary at the difficult time of her divorce. But then to never move on? To end up back in the street you were raised in? Again Caro shook her head. She and Kay had both been the first in their families to get a university education, and for her that had meant only one thing – upward mobility. But for Kay, who had been the brightest of them all (and this was undeniable), that obviously wasn't the case. She was, or was going to be, content to end exactly where she'd started. It was almost beyond comprehension. She closed her eyes, stretched her hands along the chair, felt the rough pile under her fingers and thought of her own spacious apartment with its generous proportions and clean, blank walls. Then she thought of her mother's cramped terrace. The clutter, the old-fashioned furniture, the sense of defeat that seemed to emanate from the foundations upward. Shuddering, she opened her eyes again. Sometimes she wished she could scoop Kay up and replant her somewhere else. Like she had so successfully done for herself.

'Just wanted to check. Socket on… Oh, sorry! I thought you were Kay.'

Caro turned to the voice. A man stood in the doorway. He had the clearest blue eyes she'd ever seen. They were all the more startling because everything else about him was slightly decrepit. His hair was sparse and unruly, his fleece had frayed cuffs and a grease stain, his cheeks were ruddy, his teeth yellowed, his ears creased. But his eyes? They were unclouded pools, miraculously preserved among ongoing ruination.

'Sorry,' he said again.

Caro stared at his eyes. 'Kay's in the kitchen,' she managed.

'Great.'

'I'm Caro.'

'Right. I'm Shook.'

'Shook?'

He nodded.

'And that's a name?' she laughed.

'It is now.'

She sensed his discomfort immediately. It had been meant to be a joke.

He turned to go, and as he did he came up against Kay, bearing a tea tray.

'Whoops!' Kay's voice bobbed through. 'Want a cup, Shaky?' she said, and then she was past him, manoeuvring her wide girth through the cramped furniture, as sleek and efficient as a salmon swimming upstream.

Caro sat up and recrossed her legs so her skirt would ride up just a touch. Which it did. And it was as if someone was in her head, pulling strings, making her do it.

'Three?' Kay said. She dropped three spoonfuls of sugar into a cup.

'I do hope that's not mine.' Caro laughed, tipping her head back. (Why was she behaving like this?)

'Nope.' Shook leaned forward and took the cup. 'It's mine. Thanks, Kay.' He nodded. 'Just wanted to double-check. Socket on the right-hand side, yes?'

'Yes.' Kay straightened up. 'I'll show you. Won't be a sec, Caro. Stay right there.'

'No problem,' she said, and they were gone, leaving Caro alone in the room with only the dull reverberation of her failed jokes for company. She reached for her own unsweetened cup. She felt like an idiot, a giddy idiotic teenager. And who was he anyway? Kay's electrician, who happened to have nice eyes… For heaven's sake! She sipped her tea and looked out of the window, ready to notice anything that would divert her attention. The neighbour, Mrs Newall, was tottering up the drive now, a tray of marigolds in her hand. And yes, her BMW was still there. From upstairs she heard first Kay's voice and then a burst of laughter from the electrician guy. And, inexplicably, what she felt was envy. At the very least she wanted to know what Kay had said to make him laugh.

Footsteps bumped down the stairs. Kay was back in the room.

'Sorry. That was Shaky. He lives down the road.'

Caro nodded.

'Poor old Khans!' Kay fell into an armchair. 'Twenty years they've been building their Shangri-La. Lions on the gateposts and everything, and now they're the filling in a buy-to-let sandwich. They've got half of Eastern Europe either side! Still…' She paused for breath. 'That's how I found Shaky. He's Polish.'

'He said his name was Shook.'

Kay looked at her. 'Oh, it is! I keep forgetting. It *was* Shaky, now it's Shook. He gave up drinking three months ago. He's helping me out with a job in the back room, and he won't take any money either.' She leaned forward for her own cup. 'I can't exactly buy him a bottle now, can I?'

Caro shook her head. She was thinking of the way she'd said *Is that a name?* and he'd replied *It is now.*

'Which is great, though.' Kay scratched at her neck. 'Because no other bugger will help.'

'What about Alex?'

'He's too busy building his motorcycle.'

'Still?'

'Still. And hopefully by the time he's finished building it, he'll have lost interest in it.' Cup in hands, Kay leaned back. 'So. You're going to have a baby?'

'Going to try and have a baby,' Caro corrected. She pushed back, feeling the hardness of a felted button in her spine. Kay's living room smelled of air freshener and sunshine. Across the carpet she could see lines left by the vacuum cleaner, and all she could think of was how very strange it was to hear those words spoken out loud. *Going to try and have a baby.* How resilient it seemed to make them. Because they hadn't disappeared. In the silence of Kay's living room they remained, strung out and loud. So thank God, really, that Kay had shut the door. The thought of that man upstairs hearing…well, anyone really…but no, especially him.

Kay didn't speak.

From outside she heard the electric saw again. It was out. What for so long had felt like a guilty secret was out. Her phone lit up. She glanced down at it.

'Work?'

Caro shook her head. 'Sorry. I just have to…' And she swiped the message open, talking as she tapped out a response. 'He's what we call a high net guy. But he doesn't understand investing. His father made a fortune in property and now he's splashing it around in stocks. Danny Abbott.' Caro's voice trailed off. She looked at Kay, who was staring across the room, lips pursed. 'Sorry,' she said.

Kay nodded. 'I don't know how to say this, Caro—'

'I'll be using a donated egg,' she blurted. 'And donated sperm…obviously.'

'Right.'

'Is that what you didn't know how to say?'

'Sort of.'

'It's…' Caro trailed off, looking down at her phone as she turned it through a half-circle. 'It's a complicated process. I have to… Well, I've been taking hormones. Oestrogen. In fact, before coming here I was at a scan.'

'A scan?' Astonished, Kay looked at Caro's stomach.

'It's a check. To make sure I'm ready for…for the donation.'

'Oh.'

And for a long moment they looked at each other, and then Kay said, 'But why Cyprus? Why not stay home and—'

71

'It's more complicated here,' Caro said bluntly. 'For most places, I'm too old.' *I'm too old. I'm too old...* These words, too, reverberated.

Kay didn't speak; she sat very still, nursing her mug, her eyes fixed on the other side of the room.

'It's all very thorough. There's a lot of screening.' Caro shrugged. She was talking just to fill the silence, feigning a casualness she wasn't feeling and which wasn't appropriate. 'Plus you get to match eye colour and hair. That stuff. Ethnicity, religious background, education. Everything really.'

Slowly Kay turned to her.

'Even body mass index and height.' She forced a laugh. 'Donors can't be too short or too tall.'

'What's too short?' Kay asked. She wasn't laughing.

Caro blinked. 'I don't know.'

'Or too tall?'

'I—' She shook her head. Tears pricked at her eyes. She stretched her arms out and balanced her cup on her knees. She felt a little bit sick. What had she expected? That Kay would leap up and hug her, declare it the best news ever? That was what she had done with both Kay and Helen. Every time a new pregnancy had been announced she'd been there with smiles and congratulations. But this wasn't, and never could be, the same. It was precisely why she'd hadn't told anyone.

'So how—' Kay started.

'Online.'

'You just sort of looked through…and decided?'

She nodded.

'Okay.' Kay leaned back, cup in her lap as she stared out of the window. 'Okay.'

Caro bit down on her lip. It had been hard enough convincing herself that what she was doing wasn't abominable or a heinous crime of humanity. But here, among Kay's plastic ivy and enormous TV, was her reality check. The public testing of her morality.

The silence between them intensified. She felt it in her cheeks – a strange mix of embarrassment, shame and defensiveness colouring her like litmus paper. 'I know what you're thinking,' she began. 'And—'

'Caro.'

The marker-pen emphasis Kay gave to her name stopped her short. She looked down at her cup, tears brimming. Was Kay going to talk her out of it? A moment ago she had been Caro the professional, knocking out a text to a millionaire; now she was Caro the child, lost and helpless in the face of what Kay might say. Because it was so very possible. Because she'd swayed so very much herself, it was entirely possible that one puff of righteous morality from Kay and it could all be over. This beautiful, impossible dream she'd nurtured for months, as protective of it as if it were the baby itself. She was that vulnerable. Her and her imagined family.

Kay leaned to her. 'I love you,' she said.

Caro didn't speak.

'Caro. Look at me.'

Slowly she raised her head.

'You're my *best* friend, Caro.' Kay had hold of her hand now, squeezing it. 'You and Helen. You've always been there for me, and I'd like to think I've been there for you.'

'You have.'

'Yes, I have. Even when you've been the most selfish, difficult cow on the planet.'

A tiny smile.

'But honestly? In all the years we have known each other, you have *never* known what I'm thinking.'

'Kay—'

'*I* don't even know what I'm thinking,' Kay said, and leaned back, cup at her lips.

She might as well have stuffed a dummy in her mouth.

Hand shaking, Caro put her cup down. Why hadn't she just continued her own course? Months of planning, and she hadn't ever seriously wavered from the initial decision she'd made *not* to tell them. Which had been easy, because the conversation had moved on. The 'baby' question had, insofar as it involved her, died. In recent years her childlessness had solidified, becoming set in such a way that all wondering and tentative enquiries from Helen and Kay had ceased. As if the general conclusion they'd come to was that all emotional and physiological longing to be a mother had dried up along with her ovaries. Well, it hadn't. It had simply gone into a self-imposed hibernation, and, understanding the limits of even the closest of friendships, Caro had kept this to herself. It was her own unsolvable problem, her own private sadness that no one, she'd accepted, could or would be able to heal.

Until that day in New York, at the Sustainable Futures Conference, when she'd met Alison Machowski. Fifty-six years old, CFO with one of the fastest-growing clean energy companies in the Northwest, and mother to a two-year-old son. Tucked away in the corner of the dining room of one of the most exclusive hotels in Columbus Circle, Alison had spilled her story like a river undammed. And Caro had listened, scarcely believing what she was hearing, as her eyes had flitted from the half-naked women dancing on the stage behind them to the windows beyond, where Central Park – in which she'd run that morning – was a gaping black hole in the heart of the city.

She'd flown home nurturing the very tiniest flame of possibility, which the cold light of her frenetic schedule had swiftly extinguished. Until Alison had emailed with a picture of her son, and the flame had flared again, stronger and all the more resilient. Finally, and perhaps inevitably, she'd made an initial enquiry, eased the door a crack. All of which had landed her here, so easily and so quickly, in Kay's living room, with a womb lining thick enough, a donor in hormonal synch, a baby a very real possibility. But she wasn't there yet. And the same reservations that had kept her from revealing this plan six months ago reared up again now. She folded her hands together. What she was thinking, and in fact had never stopped thinking, was that she shouldn't have asked Helen and Kay to join her. It was too complicated. It was always going to be too complicated. For the life of her she couldn't understand why she had.

Kay looked at her. 'I can see the problem,' she said. 'If you haven't told Helen.'

'I just think…' Caro whispered; she was speaking to her knees. 'I just feel it will be easier if she doesn't know until afterwards. I don't… I don't want her to judge me.'

'Do you think she will?'

'I don't know.' Caro looked up. 'Everything's been so easy for her. That's all.'

'Has it?'

'Oh, come on, Kay!' Caro shifted her weight. There was a nub of irritation in her voice. Kay going all therapist on her? Helen had been born lucky. They both knew that; they'd both, at different times, said that. 'Lawrence,' she said, 'has always earned a fortune. All Helen ever wanted was her kids, her house and her garden. Which she got. Very easily.'

A shadow passed across Kay's face. 'Losing her first baby wasn't easy,' she said quietly. 'Not easy at all.'

'No. Of course not. I was there. I remember.' Caro closed her eyes. 'I don't know how to say what I'm trying to say, Kay.'

'Start by opening your mouth.'

'Okay.' And despite herself, Caro smiled. 'You and Helen,' she said. 'You're the closest thing I have to family. But it's not the same for you.'

'Caro—'

'It's not, Kay. You have Alex and your parents. Helen has her family. You've been busy. You're still busy with your own lives. And that's life. And because Helen doesn't really understand what it's been like for me, I'd just prefer not to tell her about this until…well, until it's done.'

'Would you have told me?' Kay asked.

'Maybe.' She looked at Kay, her eyes heavy with memory. 'I told you about…you know…that time with the tablets…'

Kay nodded. 'But you never did tell Helen?'

'I was never sure she'd understand, Kay.' She fell back in the chair. 'Helen's had such a straightforward path, that's all. She got what she wanted and she was happy. And I don't deny it: I envied that.'

'Oh, Caro.' Kay smiled.

'What?'

'What we want in life changes, don't you think?' And before Caro could answer, Kay added, 'There's nothing to be envious of. What suited Helen before isn't suiting her now. That's obvious. Just as it isn't for you.'

And there was nothing Caro could say. She picked up her cup and then put it down again. Kay was right. What had suited her before did not suit her now. Because wasn't it true that for years she'd marched under the banner of chosen childlessness? Proclaiming its advantages as frequently as anyone (but particularly Kay and Helen) would listen. And it *had* suited her; it had been what she'd thought she'd wanted. Oh, the foolishness of youth. Because, of course, it was only as the option of choice began to fall away that she'd understood she hadn't *chosen* anything. She'd just deferred. And in these last few years, as the cliff edge had approached, everything she'd spent half a lifetime perfecting in order to protect herself had crumbled. All that false bravado, as unexamined as the far side of the moon. Her Brigadoon future – vanished! Her cheeks warmed. She leaned back, hands clasped together as she twisted the diamond ring she'd bought herself for her fortieth. 'I'm not prepared to tell Helen,' she said, hearing the hard edge to her voice. 'Not until it's done. It's going to

77

be difficult as it is, and... I don't want any questions...or judgements.'

'Okay,' Kay said quietly, and within the hush of the room Caro heard her words echo, and they sounded true. She didn't want any questions. She didn't want any judgements. She did not want to be talked out of it. So this really was it.

A calmness descended, silent as snow.

Kay smiled. She put her head to one side. 'Do you want us there at all?' she said.

And, hearing the deliberate kindness in Kay's voice and looking up at the familiar face – the jowls, the lines, the oh-so-clever eyes – she understood why, against every screeching voice in her head, she had asked both of them to come. She smiled back. 'It's funny. Ever since I mentioned it I've been telling myself I should have just kept quiet, but...' Her voice broke off. The back of her hand was at her mouth as she blinked away tears.

'Okay?'

She nodded, breathed in. 'Before Helen's lunch, Kay, I was prepared to do this on my own. After all, I've done everything else pretty much on my own...' Again her voice broke. 'And then Helen...the stuff about Lawrence... I mean, we used to tell each other everything, didn't we? That's how it worked. That's *why* it worked. I think over the years I've been more honest with you two than anyone else in the world.'

Kay pinched her lips together. 'Ditto,' she whispered. 'Ditto.'

'And we've gotten through.'

'Somehow.'

Her fingertips were at her chin, palms together, like hands in prayer. 'Can you,' she started, paused and shook her head. 'Can you imagine choosing the colour of your child's eyes on your own from a computer screen?'

'No,' Kay whispered. 'I can't imagine that, Caro.'

'So.' Tears streamed down her face. 'I *do* want you there. Both of you.'

Kay reached across and took her hand. 'Then we'll be there.'

Caro squeezed back. She felt as though the world had fallen off her shoulders, and she knew that on the day of Helen's lunch, somewhere, behind the chatter and clutter, deeply planted memories had made themselves heard, and this was why she'd asked them to come. Kay knew. Soon enough, Helen would. The sky hadn't fallen in, and what she had just said was true. She couldn't think of a better way to go through what she was going to go through than to have her two closest friends there. For the first time in years, she didn't feel alone.

Part Two

5

Standing at the huge windows of her tenth-floor flat, Caro listened to her CEO's phone ringing out. Turning to check the time – 6.30am – she frowned. She'd tried a couple of minutes ago, and he hadn't answered then either. A thought struck, as cold as an ice cube on her neck. She cut the call.

Matt would be on the toilet.

He'd forgotten his phone, and if she left it ringing any longer he'd waddle out to get it, pyjamas at his ankles. In fact, he was probably halfway there now. Because alongside Simon, the CFO, Caro was the only person on earth whose calls Matt *always* took. As he should, when an intrinsic part of the £100 million micro-capped public company he now owned a very healthy share of was his Investor Relations Manager, Caro. Whom he'd wooed assiduously until eventually she had relented, becoming to all intents and purposes both his IRM and his work-wife. Who else did he offload all his worries onto? (Certainly not his wife, whose calls he did skip.) And in who else's company did she kick off her Gucci loafers, slurp a cold Peroni and bitch about her day? The PC hadn't been invented and Matt was still in nappies when Caro had begun to earn her place in the sunlit uplands of city skyscrapers; even so, no one had so consistently demonstrated an understanding of the complex egos and unmitigated greed of fund managers, risk analysts and high net guys as Caro. But being young didn't stop Matt being smart. He understood completely Caro's worth. Perhaps the first who really had. Finally it felt to Caro that she had found the perfect relationship. Still, she was as far from telling him the real reason why she was taking this week off as she was from flying to the moon. Secrets and lies. She didn't feel bad; they happened in every partnership.

Relieved that she'd escaped the sound effects of Matt's bathroom (again), she slipped her phone away and went through her flight kit. Cashmere blanket, eye mask, moisturising mist spray… Then, switching her thermos to her free hand, she punched in her alarm code and closed her front door. The pile on the hallway carpet was such that residents could come and go in complete privacy. No Mrs Newalls here. Soundlessly she wheeled her suitcase across the carpet to the lift. Pressed the button. Stepped in.

In twenty years these early airport starts had never lost their thrill, and nowadays she had the act down to perfection. Handbag, matching flight bag, lipstick. Quick check in the lift mirror – not a hair out of place – and *ping!* Out into the foyer, through the doors. *Hello world!* That was how she felt. When the streets were empty and the taxi stood waiting, she felt like the earliest bird of them all –

that she could go anywhere, do anything! Not so much a lifetime as a universe away from the Caroline Hardcastle of Number 3 Artillery Terrace.

Ping!

Buzz.

Both her phone and the lift doors went at the same time.

Grabbing her phone, she stepped out. Up ahead, through the large front doors, she could see the car waiting, and inside, Helen's small head and all her hair. She always had such a lot of hair.

'Sorry, Caro. Just in the little boys' room there.' Matt's cheerful voice filled the foyer.

'Danny Abbott,' Caro said, and waved at Helen, gesticulating at her phone. 'Really, Matt?'

'Just Danny. No one else. I promise.'

'You said I had the week clear.'

'Don't give me a hard time, Caro. You sound like my wife.'

'He's an asshole, Matt.'

'He's in for 2.5 million, Caro. Besides… Wait a minute.' There was a muffled sound on the other end of the line. '*I know what time it is!*' Matt shouted.

Caro stretched the phone away to arm's length.

'You still there?' Matt said. Then, before she could answer, '*I'm not talking to you… No, it can't wait!*'

Caro sighed.

'Caro, you still there?'

'Of course.'

'Danny's away himself. You'll be fine. But if he does ring—'

'Answer it.'

'Good girl. Oh, and have a good time.'

The line went dead. 'Thanks,' Caro muttered, and dropped her phone back in her bag. *Have a good time.* How many times had she heard that in the last week? She felt such a fraud – never more so than yesterday afternoon when Mel, her secretary, had given her a hug and told her to look after herself.

Up ahead, in the back seat of the waiting car, Helen was making *hurry up!* circles with her arm. Caro's stomach tightened. With a gesture born of nerves, she smoothed her bobbed hair back behind her ear and walked towards the car.

Have a good time. What would Matt have said if he knew? Or Mel?

Helen smiled through the car window.

Caro smiled back. What would Helen be saying if she knew? In the time that had passed since she'd told Kay, she hadn't changed her mind. On the contrary, her conviction that Helen might react badly, might try to dissuade her, had only grown stronger. Her hand went to the other side of her head as she pushed more hair back. It was definitely thinning. Shiny wet slicks curling around the shower drain didn't lie. Without intervention she'd end up like her mother. Half-bald by sixty. Her fingers tightened around her thermos. *Without intervention?* When had she ever considered that a course of action? She plastered a smile on her face and walked across to the car.

'Sorry, love.' The driver had twisted in his seat to stretch his hand through his open window. 'No takeaways.'

Love? Instantly irritated, Caro looked to Helen, who nodded at her thermos.

'It's a thermos,' she said incredulously, and held it up.

The driver shrugged.

Caro leaned to his window. 'It's a thermos,' she repeated, forcing a lightness into her voice, wishing she had insisted on using her usual taxi firm. She'd tried, but Helen had insisted harder. *Leave it to me. You've got enough on your plate.* And because, in front of Helen and Kay, she always shied off from using her most used phrase – *my secretary will do it* – she had left it to Helen, who had been enthusiastic about Reg, the retired but reliable friend of a friend who did airport runs. Retired but officious, more like. She was almost surprised he wasn't wearing a high-vis vest. And this wasn't even a taxi. Clearly it was Reg's own car. A VW Passat? No takeaways in a VW Passat? 'The seal,' she said, smiling as sweetly as she could manage, 'is leakproof. It's really very secure.' And she turned the thermos upside down and shook it. 'Would you mind? I'm just hopeless without my coffee in the mornings.'

Reg hesitated. And then was conquered. Of course. Caro climbed in. How many had she met like this? Little Hitlers, scrupulously upholding the laws of their boardroom, their fiscal policy – now their VWs. God, it was tiresome. Still, it didn't take much. Not now she'd reached that age where men so easily believed women could be relied upon to behave – that was, if they'd even noticed them in the first place. She smoothed her jacket over her jeans. Clipped her seatbelt. Sipped, very discreetly, from her thermos.

Without moving her mouth, Helen whispered. 'Don't spill it…and don't mention Brexit.'

Caro looked at her.

Helen shrugged. 'He's very sweet when you get to know him.'

Caro grimaced. What she didn't say was that Reg, the bumptious old fart, could have initiated a car chase the likes of which would make *Mission Impossible* look like a *Carry On* film before she would spill a single drop from her thermos. Because it wasn't coffee. It was the booster juice she'd been drinking for weeks now. Foul-tasting and foul-smelling, but highly recommended by Alison Machowski herself. And the only way she could get it down was sip by tiny sip, minute by minute. What she wouldn't actually give for a strong black coffee. Thankfully, the leakproof seal also kept it aroma proof.

Beside her, Helen was giggling.

'What?' Caro turned, her voice low.

'Do you remember that time at uni, when we missed the last bus home one night and ended up having to take a taxi? The driver didn't want us because Kay had chips – remember? He didn't want them in the car?'

Caro smiled.

'And when he gave up, Kay took one step inside...' Helen broke off laughing. 'One,' she said raising a finger. 'And tripped! Chips everywhere! We couldn't speak for laughing! Do you remember?'

Caro smiled. She did remember, although she hadn't thought of it in years. 'He threw us out, didn't he?'

'He did. We walked in the end. No chips, no cabs, no coats.' Helen leaned back and sighed, a huge smile on her face. 'I cannot tell you how much I'm looking forward to this, Caro. Really I can't. It'll be just like old times.'

Leaning back in her own seat, Caro looked straight ahead. She had a sense of foreboding as the gulf between what they were both expecting showed itself for the first time. Old times? The night Helen was talking about was another lifetime ago. All her energy was focused on the possibility of a new life.

'Are you okay?'

She blinked and, looking down, saw Helen's hand on hers, unpeeling her fingers one by one. She'd been gripping the thermos so hard her knuckles had pooled white. Flinching, she pulled her hand back.

'Caro?' Helen's face was serious. 'Are you okay?'

'I'm fine.' Caro smiled. She opened her mouth, ready in the warmth of the moment to confess, to spill it all out… and then she closed it again. Kay's measured and cautious response had been enough of a canary in a coal mine. And that was Kay. Helen, she knew, wouldn't hold back on what she thought. 'End of a stressful week, that's all,' she said, and turned to look out of the window. It was funny. She knew when and with whom Helen had lost her virginity (although Helen had no idea when Caro had lost hers, and *that* was a secret she'd take to the grave), how she voted (Labour at uni, Lib Dems for a while, Labour again and last time, Green), what made her collapse with laughter (fake dog poo, whoopee cushions), and what reduced her to impotent, angry tears (news stories about child neglect). But she had no idea how she might react to the news that she intended to carry and give birth to a child to whom she was not genetically related, and long after her body should have been capable of doing so. It was all so new, wasn't it? Who could have imagined, when they met all those years ago, that this was something they should discuss?

Helen tipped her head back against the seat. 'Well,' she said, 'this will do you a world of good. And me. And Kay. I'm so glad she decided to come. I'm sure Alex will be fine. In fact, I think it will do them both good. A little space.'

'I'm glad she's coming too,' Caro murmured. She was. In her mind, Kay's arrival in Cyprus was the finish line. The real destination of this trip. By then the treatment would be over and, with Kay's support, she'd be ready to face Helen. Then everything would be okay. Two days. She had only to get through the next two days.

'So you two ladies off to Cyprus?' Through the rear-view mirror, Reg grinned at them. 'What's the big attraction there?'

Helen laughed. 'I'm not sure, Reg. Caro's the expert.'

Looking up, she caught Reg's eyes, flashed a tight smile back and sipped carefully from the thermos.

Three thousand miles and several hours later, Helen turned to look across the courtyard of the small hotel that was to be her home for the next week.

Wow!

She stuck her thumbs in her waistband and hitched her jeans free of her knickers. Wow! Across the white boundary walls bougainvillea scrawled like magenta graffiti, and beyond them fat limestone mountains rose to fill the horizon. On the lower slopes, a hundred thousand blue-black grapes glistened like tiny pigs on tiny spits. Above, the vegetation was scattered and stubbly, as if, left to itself, the mountain had decided it couldn't be bothered to shave. And then way up, across the blunt summits, green-black cypress trees fringed the skyline. Soldiers, every one of them. Wow, wow, wow.

She let out a long, low whistle. No, this wasn't England. She wasn't in the garden of her house, The Old Vicarage, with its green lawn and green shrubbery and its spring pastels of hyacinth and lilac. She was here and it was perfect. Understated and exclusive. Just like Caro, really. Beyond what she had been expecting, and surpassing every internet image she'd viewed. Yes, finally Caro had arrived. Wherever it was she'd been striving for all her life, judging by this, she had arrived.

Smiling to herself, Helen turned. In the middle of the courtyard stood a small fountain, yellow lotus flowers drifting in the green-blue water. So perfect! She stretched her arms forward, linked her hands together and let them fall. If Caro had arrived, where did that leave her? Still on a wet English beach with a pile of egg sandwiches?

Helen, Helen, Helen… She turned away to look in the opposite direction and there was the Mediterranean, all its eternal romance and epic history reduced to one long, irreverent wink. Sighing with pure pleasure, she put her hand inside her blouse and yanked her bra strap up (it still felt three sizes too small, this balcony thing). Caro had been right! Mountains to the east, Mediterranean to the west. And one whole week. No laundry. No cooking. No shopping. No cleaning. No… Lawrence.

As she reached her arms high above her head to stretch,

her blouse rose up, exposing her belly. The movement and the breeze on her skin felt good. It had been a long day, one sweaty hour after another – trains, planes, taxis. She needed a cool shower and she needed to stop thinking about Lawrence and Jack. They were fine. This was fine. Her son was capable of washing socks and her husband was on his way back.

Of course, he'd said when she had finally told him, making it sound as if she'd asked permission, which she was sure she hadn't. Then: *You'll be back before me, won't you?*

From a little distance behind, she could hear the man from the hotel chatting to the taxi driver. Turkish? Or she thought it was. She watched as they laughed together, their heads thrown back, the man from the hotel crossing his arms as he shook his head. Suddenly shy, Helen smoothed her blouse back over her stomach and, shielding her eyes from the sun, turned back to the mountains.

Across to the west, a village had sprouted from the deep fold of the land – who knew when? – scattering itself upward like a handful of square pebbles. Orange-tiled roofs, white cubes of houses, each with its own slash of balcony. And the pinnacle of a church, a four-sided bell tower, protected by a doll-sized railing. She sighed again. It really was perfect.

The men were still talking, and it seemed amazing to Helen as she stood and listened that they too weren't taking in this wonderful view. Did they even see it any more? This tranquillity? The taxi driver had almost snoozed his way from the airport. His elbow resting on the door frame, his hand cupping his brow as if to actually hide the scenery.

Strangely subdued, Helen put her hands in her pockets, scuffing her sandal through the dust. Wasn't that what she did too? Coming home, wrestling with shopping bags, exhausted after work, hadn't she too adopted a habit of not looking? Yes, she had. And from this distance, she saw for the first time just how true that was. Because *if* she looked, if she ever really looked at her house these days, she knew that where she had once seen romantic French doors to leave half-open on summer evenings, she now saw wood that always needed painting; where she'd once seen the perfect drive in which to park sleeping babies in elegant prams, she now saw gravel that always needed weeding. The original sash windows didn't let enough light in; the charming kitchen alcove was draughty; and the pantry, where she'd once imagined jars of home-made jams, was cold and nearly always empty, a packet of waxed lids slowly fossilising on a top shelf. What she saw when she looked at her house now was a mirror of her own dissatisfaction.

So yes, she could quite understand why the taxi driver hadn't bothered to look at this tremendous and beautiful view. Hands on hips, she squinted up again at the neat cube-houses of the village. They offered a vision of life that really did look perfect, but then, she hadn't invested anything more than this moment in them.

The harsh scrape of wheels scrunching on gravel had her turning and, so lost had she been in her thoughts, she was almost surprised to see the taxi leaving. When she turned back she saw that the man from the hotel, the one who had unloaded their bags, had now carried them to the door. He stood wiping the palms of his hands.

'Dusty?' Helen said. Everything was dusty. She was covered already.

He glanced up at her.

'Dusty,' she said again, and turned her own hands over to explain. But her hands were pink and plump – nothing like his.

If he saw the comparison, he was too polite to show it. He nodded. 'Always,' he said, and raised his arm in a chivalrous gesture, inviting her into the cool of the hotel lobby.

The glass doors slid open as she entered an oasis of cool light. The floor was a smooth sea of polished white marble, the desk a pale maple. By the stairs, in a pot so large it could have housed a human, stood a large olive tree twisting almost to the ceiling. To her right, a settee and chairs in sand-coloured pastels had been grouped around a glass coffee table. It was all as painfully tasteful as she'd expected of Caro. In fact, it looked like Caro's living room.

She looked across to the desk, where Caro, who had gone ahead, was still trying to get them checked in. The woman she was talking to reminded her of Kay. Short and broad, with a severe bowl haircut. On the desk next to her stood the most wildly beautiful orchid Helen had ever seen – blooms of rich butter-yellow, cupping inner lips of fiery orange. Like looking at a bunch of pouting mouths.

There had been a mix-up with the booking, apparently. That was all Helen knew. The extra room for her and Kay wasn't going to be available for another two days. Someone somehow had got Kay's arrival date mixed up with her own. The woman at reception, Caro said, had suggested that they share. Which had been fine by Helen but not with Caro, who'd become so disproportionately angry that Helen had had to walk away, back out to the courtyard.

And ten minutes later there she was in the same spot, still arguing their case, still wearing huge round sunglasses and the floppy hat she'd had on from the moment the plane touched down. She looked like a bug under a mushroom.

Helen wanted to laugh. She hadn't been away with Caro in decades, but clearly not much had changed. Thirty years ago, hadn't she turned up to catch the bus to Stonehenge with a suitcase on wheels and pearl drop earrings? They'd nearly wet their knickers. Kay had been in dungarees, Helen in an oversized plaid shirt. The bus had been stuffed full of filthy backpacks, string jewellery, braided hair and sweet petunia oil. It had been heading to Salisbury, for God's sake! Summer solstice at Stonehenge. *Give it up*, Caro she murmured as she watched the ongoing discussion. This, she thought, was probably what happened when you'd lived so long on your own. You got very used to your own space.

'Typical!' Caro's voice was loud and sudden. So loud, it made the petals on the orchid shake.

And from the corner of her vision, Helen saw the woman behind the desk reach a hand to slide it away out of danger.

'It really doesn't matter,' Caro exclaimed as she turned towards Helen, 'how many times you check and double-check! You can almost guarantee there'll be a cock-up somewhere along the line. I just hope—'

But Helen had switched off. She was looking over Caro's

95

shoulder at the woman behind reception, whose black eyes were boring into the back of Caro's head. This wasn't a good start. She waved a hand to cut Caro off. 'I'll just wait here,' she said, turning away. 'There…by the doors.'

Did Caro even notice? Helen wasn't sure. She hadn't paused for breath, turning back to the desk now to continue the tirade.

Helen went over and collapsed into one of the plump chairs. She leaned towards the cool of the window and took a deep breath. A few hours in and it was already difficult. *Caro* was difficult – far more so than usual, actually, and right now all Helen could think of was that if she could only keep looking at all those tiny houses, those little balconies with their neat tables and neat chairs, she could avoid the storm in a teacup of mixed-up bookings and hold on to the feeling of peace she'd experienced when standing in the courtyard. The feeling that this was a wonderful place and she was going to have a wonderful time.

Tipping her chin up, she closed her ears. The difference between her and Caro was simple. Caro still believed, and always had, that life could be planned. Would actually respond if she shouted *Sit!* When, Helen thought, as she closed her eyes, was she ever going to learn that it didn't work like that? That things went wrong, and sometimes it wasn't a big deal and other times it was. A tiny tear escaped her left eye, as it always did when she thought of the biggest wrong deal in her life. Her perfect, dead, baby boy. She pressed the tear dry. It was always the left eye. Then tilting her head to the sun that streamed through the window, she breathed out and let the sunlight warm her face.

96

*

'Right then!'

Minutes later, or seconds – really she had no idea – Helen opened her eyes to the sight of a large oval plate looming above her. Caro's sun hat. It had her thinking of circus acts – plates on sticks.

'Finally,' Caro breathed, as if she'd just completed a marathon or merged a conglomerate of banks. 'I've got it all sorted! You need to come and fill a form in. Me too.' She turned back to the reception desk. 'I'm afraid we will have to share tonight, and probably tomorrow. Is that okay with you?'

'Of course,' Helen shrugged. It had been fine half an hour ago when the scary woman at reception had first suggested it.

'Oh, and they've given you and Kay an upgrade. As they should. You've got a jacuzzi now.'

'Lovely.' Helen pushed her sunglasses back on her head. 'But don't you want to take that? It was your holiday in the first place.'

'No, no.' Caro took off her hat and began fanning herself. 'God, it's so hot.'

'Caro.' Helen reached out and put her hand on Caro's arm. She did look flushed. Then again, she had all day. 'Relax,' she said. 'We're here now. I'm perfectly happy to share.'

'Okay,' Caro managed unconvincingly. 'Okay.'

Helen frowned. She'd spent her entire adult life surrounded by first boyfriends then a husband, babies, toddlers, children, teenagers, dogs, cats, rabbits. For years she hadn't even been able to do a poo in peace. Sharing was a breeze. But for Caro? She felt a pang of guilt. For someone so accustomed to their own space, sharing must be hard. 'It'll be like old times,' she tried.

'Old times?'

'You know? The flat on Sydney Road?'

Caro looked at her. 'God, Helen, that was several lifetimes ago.'

'I suppose.' And her smile faded as she watched Caro struggle to stuff sunglasses and papers into what looked like an already hopelessly crowded handbag. Her hands were actually shaking. As if the uncontained nervousness were contagious, Helen took a step back, slipped her hands into the back pockets of her jeans, and stared down at the floor.

Over the years there had been many times when Caro had gone on for so long about the stress of this or that deadline, the travelling, the massive responsibility of truly eye-watering figures, that she'd just switched off (as, she suspected, had Kay). Hadn't she had pressures of her own? Hadn't Kay? Life was what it was. But standing here now, watching Caro's fluttering hands, a warm shame swept through Helen. Perhaps she hadn't understood at all the kinds of pressures Caro faced on a day-to-day basis? What was clear, what couldn't be missed or misinterpreted, was that Caro really needed this break and had obviously been counting on a space of her own. On top of which was the undeniable fact that she wouldn't even be here if it hadn't been for Caro's kind and spontaneous invitation. She'd be standing by the sink, looking at the debris of dinner, shouting *be careful!* or *ring me!* at the front door, Jack already halfway down the driveway. Or stalking Libby on Facebook (which was hopeless, not least because Libby never touched Facebook and had been at least three steps ahead of her on social media since she was fifteen). She took a few steps over to the window and looked up at the wonderful view, and it hadn't changed; it was just as wonderful as it had been five minutes ago. Tears welled. 'I'm just so happy to be here,' she murmured to herself, and repeated in a louder voice as she turned to Caro, 'I'm just so happy to be here!'

Caro gave a small smile. 'It is nice.'

'Oh, Caro.' Helen rushed over and threw her arms around Caro's neck. 'It's perfect. It's bloody perfect. Thank you for inviting me.'

For a moment Caro stood as stiff as a key. Then, with an awkward pat on Helen's back, she said, 'Well, thank you for coming.' And her voice, ragged at the edges, was so at odds with the imperious confident tones of just a few moments ago it might have been a different person.

Keeping her hands on Caro's shoulders, Helen pulled back. 'You really do need this week, don't you?'

'Pfff.' Caro brushed her off. 'I'm fine. Let's get these forms done.'

'Right. Yes.' She turned to the reception desk and was surprised to see that the scary woman had been replaced by the man who had carried their bags in. He smiled as they approached, and handed them a check-in form each and a couple of pens.

Then, feeling oddly self-conscious, Helen stood side by side with Caro as, heads dipped, they filled in the blanks.

99

First, Caro couldn't remember her mobile number. 'I never ring it!' she muttered, rummaging through a handbag of leaflets and tissues and, now that she was closer, what looked to Helen like a lot of medication. Then she got her postcode mixed up. Did it end '4NC' or '4NP'?

With her own form completed, Helen stood aside and watched Caro struggle to remember the details of her life. Never had she seen her friend so agitated. It filled her with a thin layer of worry. From the outside, Caro's life always seemed so smooth – which, of course, didn't mean a damn thing. Once again Helen moved away to the front door. She didn't want to think too much about the stresses Caro might be under. Just like she didn't want to think about her own problems. They were here, in paradise, and a week should be long enough for the sediment of time and distance to gently wash away. For them to talk. She was looking forward to it.

Over to her right, on the glass coffee table, she caught sight of a stand displaying brightly coloured flyers. Willingly distracted from Caro's faffing, she picked one up, skim-reading what was an advertisement for sailing lessons.

Beginners welcome.

Sailing? As Helen leaned forward to put the flyer back, the idea seemed to jump clear of its A5 margins and land on her nose, both tiny and huge, *very* close up, impossible to ignore. Sailing? Even the word made her smile. Slowly she walked back across to reception, where the man stood reading her completed form.

He had, she couldn't help noticing, a noble face. Weather-beaten in ways that made men more handsome, as if he'd survived hand-to-hand battles or sailed oceans. His nose was strong – a Roman nose – and he had high, clean cheekbones, and the greyness of his hair wasn't grey at all but the silver of molten mercury. Silver hair, copper skin. She couldn't stop looking, and the longer she looked the warmer she became. Which hadn't happened in... well, she couldn't remember. Not this century, anyway. She couldn't, she realised, take her eyes off him.

His head was down, reading through her form, and standing there Helen knew that he knew she was watching, and it felt as if he was reading her life. All her secrets, her unspoken desires rising up from the page. Her face – she could feel it – had flushed a deep magenta-red. She had been on HRT less than a week. Was this the effect? When, finally, he looked up, straight at her, she nearly imploded.

'Ready?' She turned to Caro, her voice a busted squeal of embarrassment.

6

Kay's Bag for Life was on its last legs. Overloaded with thirty Year 11 maths papers, the handles had thinned to wire, cutting angry pink slashes across her palm. She switched hands and used her shoulder to push through the unlocked porch door of her parents' house. Before she went in, she took a quick look up the road towards her own house. The front window was dark, which meant that Alex would still be at work at the garden centre. She breathed a sigh of relief. She might get home to a silent house, might have half an hour on her own.

Manoeuvring her way through her parents' front porch was to manoeuvre her way through her mother's decline. Hanging on the wall were the walking sticks she no longer used, one with a fold-out seat. Tucked under the bench was her Walker on Wheels. Waiting by the side of the door, as forlorn as a jilted lover, was her wheelchair. It hadn't been used in six months, and everyone was now past the point of believing it ever would be. She turned her key in the inner front door and was immediately hit by the unmistakable scent of ill health – that blend of still air, urine and disinfectant. Since the nurse sent by the council had deemed her mother ineligible for free incontinence sheets, it had fallen on Kay to source them, order them, keep them stocked. Sometimes she forgot, and when she did, the pads her mother wore weren't enough. Then the mattress got soaked and had to be sponged, and the smell permeated, infiltrating curtain fabric, settling on cushions.

The hall was dark. She could make out the shape of her father's jacket and cap on the peg, the rectangle of the frame that held an aerial view of her parents' pride and joy – this bungalow. At the edge of the photo Kay's own house was actually visible, and sometimes on her way out she'd stand and look and wonder why it was she'd never made it out of the frame.

She put her bags of books on the floor, shoved her hand deep in her pocket and pulled out her phone. It had been buzzing like a trapped wasp all the way from the bus stop.

A text.

Three.

From Caro.

Mix-up here. Having to share with Helen tonight and tomorrow. Will all be sorted before you arrive, but it's hard.

Helen's at the bar. Time for a quick chat?

Kay dropped the phone back into her bag. What she wouldn't give to be at a bar! But it was Thursday evening, she still had one day left of what was turning out to be her worst term ever, and she wasn't joining them until Saturday. So right now she had as much time for a quick chat as a fox running from hounds.

She checked her watch. Her father would be in the living room, watching his quiz show. And sure enough, as she peered along the gloomy hall she saw the unmistakable blue flicker of a television screen coming from the open living room door.

She ran her hands through her hair, winced at her reflection in the spotted hall mirror and walked to the doorway. Across the room her father sat in his favourite chair; she could see the back of his head, speckled with sunspots, his fingers tapping together on his lap. Leaning against the door frame, Kay waited. Disturbing him felt wrong, dragging him back into the twilight of his life unnecessary.

'Hello, love,' he said without turning to her.

Kay smiled. Sometimes there was no need for any dragging. Sometimes he just sensed she was there.

'Hi, Dad.' Moving his spectacles, she perched herself on the arm of his chair. 'Have you had your tea?'

When he looked up at her, his eyes were watery. 'Had a lovely lasagne,' he said, and took a handkerchief to wipe the corner of each eye. 'Craig popped it in the microwave for me.'

'Is he still here?' Kay said, and she looked out to the hall. 'He should have gone ages ago.'

'He said he'd wait to see you. I told him to go, but he said he'd clear up and wait.'

'Okay,' Kay nodded. Craig still here was the only good news in a day filled with seven shades of shit. He was the human equivalent of a Malteser, light and moreish, designed to make you feel better. He was – after the email she'd just received from Nick, her headmaster – exactly what she needed. Who, she thought for the 700th time, sends an email like that, Thursday afternoon before the Easter holidays? Especially when he wasn't going to be available to discuss it tomorrow. God, she missed Lizzy, her old headmistress. Back in the day, Lizzy finished off terms with drinks to '70s hits in the staffroom, not pompously worded emails that outlined parental *concerns*.

'Would you look at this.' Her father waved a hand at the TV. 'This idiot calls himself a scientist and he can't name the chemical symbol for calcium.'

'Maybe he's a different type of scientist.'

'Like what?'

'I don't know. Political science? Social?'

'Pfff.' Her father shook his head. 'That's all gobbledygook to me.'

Kay stared at the TV. 'It is a bit to me,' she said. '*Ca*. Calcium is *Ca*.'

'That's my girl.' Without turning away from the screen, her father patted her knee. 'That's my smart girl.'

'I'll check in on Mum.'

'She might be sleeping already. Craig said she'd slipped off.'

'Okay. I'll take a quick peek anyway.' And she leaned forward and kissed the top of her father's head, eased herself up and went out into the hall.

Craig, her mother's carer, came mid-mornings to make sure both her parents had taken their medicines, to help her mother shower and, if there was time, prepare a light lunch. In the early evenings he came back, to help her

105

mother get ready for bed and to check they'd eaten the light lunch. Sometimes they forgot – medicines, food…just as she sometimes forgot the incontinence pads. Of course her mother couldn't remember anything, but her father? A man who could name the entire periodic table but couldn't be relied upon to eat? It wasn't memory, she knew that. It was lack of interest, which was worse. Hand on the doorknob, she stood outside her mother's bedroom.

'She's sleeping,' Craig whispered. Standing in the rectangle of yellow light that came from the kitchen, he was drying a saucepan.

'Already?'

'We had a traumatic start to the day.'

'And I had a traumatic end,' she muttered.

'Mrs Patterson!' Craig waved the tea towel at her.

Kay looked at him, and despite everything there was the bubble of a laugh in her throat. 'Will you stop calling me Mrs Patterson!'

'Sorry.' He was trying not to laugh as well. 'Let her sleep,' he said. 'She really was exhausted.'

'Okay.' Reluctantly Kay released the door handle. Just a year ago she would have come in, sat down next to her mother and told her all about her day. About Nick's email, the likes of which Kay had never received. The cold shock of reading it and the outrage she'd felt, which had morphed into disbelief. And her mother, an ex-teacher herself, would have understood, would have known what to say and would have been able to help calm the storm of emotion that raged inside. Was it only a year? Now her mother was as unreachable as a photograph. Silently she touched her fingers to her lips and blew a kiss through the closed door, yanked her jumper down her hips and came into the kitchen. 'It's been fifteen years, Craig,' she said. 'And I've been divorced from Mr Patterson for eleven of them.'

Craig giggled. 'I can't help it,' he said. 'You'll always be Mrs Patterson to me.'

Ah, he was definitely as sweet as a Malteser. This goofy, lanky kid. Hopeless at maths, as quiet as a dormouse, equally ignored and abused by his contemporaries. He had obviously found his calling in life, and Kay couldn't be more thankful. In the last three years, since they'd been paying for daily help, they'd been through more carers than she cared to remember. Sometimes they didn't speak English, which made communication difficult. Sometimes they didn't speak at all, which made communication very difficult. Sometimes they were competent but cold and sometimes they were over-the-top friendly but completely useless. Like the girl, who never once checked whether her father had taken his blood pressure medication. She'd only found this out when he complained of feeling dizzy and she opened the kitchen cupboard and found the source of the problem.

But now they had Craig, who'd been with them a full year and whose company was often the highlight of her day. They'd recognised each other straight away, teacher and ex-pupil, and it was a source of joy for Kay to see the man he'd become – selfless and generous, funny, kind, with an endless pit of intuitive empathy. It had actually affected her teaching, softened her stance in the classroom, because she couldn't help thinking the world would be a better place

– much better – if there were more Craigs, for example, and fewer like Zachery Woods.

Ouch! The name had her screwing her face up, as if she'd just eaten a lemon. She'd do better not thinking about it. Zachery's mother, Amanda, was the reason for Nick's email. And although he'd been careful to label the points that she'd raised as 'concerns', Kay wasn't fooled. It was a thinly veiled complaint. Not official, but still there. The first she'd had in nearly thirty years of teaching, and sent less than forty-eight hours before she was flying out to her first holiday this century. Timing, Kay, timing.

'Gawd, you look like me at the end of a Saturday night,' Craig said, interrupting her thoughts. 'Want a brew? Or something stronger?' He rubbed his palms together, singing, 'Someone's going on holiday!'

And before she could respond, he'd skipped out of the room.

She collapsed into the nearest chair. She really needed to put the issue out of her mind, if for no other reason than that there was nothing she could do. Nothing at all – which, of course, hadn't stopped her thus far chewing it over and over, as relentless as a dog with gristle.

It was true that Zachery Woods wasn't doing as brilliantly as he should. This was down to his fluctuating discipline and not, as his mother was suggesting, Kay's dislike of the boy. Mrs Woods had even gone as far as suggesting that Zac move class, which had shaken Kay to her core. She was a good teacher. And she prided herself on her patience and impartiality. So why, very deep down, had the thought that Amanda Woods could be right implanted itself in her mind as firmly as a tiny, fat Buddha?

She knew why. She *didn't* like Zac – hadn't since she'd first met him as a tiny Year Sixer. Sometimes – not often – this happened. Every teacher she had ever worked with had experienced one or two children they could never bring themselves to actually like. But voicing this was strictly staffroom chat among only the closest of colleagues. It never manifested itself in the classroom. Except... She leaned forward and rested her chin on her hand. Except the last five years had taken their toll. She was exhausted. She didn't have the energy she'd once had for smart-arse kids bent on disrupting the class. She'd snapped, shouted louder and reacted more strongly than she might have done in the past – all of which had been water off a duck's back for Zac. Or so she would have thought – if she'd actually had time to think, that was... Dropping her head into her hands, Kay rubbed her eyes. If she was at fault, if she was holding the boy back...that was unforgivable.

'Here we go! This will see you right!' Craig was standing in the doorway, a huge grin on his face, a bottle of whisky in his hands.

Kay frowned at the bottle. 'What's with the lines?'

He held it up. Thick black marker lines had been drawn across the outside of the bottle. 'I like to keep an eye on how much your dad has. He's allowed a nip before bedtime and that's it.'

Kay smiled. She knew this. Knew that her dad had a sip of whisky at night. What she didn't realise was that Craig had been monitoring it. Her eyes pricked with warm tears. What did it matter in the end? A* or F, Oxford or Luton Tech.

None of it would be worth a sod when the likes of Amanda
Woods reached her twilight years and couldn't wipe her own
arse. Then she'd consider herself bloody lucky if Zac turned
out to be an inch the person Craig had become. Like she was
bloody lucky herself to have a son whose day was complete
and happy working at the local garden centre and eating his
tea with his mum. Alex hadn't even got an F. In anything.
And Craig? She pursed her lips together, trying to remember.
'What did you get in GCSE maths again?' she said.

'F,' he said. 'Five per cent of which was for getting my
name right.'

Kay let out a raw, short laugh. Yes, Mrs Woods would
be very lucky if, when she needed it, she found a Craig in
her life. The thought cheered her enormously.

He leaned forward and poured Kay a slug, screwed the
lid back on and lifted his own teacup. 'Cheers,' he said,
nudging his mug with her tumbler.

'How come you're still here?' She glanced at her watch.
Craig was now ten minutes over his allotted half hour.
'Hope you don't think you're going to get paid for watching
me drink whisky?'

'My 7.15 died,' Craig said, wide-eyed over the rim of
his mug. 'Svetla found him this morning. Stiff as a plank,
sheet by his chin. Very neat.'

'Oh God,' she laughed. It was the way he said it.

He shrugged. 'Perils of the job, Mrs Patt... *Kay*.' He
winked. 'You never know what you're going to find when
you open that door.'

'They should pay you danger money.' Kay smiled. 'Or
trauma money.'

'They give us 10.8 minutes' travel pay instead,' Craig said, deadpan. 'No matter how long it takes.'

'10.8 minutes!' Again she laughed. 'How did they come to that amount?'

Craig raised his eyebrows, pretended to think. 'Perhaps they were in your maths class?'

And *again* she laughed. She'd laughed more in the last five minutes than she had in the last five days.

He stood up and went to the sink. 'Anyway, it's a blessing.' He swished his mug out and turned, wiping his hands on a tea towel. 'Until the slot gets filled I've got a bit of extra time to chat. And after the day I've had!'

'Was it long?'

'Long? It's lasted a week, and it's not over yet. This afternoon I've had two sits, four tea calls, two medication prompts, three undresses and three put-to-beds, and I've still got a catheter to empty.' He was using his fingers to count, all over the place.

Kay sat watching in a glow of whisky burn and affection.

'Oh! And last night some lazy arse night shift dickhead went and left a commode by the side of one of my ladies' beds. The stink! I nearly keeled over! Plus your mum had a right cob on this morning when I tried to get her into the shower.'

'Cob on' was Craig's code for 'aggressive'. A word that shouldn't be possible to use in the same sentence as 'your mum'. And yet here they were. Keeping her voice low, she said, 'Did she hit you? Tell me the truth.'

'I ducked.'

'Oh, Craig.' Kay put her tumbler down.

'Don't worry.' Craig shrugged. 'I'd be miffed too if someone made me get up and then tried to get me straight in the shower!'

Kay's smile was weak. This was the third time in as many weeks that her mother had become...violent? She swallowed hard. Just thinking the word was a violence in itself, but she'd seen it with her own eyes, and it was *violent*. The fury and strength her mother seemed to be able to summon.

'I'm really sorry to say this,' Craig started, 'but I'm not sure how much longer your dad will be able to cope.'

'I shouldn't go.' She shook her head. 'I'll ring and cancel. I can't go and—'

'*Mrs Patterson!*'

'*Kay*, for heaven's sake!'

'Kay, then! That isn't what I meant!'

Kay's lips twitched. 'Are you telling me off, Craig?'

'Yes, I am.' He laughed. 'Feels odd, doesn't it?'

'Okay.' She put her head to one side. 'Okay.'

'And I haven't finished.' He came and sat down next to her. 'You need this holiday more than anyone I know. Except for your dad, of course. I think he might need one more.'

'Has he said something?'

Craig nodded.

And she was so surprised she didn't speak.

'He won't say anything to you, of course, but he's really looking forward to the break. As much as you should be. Your mum will be fine. Ashdown Home is a really nice place. I'll still come in every day. And I'll be taking him across to see her Tuesday and Thursday. He wants to have a pub lunch out. Did you know that?'

Kay shook her head. 'No,' she said, 'I didn't.'

'So! You can keep your Cyprus, thank you very much.' He patted her arm. 'And your Club 50. Or whatever it is.'

'Did...did he really say that?'

'Yes,' Craig said simply. 'He did.'

Kay turned away. She hadn't anticipated this. Hadn't understood how much her father needed and wanted a respite. He'd never given any indication that this was the case. Then again, how could he? Family was everything, until it really *was* everything.

'Right then.' Craig stood up. 'As my eight o'clock is still alive, I suppose I'd better get on. There's a little bit of lasagne left if you want to take it home?'

She shook her head. 'I'm going for a big shop after school tomorrow. Make sure everyone's stocked up while I'm away.'

'There's enough cream of tomato to fill Kielder Water.'

'Alex as well. You know how he is, Craig.'

'Right.' Craig picked up his bag. 'Well, if you're going, make sure you get some Club biscuits in then. Orange. Not those purple fruit and nut things.' And with a last Malteser-light smile he was gone.

Back home her house was silent, filled with a few swirling dust motes and the beep of a washing machine long having finished its cycle. Alex's laundry. Which she would leave, all the socks having to be hung from the clothes horse in a way that only Alex understood. She switched the bleeping off (whoever was responsible for programming an alarm into a washing machine deserved to be shot; she'd pull the trigger herself), filled the kettle and stood looking out of the window, thinking what she always thought when she looked at the hulk of tarpaulin that had taken over her back lawn.

Who, apart from Alex, would buy and attempt to renovate a decrepit old motorcycle off nothing more than a few *Rust to Riches* episodes on Netflix?

It was just like the raspberry tea he had come home with a few months ago. She'd never (as far as she could remember) said she liked raspberry tea. True enough, she liked raspberries – very much – and she drank tea. Alex always got from A to B without a single diversion – always had and always would. Like the French thing. When he was eight years old and they'd watched *Lady and the Tramp* and he'd then gone into school and told his whole class he could speak French. *Tell us*, the teacher had said. So he did: *Oh la la pussycat!* Even the teacher had laughed. He experienced the world literally, and as long as she could keep him safe, the simplicity of his needs would surely mean a contentment with life that was enviable. *As long as she could keep him safe.* She closed her eyes against the dark lines of the tarpaulin, underneath which lay the beginnings of a motorcycle. A digestive biscuit and a long cuddle on her lap weren't going to be much help when he took a curve too fast or hit a barrier at ninety, which she was so terribly sure he would, sooner or later.

The rise of the kettle's whistle had her turning, switching it off and reaching for... She pushed her Yorkshire tea aside and took instead the red foil packet at the back of her

114

cupboard. It wasn't even open. In six months she'd never even tried it. She tapped the contents loose, cut open the top and spooned a large teaspoon of raspberry-flavoured tea leaves into the pot.

Upstairs in her bedroom she stretched out on the bed and flicked on her new reading light, made possible by the new electric socket that Shaky – that Shook (she must stop getting it wrong) had put in. The last of the evening sun moved across the wall opposite, and Kay leaned her head against the quilted headboard and looked around her bedroom. Her personal oasis. After her divorce from Martin, she'd papered these walls with looping flowers that had long, slender stems and fragile petals. She'd chosen gauzy, impractical curtains and artificial orchids, and in this way had unconsciously set about creating a space for herself that the mere company of a man could not hope to compete with. It never failed to restore her. She reached into her handbag, feeling for her book, but her hand found her phone instead. She pulled it out, reread Caro's message and batted out a swift response.

Sorry. All done in. Talk tomorrow. You'll be fine.

Finding her book and opening it at the page last read, Kay settled back. Her eyes had closed before she'd turned the page.

7

Helen was up before sunrise, tiptoeing around the room, pulling on jogging pants and T-shirt, fishing out the teabags she'd brought from home. She felt energised and excited, a wholly novel way to start the day. She'd slept like a baby and, judging by the gentle snores coming from the other twin bed, so had Caro.

Moving quietly, she made her tea and slipped through the lightweight curtains out onto the balcony. Here the air was fresh and cool and dark. She settled into a chair, pulled a blanket around her shoulders and watched as perpendicular lines grew into houses and mountains reclaimed their mass, as the ink sky paled and a rising line of light pushed heaven away from earth. The new day was revealing itself, as shy and slow as a child peeling hands from face.

Across the foothills, sunrays the colour of fresh honey transformed the church bell into a nugget of poured gold, and dusky roof tiles lightened to a fresh salmon pink. Birds swooped high, gliding back, stretching their wings. A dog barked, shutters were thrown open and the first car trundled past, heading for the coast.

Hands wrapped around her cup, bare feet tucked under the blanket, Helen sighed, and it was nothing like the way her mother used to sigh. The distance between herself and her normal life could not, in that moment, have been greater. She felt rejuvenated, as if she'd bathed in the fountain of eternal life...something like that, something tinkling and silver and light against her eyelids, which she closed now, as she turned her face to the rising sun.

She'd been there a minute – perhaps not even that – before Caro appeared, stalked across to the balcony and leaned over.

Opening her eyes, Helen felt a tremendous surge of affection, as if she would get up and hug Caro, even though Caro hated hugs. Because if Caro hadn't insisted, she never would have come, and now she was here she couldn't imagine being anywhere else. It was all so magical.

'It's a bit disappointing.'

Disappointing? Helen turned and looked back across the valley. Were they seeing the same thing?

'I thought we'd get more of a sea view.' Wrapping her arms around herself, Caro turned to face her. 'And it's freezing.'

Helen didn't answer. Instead she dipped her chin and sipped her tea. It was true the day hadn't yet begun to warm, which for her made it all the more delicious. So ripe she wanted to leap into it. Run down to the ocean (however far away) and plunge herself in. 'We can see it,' she murmured.

'The sea?' Caro turned back to the view, hand at her eyes as she strained to look. 'Only just.'

Just? Helen stood up. The moment had been spoiled, a

moment more perfect than any she'd experienced in a long time…a very long time. 'I'm going to take a shower,' she muttered.

Back in the room, she snatched up her toilet bag and a towel. Before she closed the bathroom door she glanced out at Caro, and the idea struck her that this would have been exactly Lawrence's reaction. That he too would have been disappointed – the sea view not being the sea view he had been expecting. Not enough of a sea view. That he and the sea could, and should, have done better.

She shut the door, took off her bathrobe and, ripping open the foil packet, took out her Novafem. If she could, she would have swallowed a week's worth in one day. The irritation she was feeling right now, she hadn't felt…well, for a few days, actually. She stared at herself in the mirror. Perhaps they were both going to need their space – Caro from her and she from Caro.

But any bad mood that might have lingered slipped away when she came downstairs into the dining room and saw the breakfast buffet laid out like a gift from the gods. So beautiful, so prepared, it took her breath away. Glistening black olives and virgin-white crumbling cheeses. Sliced melon, so ripe it melted into the plate. Grapes, oranges. Yogurts, cereals. Crispy bread, fluffy bread, seeded bread, dark, serious-looking bread. Eggs, scrambled and boiled. Strips of streaky fat bacon, hams, tomatoes… The sight of it all, with not a pan or a spatula or a sulky teenager taking the best bits first, paralysed her.

'Helen.' From behind she felt Caro's nudge. 'Today would be good.'

Helen took a plate and walked the length of the buffet and back again. She stopped in front of the tomatoes and became wholly distracted by the pastries, where pains au chocolat and gloopy custards competed with exquisitely fine baklava. She was a kid in a sweet shop, a dog outside a butchers.

She filled her plate, joined Caro at the table and wolfed the food down.

Caro picked at a boiled egg.

Returning to the buffet, she filled her plate and once again emptied it.

Caro ate half a tomato.

The third time she went back, she headed straight for the baklava. Exquisite. There was no other word to describe such a creation. She put two on her plate and one in her mouth, turned, and bumped into the silver-haired man who had signed them in yesterday.

'It's good to see such a healthy appetite,' he said, and smiled at her plate.

As if she had a scarlet light bulb behind each cheekbone, Helen went pillar-box red. Syrup leaked from the side of her mouth. The silver-haired man turned and took a paper napkin, which he handed to her. Was there a colour of mortification deeper than red? Purple? Magenta? Whatever it was, her cheeks found it. She nodded a thank you and mopped her mouth. The amount she'd just eaten wasn't healthy – unless you were a horse – and somehow it was a thousand times worse that it was this man who'd noticed her stuffing her face. Already the waistband of her elasticated jeggings was cutting into her belly. Back home she usually had a cup of tea and a bowl of Bran Flakes for breakfast, and she really wanted to tell him this. But with a mouthful of baklava it was impossible. And then what would she say anyway? That she'd got overexcited?

'Did you sleep well?' he asked.

With the back of her hand at her mouth to disguise the fact that she was swallowing huge chunks of pastry, she nodded. 'Very well, thank you.' Then, because she had an inexplicable need for him to see beyond her appetite, she added, 'I was up early enough to see the sunrise.'

He nodded. 'Me too.'

'Really?'

'Yes. Every day.'

'Oh.' Helen didn't know what to say. She felt a little foolish. As if she was the last to discover something everyone else knew. 'It was so beautiful,' she managed.

'Yes,' he said. 'Every day is beautiful in the beginning.'

Stunned, Helen stared at him. In twenty-five years of marriage she'd never heard her husband say anything that came even close.

He lifted his arm and, in the same chivalrous manner as yesterday, indicated that she should go ahead of him.

Back at the table, Caro was now picking her way through a pot of strawberry yogurt. Helen sat herself down. Her appetite had evaporated, swept away by what could only be described as excitement. The silver-haired man had disappeared and, sipping her coffee, she found herself wondering what was making her feel like this. The man? His poetic way of speaking? She put her cup down and looked at the baklava on her plate. One thing she was sure of – it wasn't the pastries that had got her worked up. She pushed them aside and, opposite, Caro did the same with the yogurt pot. Helen glanced at it. Barely a teaspoon's worth had been eaten. Added to the slice of egg and half a tomato. Then there was the tiny bowl of soup Caro had had for dinner last night… Helen picked her cup up again. Something was wrong. Caro had always been whippet-thin, but she still ate. Sipping her coffee, she watched as a woman at the neighbouring table lifted her handbag and took out sunglasses. It made Helen think of the medication she'd seen in Caro's handbag yesterday, and although Caro had always nurtured symptoms, depending on them the way grass depended on rain, Helen felt suddenly and strangely fearful. None of them was getting any younger. This was the time of life when it started. She put her cup down.

'Caro?'

From under one stiffly arched brow, Caro looked up.

'If I ask you something, will you be honest with me?'

Now Caro's other eyebrow arched.

'Are you really okay? I mean, apart from the normal stuff?'

Something passed across Caro's eyes – Helen was sure of it. It wasn't anything more than a shadow, a weight that seemed to tug at her lids, like a reluctant shade pulled down to block the sun—

'Is that it?' Caro said brightly.

—and then whipped back up again.

'Yes,' Helen said carefully, 'that's it.'

'I'm fine. Why?'

Helen shrugged. Now she was struggling. The moment had been so brief she wasn't sure it had happened. 'Well,' she said, 'for a start, you've hardly eaten anything since we got here.'

Caro smiled. 'It's the travelling, Helen. It always takes a bit of time for my stomach to settle.'

'Okay.' Stalled, she picked up her cup. Something felt off. A semitone out of tune. She hadn't been away with Caro for many years, and people change; even so, she could spot the sliver of inauthenticity in her friend's responses. They'd known each other too long for her not to. 'Plus,' she started, and – glancing sideways – saw Caro flinch. 'I couldn't help noticing, yesterday at reception. You have a lot of medication with you...in your handbag.'

Caro didn't answer. She took the filmy lid of the yogurt and pushed it back into place.

The action was infuriating. Was Caro sick? And if so, why the hell wouldn't she say? Helen leaned across the table. 'Is it anything I need to be worried about? You would tell me, wouldn't you? You would say?'

Smiling, Caro looked up. 'Helen,' she soothed. 'There isn't anything to tell. Apart from hay fever, indigestion, HRT, allergy tablets, what's in my handbag is just the normal essentials of a middle-aged woman. That's all.' She smiled again. 'And a few supplements.'

'You sure?'

'I'm sure. Now, we're on holiday, aren't we? Relax!'

Relax? Helen finished the last of her coffee. Caro had been a cat on a hot tin roof yesterday. And really? The normal essentials of a middle-aged woman? She was just as middle-aged as Caro, and stuff like that didn't rattle around in her handbag. Then again, it never had. Helen stretched her arms behind her head. One way or the other, Caro had been "sick" with something all her life. Allergic to cats, allergic to candles. Stress headaches, sensitive stomach. Heartburn, PMT. Her symptoms were as real to her as the tooth fairy to a child. She'd just forgotten, that was all. It had been so long since they'd spent any real time in each other's company, she'd forgotten. That poky bathroom cabinet in the Sydney Road flat, for example. It had been stuffed full of Night Nurse and aspirin, paracetamol, Rennies, and always a bottle of something bright pink. She yawned, hands across her very full stomach, a little bit queasy and full to the gills. Night Nurse! How silly to have even been worried. Caro was as Caro was, and the only course of action was to leave her to heal herself in whichever imagined way she believed she needed.

'Now!' Caro folded her napkin in half and placed it on the table. 'What would you like to do today?'

'What would I like to do?'

'Yes. This is your holiday too! You can choose. Except...'

'What?'

'We're not buying milk!'

Helen laughed. 'No, no milk.' She leaned back in her chair and looked out over the swimming pool. Her. Helen Winters. Mother of three, two living. (Never, ever would she allow herself not to include all of them.) Wife of one. Part-time health centre receptionist, avid gardener. BA in History. Former assistant marketing manager and a one-time shared recipient of a Heritage Society *Enhancing*

Customer Experience award. What did she want to do today? She looked up. 'Sailing,' she said. 'I would like to go sailing.'

And if only it had been as easy as that.

She watched as Caro digested her answer.

It was taking some time, and the moment reminded Helen of her birthday lunch – the pauses she'd allowed to mature without feeling any need to apologise or excuse or explain herself. Caro had asked her what she wanted to do and (knowing it would not be the expected response) she'd answered honestly. And yes, last night over dinner they had talked about visiting the castle, but actually what she really wanted to do was go sailing.

'Mmm.' Caro picked up her cup.

Still Helen didn't speak. She stretched out her legs and stuck her hands under her waistband, relieving the pressure (she really had eaten too much). The moment wasn't without its tension. *Answering honestly* felt raw, like losing a skin, the layer of herself that always put everyone else first. But it was funny, the change she felt inside. As if, waking up on her fiftieth birthday, her mind had run a quick tally of the days left, and in response had shaken itself like a wet dog to come away lighter. Far less inclined to get weighted down in niceties.

Caro put her cup down and glanced away towards the pool, and Helen couldn't help smiling the smallest of smiles. *She had answered honestly.* It was radical and different and it had her wondering why she'd never felt able to do it before. Where might she be, who might she be, if sometimes, just sometimes, she'd put herself first and answered honestly?

Have you thought about what you're going to do after university, Helen?

I'm going to take a gap year, Dad. Travel.

Where shall we go on holiday this year, Helen?

Pompeii, Lawrence. Florence. Anywhere but bloody Cornwall.

But even in her imagination, these conversations felt too far-fetched to have ever been real.

'There were some flyers,' she said now, because someone had to break the silence. 'Yesterday at reception.'

'Were there?' Caro turned to her. 'I didn't see.'

'I can pop up and ask.'

'And you want to go today?'

Here it was. She stood up. Even if her twenty-one-year-old self had had the courage to say out loud all the things she'd wanted to say, her father would never have heard. *A gap year? Along with all the other hippies and wasters?* In twenty-five years, Lawrence had never heard. *What's wrong with Cornwall? The kids love it.* And now – she might have known – Caro had gone deaf too.

'I thought we could take a trip into Kyrenia,' Caro said. 'Take a coffee. And I was reading in *The Sunday Times* about a lovely restaurant there – maybe for lunch?'

Helen hitched her jeggings up. 'Sounds great,' she said. She was talking to her waistband. Something about the casualness of Caro's refusal to hear her had lit a bit of a fuse. She *would* do what she wanted. *Today.* Or she would at least try to do what she wanted. 'Let me just grab one of those flyers.' And as she left the table she had a vague image of Caro's face, the stamp of surprise upon it.

This was not typical Helen behaviour, but already she

was halfway up the stairs and that long-ago, never-forgotten conversation with her father was replaying itself over and over. What might have happened if she had actually spoken up? Would she have gone on her gap year? Would she have had wild affairs with Australian outdoorsy types? Had a lover who whispered Spanish in her ear – *Quiero hacerte el amor en la playa...?* Would she have got to teach English to a room of Peruvian mountain kids? She reached the top, hands on hips, almost breathless with the headiness of rewriting the past. She was fifty! And amazingly, quite wonderfully, that meant that she seemed to have crossed into a different land with a whole different language. *I want. I can.* If only... Oh, if only she really could go back to her twenty-one-year-old self, tap her on the shoulder and whisper this magical secret.

The reception desk was empty, and the hotel foyer so quiet she could hear her own quick breath. She walked over to the coffee table and read again the sign in its A5 holder.

Sailing lessons. Beginners welcome. Kyrenia Harbour. Private lessons at your convenience. Ask for Kaveh.

'Kaveh,' she said, testing the sound out loud.

'Your wish is my command!'

The voice, which came from behind, had Helen spinning round in surprise.

'You called?' It was the silver-haired man again.

On went the scarlet light bulbs! Where had he come from? She hadn't heard a thing.

For a moment he didn't speak. He was looking at her intently, his mouth turning up as if he was waiting for

126

permission to laugh. 'Is there anything I can help you with?'

She turned back to the safety of the table and the flyers and bit down on her lip. This was ridiculous; she felt like a schoolgirl. 'I just came to pick up one of these,' she said and, picking up a flyer, jiggled it to reinforce the point.

'You would like to go sailing?'

'Umm…' Her head was down. She read the first line three times without making sense of it at all. 'Umm… I'm thinking about it.'

Kaveh dropped his head to one side. 'My advice? Don't think too long.' And, smiling, he turned and walked over to the reception desk.

Behind her the front door opened, her flyer wobbled in the breeze. She looked across at Kaveh. 'Yes!' she called.

He turned.

'Yes… I want to try it!'

For a moment he looked surprised, or perhaps impressed. Either way, his expression pleased Helen immensely. 'When would you like to go?' he said.

When would she like to go? Panicked, Helen scanned the room as if she was expecting someone to jump out from behind a table and save her (from what?). But the door that had opened a moment ago, had opened to let a guest leave. So it was just the silver-haired man and her, and she felt as if she was in a time warp. As if she'd been picked up and zapped forward light years without her feet touching the ground. Back at the breakfast table it had all seemed so simple, so controllable, including Caro's less than enthusiastic response. A walk upstairs to pick up a flyer, a navigable timescale and landscape of checking out the

details, availability, costs, etc. Small steps into this new
territory, safe little hurdles between her and commitment,
all of which had been tossed aside by this man. This silver-
haired, copper-skinned man who turned her inside out just
by looking at her. So, Helen – again she bit down on her
lip – *when would you like to go?* 'Today?' she managed and her
whisper was so small she wasn't even sure she'd breathed it.

Kaveh smiled. He turned to the clock on the wall
behind the reception desk. 'I am free in about an hour,' he
said. 'Does this suit you?'

Every part of her lit up with excitement and fear and
embarrassment and desire. She nodded.

'Good.'

'But I've never done it before,' she blurted.

Kaveh smiled – such a knowing and deeply sexy look
she had to dig her nails into her fists, will the light bulbs in
her cheeks to dim their wattage.

'Don't worry,' he said. 'I will go very gentle with you.'

Back in the room, Caro hadn't given up. She was lying on
the bed, reading out loud from her Kindle. '*Notwithstanding
the fact that the castle has been rebuilt several times, The Ottoman
Influence can be seen through the many architectural modifications in
the interior.*' Frowning, she let the screen drop onto her lap.
'Helen? *Helen!*'

Helen popped her head out of the bathroom.

'I really thought this was something you'd be interested
in.'

'I am,' Helen said lightly. 'Just not today.' And she
disappeared again.

Caro tossed the Kindle aside. 'I'm going to do my yoga,' she said to the ceiling, and, when the ceiling didn't reply, got up and went out to the balcony.

And because she'd been waiting for this first sign of surrender, Helen immediately leaned around the bathroom door, saw the room was empty, and sighed. It was done. Fait accompli. Nearly.

Kaveh was to drive them to Kyrenia. Having accompanied Helen back to the breakfast table, he'd informed Caro that the restaurant she was intent upon visiting was an overpriced tourist trap. He knew a local place, he said, and would be happy to invite them both for lunch after Helen's sailing lesson. Would Caro like to join them on the boat? No? Well, Kyrenia was full of interesting shops and historical sights – more than enough to keep Caro occupied during the short time Helen would be at sea.

At sea!

All the way back to their room, Helen had tried to ignore Caro's stiff displeasure (the lesson was one hour!), concentrating instead on those words. At sea. *She* was going to be *at sea*. Like a sailor. At sea. At sea, at sea, at sea...

But Caro had kept trying. Listing the historical wonders of the town and mentioning at least three times that the restaurant *she* had had in mind had been featured in *The Sunday Times*. Hiding away in the bathroom, Helen had done her best not to hear. And, of course, her excitement was tempered with guilt. This was Caro's holiday, etc, etc. But it was one hour. One tiny hour! If she thought of all the times she'd had to rearrange or postpone because of

Caro's busy schedule… Once she'd even waited seventy-three minutes while Caro took a work call. She knew exactly how long, because she'd been sitting in her own kitchen, drinking wine, trying to hide from her children, while Caro had paced and pulled faces and wittered on about *healthy pullbacks* and *moving averages*. They'd found her in the end. Her kids. (Lawrence couldn't keep a lid on fresh air.) Consequently, she'd started a rare evening out half-drunk, with orange Wotsit stains on her jacket. Had she said anything? Had she stomped and huffed around the kitchen like a spoiled child? No, she had not.

She slipped back into the bathroom and looked at herself in the mirror. Now Caro had given up, the only thing standing between her and the open sea was…what to wear? That was, what to wear for her first sailing lesson with *him*? So far nothing was working. Not that casual but chic Boden thing…or that cheap, bejewelled Primark vest thing… And definitely not this! A frumpy floral blouse she couldn't believe she'd bought in the first place. She tore it off and stared at her reflection, frustrated, panicky and damp under the armpits. Beyond, the room was still quiet. Easing back around the bathroom door, Helen looked out to the balcony. There was Caro in an impressive upside-down yoga pose, wearing a ribbed vest and clingy short shorts so Helen could see both the slenderness of her limbs and all the sinewy strength of them. Sweat pricking at her hairline, she looked down at her own body. She was as rounded and plump as a peach. She was soft, Caro was hard, and this, she considered now, might be the fundamental difference between them. Caro was strong, tough. Of course she had always had the confidence required to keep pursuing her agenda.

Subdued, Helen picked up a pair of boring but safe navy shorts. It hadn't always been that way. That was what she was thinking as she clutched the shorts to her chest and watched Caro swoop forward into a plank, like some kind of wooden eagle.

So when had it changed? Because at university it was Caro who had been so painfully shy she could barely leave the room. And it was Helen who'd had seams and seams of unmined confidence. When had all that changed?

Caro lunged forward and stretched herself into The Warrior.

Helen went back into the bathroom.

She got the shorts up, but baklava-shaped lumps spilled out over the waistband. God, it was hopeless. Warm weather clothing was unforgiving; it just meant extra flesh squeezing out everywhere. Like the toothpaste when her kids were younger. When, last thing at night, exhausted, she'd pick it up and the paste would explode sideways. That's what she looked like – an overused tube of toothpaste. The hem of the shorts was so tight her knees had spread to twice their width. Wet, cold British summers had advantages.

She padded back out to the bedroom and looked at the strewn contents of her suitcase. Her only safe option was a maxi dress. Those lovely swaying tents she'd bought from Matalan. But that really would be *ridiculous*. She must at least try to look sporty.

Sporty? The word had her sitting down so heavily the bed groaned. Out on the balcony, Caro was now in a headstand. Eyes closed, in a headstand! And the unavoidable comparison between them became painful, because once upon a time she too had been lithe and slim and strong and sporty. Very, very *sporty*. She'd been a devil-may-care, sporty kind of girl. She looked back out at Caro. It was as though for the last thirty years she'd allowed herself to be smoothed into such a blob she had no edges left – the slow erosion wrought by motherhood and marriage. But Caro? All this time Caro had been sculpting herself. They had both undergone a metamorphosis.

It took a great will of effort for Helen to stand up, yank her elasticated jeggings back on and settle on a floral T-shirt, with a neckline low enough to display all the goods displayed by her new balcony bra. This made her feel better, but my goodness, she'd been close! So close to calling out, *Okay. Let's do the castle.*

'What do you think?' she said now.

Upside down, Caro opened her eyes. Her legs stretched heavenward, her arms were perfect right angles, her stomach as flat as an ironing board. 'I think,' she said, 'that he's wrong. I've never been disappointed by the recommendations in *The Sunday Times*.'

Helen sagged. 'I meant me!'

'Oh.' Caro let her feet drop, pushed back with her hands and slowly, vertebra by vertebra, rolled up through her spine. 'It's just a sailing lesson, Helen,' she said as she wiped her palms together. 'Why are you so bothered?' And she swept through, grabbing a towel as she passed. 'Bathroom free now?'

Long after the bathroom door had closed, Helen

stood watching it. This morning, for a myriad of reasons, felt like no other morning she could remember. It wasn't just a sailing lesson, it was her giant leap, and Caro didn't understand. Then again, why would she, when she criss-crossed continents on a weekly basis, when a sailing lesson for her would signify nothing more than the smallest of steps? Eyes smarting, once again Helen felt the gulf the years had gouged between them.

8

'Car!' Two feet ahead, Kaveh shouted the warning without turning round. Necessary because Kyrenia's ancient streets were narrow and cobbled, built for the *clip-clop* of an ox and cart, not the stealthy purr of the internal combustion engine. In these streets, hatchbacks became tanks and wing mirrors cut through tablecloths, clubbing the innocent heads off trailing petunia. Whenever the alert was shouted – *Car!* – there was nothing to do but hop into the safety of the nearest shadowed doorway. Which they did now.

Breathing in, Helen found herself squashed behind a giant terracotta vase stuffed with white cyclamen. As she inhaled the fresh green water scent, she watched the car inch past, hermetically sealed, windows up, with air con on.

On the other side of the vase, Kaveh grimaced. 'Americans.' He pointed back up to where he had parked his car a few moments ago. 'It's too far for them to walk.'

Sweat dripping down her neck, Helen smiled. The heat had her thinking the same – it really was too far to walk –

but she wasn't about to admit that in front of Kaveh.

They continued on. Past raftered houses three or four stories high, where iron-railed balconies held terracotta pots that balanced precariously. Helen clung to the shadows. The balconies looked like rows of loose teeth, hanging by threads. She looked down at her T-shirt and her own volatile balcony of flesh. Perhaps it hadn't been such a good choice.

They passed children hovering in doorways, old men sitting at cafe tables, the dregs of a bitter coffee belying time spent doing nothing at all. Kaveh seemed to greet everyone.

'Have you lived here a long time?' Helen was breathless (Kaveh walked quickly). 'You seem to know a lot of people.'

'On and off, all my life.' He disappeared around a corner, hissing gently at a cat that lay stretched on a nearby doorstep. The cat didn't move, and looking at it, Helen thought two things. That for an older man, Kaveh was very nimble. And that the harbour had better be around the next corner. It was.

'Oh, wow!' As she turned the corner she stopped short.

Caro, who had been a step behind the whole time, bumped against her, which knocked her sunglasses off her head. 'Oh, wow indeed,' she said, scrambling for her glasses.

Ahead of them, cradled by a sea wall and coloured the exact turquoise blue of every holiday brochure ever printed, lay Kyrenia harbour, alive with the noise and movement of a thousand sailboats. Row after row straining and pulling at their creaking ropes, masts jingling, booms humming. Canopies of bright blue fluttering like ribbons, white-scripted names waving. *La Lula*, *Vagabond*, *Yacht's All Folks*. And the water…it danced too! Cheek to cheek with a million silver stars thrown down by the sun. Helen felt the breeze on her face, heard the percussion of the boats and turned to Caro. 'It's so beautiful,' she breathed.

And Caro just shook her head, because it really was.

'My boat is this way.' Kaveh, who had been watching them, raised his arm to indicate the other end of the harbour. But it seemed to Helen that there were literally a thousand boats, all shapes and sizes, tethered along the crescent-shaped waterfront.

She smiled. Boats, not ships and if she could launch just one today she would, she felt, finally live up to her name.

'After you,' she laughed and they continued on, following Kaveh, neither of them speaking, both of them soaking up the myriad sounds and smells of this extraordinary place.

Along the narrow waterfront, they stopped in front of a dark, cave-like cafe, where Kaveh named the sticky slices of *pasteli*, the piles of dusty cubed *loukoumi* and his personal favourite, sunshine slabs of *shamali* cake. Next to the cafe a large clinical-looking restaurant spilled across the pavement, *Penne el Pesto* and *Spaghetti Marinara* chalked on the specials board. A pale couple, self-consciously seated at the foremost table, sipped long, pale coffees, and a Chinese chef in starched white bent over a large stainless-steel wok. On they went, past tiny craft shops stuffed with cotton candies and rings, beads, bracelets, snoods, scarves. Past glass-fronted displays of Kütahya tiles, evil eyes, colourful lamps…until finally, towards the eastern end, with necks stiff from twisting, they came to a stop in front of what looked like a water sports hire shop.

'I just have to pop in here,' Kaveh explained, and he disappeared through the door.

Helen stood, lazily reading through the signs in the window: *Waterski hire, Goggles*. She didn't notice Caro reach into her handbag and take out her guidebook.

'The thing that really struck me about the castle,' Caro began.

In disbelief, Helen turned to her. Was she really going to start all that again?

'Is how well it worked as a point of defence. Considering that it was built by the Byzantines in the twelfth century…' Caro pushed her sunglasses back and looked up. 'There it is! You can't miss it!'

Reluctantly, very reluctantly, Helen glanced to where Caro was pointing. Yes, there it was. And yes, it was hard to miss. Impossible, actually. A great rectangular sandstone block, with arrow slits and a rounded tower, like a giant empty toilet roll, right on the edge of the sea. And it did look effective as far as defensive went, but she did not want to traipse around it. A feeling of irritation crept over her. In truth, she was still smarting at Caro's dismissal of *just a sailing lesson*. 'Mmm,' she said, as non-committal a response as she could manage.

And before Caro could counteract, Kaveh came out of the shop carrying a blue life jacket. Instinctively Helen looked down at her bosom.

'Can you try this on?' he said.

Blushing, she took it. 'I'm sure it'll be fine,' she said. (*Why, why, why* hadn't she worn her sensible T-shirt bra?)

'I'll get a spare, just in case.' And Kaveh ducked into the shop again.

'What do you think, Helen?' Caro said quickly. 'We could just take a very quick tour first?'

Helen stared at her. 'Of what?'

'The castle!'

So there was her answer. Yes, Caro was going to start all that again. She was astonished and at the same time she wasn't astonished at all. Caro was tenacious. She'd just forgotten quite how tenacious she could be. It had been so long since they had spent this much time together, but of course Caro had form. On Kay's fortieth, she'd overruled Helen's choice of restaurant. On her own hen night, when Caro had asked her what she'd wanted to do (an overnight in a haunted castle), she'd gone and booked a spa trip instead. And then of course, there was Stonehenge. Something Helen had never forgotten. She'd been determined to camp out with all the other hippies, under midsummer stars as close as possible to the ancient stones... But spooked by the police presence, Caro had insisted they leave for the B&B, and Caro had won. *No one*, she'd argued, *wanted to start professional life with a police record.*

It was, Helen thought, irritation prickling, how high achievers became high achievers. You couldn't achieve anything if you took no for an answer, and no, she didn't have a police record, but then again, she'd never once slept under the stars.

Kaveh reappeared, holding another life jacket.

Caro turned to him. 'We were just thinking of doing a quick castle tour,' she smiled. 'Very quick.'

138

He raised his palms and shrugged.

And Helen watched in horror. If she didn't speak up now, the whole day would be swept out of her control. This half of her life would be just like the first half. She opened her mouth, but as she did Kaveh cut her off by raising his arm and sweeping it across the arc of the harbour.

'Or,' he said, with a smile, '*I* can give you your history lesson?'

Caro's face froze.

'This, for example,' he continued without pause. 'We have your people to thank for this.' He was pointing to the breakwater up ahead.

'I...' was all Caro managed.

Helen didn't even try. Mouth turning up in a small smile, she watched Kaveh carefully.

'It was built during the colonial period,' he continued. 'Is that what you say? Colonial times? Is it colonial?'

'Colonial. Yes,' Helen prompted.

Kaveh winked at her.

(Did he? Did he really do that?)

'So yes, in colonial times they closed this north part and they built a new opening. The custom house there and the dock – this was also when they were built. They did a lot of building.'

For a brief moment, no one spoke.

Then Caro nodded tightly. 'Very interesting.'

'And before that, all the warehouses were a shelter for animals. Lions for the Romans! Here in Kyrenia. Imagine that? Lions and bears. It was a very important town, right in the middle of everything. All the trade routes between Europe, Middle East and North Africa.'

It was then that Helen had to turn away. Kaveh was doing to Caro what Caro had been doing to her all morning. Railroading her, steamrolling over all resistance, so that now Caro's face had pinched with irritation, and it was only manners, Helen knew, that restrained her. (And didn't Helen know all about that!) The relief she felt was tangible. He'd grasped what was happening and had jumped in and saved her. He might as well have thrown his cloak at her feet, and she felt that in this one moment of gallantry he had understood her better than her husband had ever done. Of course. Because how would Lawrence ever have jumped in like this, when it had always been him behind the wheel of the steamroller in the first place? *What's wrong with Cornwall? The kids love it.* And again she was struck in a way she never had been before by how similar they were, Caro and Lawrence.

'Of course' – Kaveh was still talking – 'the harbour is used for yachts now. It's only tourists who come.' Finally he paused. Was that a pause? She turned, but Caro had jumped straight in.

'Yes,' she said. 'I read that. What a shame.'

'Do you think so?'

'Don't you?'

Helen watched. Caro's jaw was stiff with suppressed frustration, and the air between her and Kaveh fizzed with tension. She looked down at her sunglasses, twisting them in her hands. It was all well and good, this being fifty and pleasing herself thing, but it wasn't natural. She was torn.

'What I think,' Kaveh was saying, 'is that it can't be a

bad thing that we have time now to sail just for the fun of it.' He smiled at Caro. 'Are you sure you won't join us?'

'Quite sure.' Caro dropped her book into her bag and stood, hands entwined, knuckles white.

Helen turned her sunglasses over, opening up the arms and folding them in again. Caro, she could see, was hurt, but what was she supposed to do? *What do you want to do, Helen? Mum? Darling? Daughter?* A tremendous urge rose through her. She wanted to shout, stamp her foot. Because Kaveh was absolutely right. Sailing for the fun of it? She couldn't think of anything better to do and, Goddammit, she wanted to have fun! Wasn't it time that *she* had some fun? She turned to Caro and, with a loud buzzing in her ears, said quite firmly, 'I'm sorry, Caro, but I do want to go sailing. Can't we stick to the original plan? You do what you want to do and we'll meet you back here in an hour?'

Stiff-jawed, Caro agreed.

They said their goodbyes and arranged a meeting place. And although, watching Caro walk away, Helen felt as if she'd just drowned a puppy, she did not go back to save it.

The moment Helen stepped on board Kaveh's boat it tilted – violently. Shifting her weight only made things worse. The boat shifted with her and then the other way...and back again. Legs of jelly, she grabbed the only thing that seemed sober – the mast – and planted her feet as wide as she could. Kaveh had called the boat a daysailer, and said it could hold four; but, looking from one end of it to the other, if Caro had decided to join them, quite where she would have fitted Helen didn't know.

141

Behind her, still on the bridge, Kaveh was untying knots.

'I thought it would be bigger,' she called, trying not to sound petrified. And as if it were activated by voice (hers), the boat turned, so now the bow faced seaward – ready to go! If it hadn't still been tied to the dock, it might have floated off altogether. She was seriously unnerved. Every other boat she'd ever been on had behaved like every other means of transport she'd ever been on. That is, they'd remained still until someone had turned a key. This thing had a mind of its own. Now she wasn't sure at all about sailing. Aware that one false move might see her in the water before they'd left the shore, she wrapped her arms around the mast and stayed as still as she possibly could.

Kaveh was *still* untying knot after knot.

Cautiously she peeled her cheek from the mast and turned her head to look out at the port. Close up like this, the water didn't seem quite so holiday-brochure-ish. It looked darker and deeper, and certainly colder. She gazed out at the expanse of sea beyond the breakwall and her stomach liquefied.

'Okay.' Kaveh stepped on; the boat lurched and he didn't even notice.

Helen pressed herself against the mast. 'It's wobbly,' she managed.

He smiled. 'Hold on.' He took a large board and slotted it through a space in the middle of the hull. The boat responded immediately, contenting itself with the gentlest of nudges this way and that.

'What's that?' She nodded at the board.

'The centreboard,' Kaveh said, and he used his hands as he explained how the board slipped deep under the boat, stabilising it.

Slowly, as the rocking settled and the boat stilled, she relaxed her grip. It was just like sticking a dummy in a baby's mouth.

'Okay, Helen. Start with this, please.'

Helen looked up to see Kaveh holding the life jacket she'd left on the pier. She could put it off no longer. She took it from him and he turned away, busying himself with more knots. She shrugged it on, but with her balcony bra doing its job so well, she only just managed to get the buckle fastened. The strain was enormous – for her and the buckle. Clearly one of them would have to give. 'Umm,' she began. 'I—'

'Try this one?' Kaveh said. He was holding out the second life jacket. The one he'd gone back in for – the larger one.

'Thank you,' she mumbled, released the buckle and breathed again. Then she strapped herself into the larger life jacket. 'I feel like a sumo wrestler,' she joked.

He turned and looked at her, his eyes dancing. 'A sumo wrestler who won't drown,' he said seriously.

What an idiot he must think her! Her blush deepening, Helen handed back the too-small life jacket. And standing there, sweating, swaying, a part of her began to vehemently wish that she'd stayed and traipsed around the castle with Caro.

And then he said her name. 'Are you ready, Helen?' Separating it into two rich syllables, as thick as double cream. It was a stroke, not a sound. She nodded, and although she was about as ready as the prisoner is for the rope, she also felt that she'd go anywhere with this silver-haired man.

'You sit here.' Kaveh, holding the tiller, indicated a spot further up towards the front of the boat.

She inched past him, chest to chest, barely able to meet his eye.

'I want you to take this.' He held out a rope to her. 'This works the front sail. The jib, you call it.'

'Me?'

'You English,' he said, and smiled. 'It's going to be okay, Helen. That's all you're going to be doing today, and we're going to start here.'

She looked to where he pointed.

'In the harbour?'

'Just up and down, until you get used to the feel.'

Helen swallowed. It hurt.

And once again, just like yesterday in reception, he seemed to read her thoughts. Gently he put his hand on her arm. 'It's easy. Like riding a bike. You can ride a bike?'

'I can ride a bike,' she said.

And although she wouldn't have used that word – *easy* – she couldn't have said it was hard either. The water was calm, the wind tame. Kaveh steered across the width of the harbour several times, handling the tiller and the mainsail. Helen took care of the jib. He taught her how to use the shoreline to orient herself, how to watch for darkened patches of water which signalled wind ahead. He explained how to read the sails with both her ears and her eyes, so that soon enough, when the jib started flapping, she was pulling back or slackening on the rope accordingly. She forgot about the embarrassment of the life jacket. She forgot about Caro. She even forgot she was in Cyprus. Her hands chafed, her eyes strained, and with every nerve on alert and every muscle braced she grew bolder, bigger, braver. And when a sudden gust surprised them, speeding the boat forward, and Kaveh threw himself backwards from the rail and yelled, '*Hike out, Helen. Do the same!*' Helen didn't hesitate. She sat up on the rail, dug her heels under the seat and pulled the jib sheet for all she was worth, leaning her body back to the sea, hair falling, eyes open to the sky above, every nerve pulsating with life.

And then he asked if she felt ready to venture further. 'Yes,' she said, with a smile as wide as the horizon, seawater drenching her face and arms. Of course she wanted to venture further. She wanted to keep it going, this adrenaline rush, these feelings she hadn't felt in more than half a lifetime. So Kaveh steered the boat past the breakwater and Helen held onto her rope, gazing at the mountains that rose up behind Kyrenia. How alive she felt! Just like Lawrence had always said. No wonder he kept going back. She wrapped the rope tighter around her knuckles, pulled harder, and the boat responded. It was thrilling, and for the first time in twenty-five years of living together she felt she might have stumbled across a genuine understanding of her husband. The next thing she thought was that it had come too late.

'It's fun, yes?' Kaveh turned, the wind blowing his beautiful silver hair forward.

145

'Yes,' she said. 'It's really fun.' But she was thinking about Lawrence again – the way he always dumped this part of his life, along with his holdalls and rucksacks, at the front door – and she had to look away to hide the tears at her eyes. Not once had Lawrence ever said, *It's fun, yes?* Not once.

The wind fell away, the rope went slack in her hands, the current cradled the boat and they bobbed out into open sea.

9

Long after her decaffeinated coffee had turned cold and filmy, Caro remained at the table, her eyes straining to keep the boat in view. But the harbour was busy, and Helen and Kaveh kept disappearing. Every time this happened, the napkin which she'd twisted around her fingers tightened and she leaned further forward, squinting harder.

It should have been easy. With Helen gone, she had the space to mentally ready herself for the clinic tomorrow. To relax, sit in the sun and watch the world go by. But the one thing Caro had consistently failed at in life was relaxing, and her nerves were now so tightly wound she twanged. At least with Helen she'd had a distraction. Without her there was only the churning of her own unsettled thoughts, a complication she hadn't really considered. Plus Helen had offered protection. Alone now, surrounded by groups of holidaymakers, her lone status in the world was horribly highlighted. She felt exposed and vulnerable, as if every face she passed could see through the façade and knew she wasn't in Cyprus for the sun.

Kaveh's boat reappeared from behind a larger vessel. Caro lifted her sunglasses. Was it them? Yes, she could see the small cloud of blonde that was Helen's hair, and even from this distance she could tell that Helen was laughing. She smiled. It was good that Helen had agreed to come, for her own sake. It wasn't like her to be unhappy or bored. Helen had always had fun easily, far more so than either herself or Kay – which, truth be told, was something Caro had been envious of – and, cheese melter aside, her dinner parties were always the ones she'd most looked forward to. Or they had been.

She picked up her cup and took a mouthful of coffee, wincing at the sourness. It was funny she hadn't really noticed the fact there hadn't actually been any parties of late. How the fun had dried up. Placing the cup back in its saucer, she stared at it. She'd been so caught up in her own world, so transfixed with the unhappiness reflected back in her own mirror, she hadn't noticed the same in Helen.

Taking out her purse, Caro found a €5 note – twice as much as the coffee had cost – and tucked it under her saucer. Before she stood up, she looked again to the harbour. It seemed as if Helen and Kaveh were heading further out now. Their sails were fully unfurled and they were moving fast. Hand shielding the sun, she watched, astonished, as the boat tipped and Helen threw herself back to counterbalance. Yes, she'd been right, they were definitely heading out towards open water. Caro's head moved from side to side as she smiled and mouthed, '*Go, Helen. Go.*'

Still smiling, she turned back to the table and picked up her sunglasses. She was thinking about those dinner parties again. Helen was right. Because not only hadn't she noticed how they'd melted away, she hadn't noticed either how they had always ended the same way: Helen in the kitchen, Lawrence fiddling interminably with the remote control of the smart TV. (At least in his projector days he hadn't been able to skip back and repeat as easily.) She hadn't noticed because she'd always had somewhere to be the next day, and the only image that seemed to present itself now was that of Helen leaning against the kitchen door frame, flushed with alcohol. Turning back to the harbour, Caro took a deep breath. Well, today Helen was framed by an ocean; and watching the tiny boat bob away, Caro felt both a resigned envy (she knew the limitations of her own physical timidity) and admiration. *Resigned envy.* It took her a long moment to understand that – to fully comprehend the harmlessness of the emotion. Because to be envious of Helen sailing an ocean was one thing, but to be envious of her stranded against the kitchen door frame was quite another. Her manicured fingertip tapped against the arm of her sunglasses. Had she really been envious of that?

Yes, she had. Long ago and far away, Lawrence had chosen Helen. And although Caro had moved on, what she'd never quite been able to escape were the mists of *what-might-have-beens*. The wistfulness that had clouded around her ankles, sitting in Helen's lovely house, hearing about her children's accomplishments or Lawrence's latest adventures.

She bent forward to smooth the creases from her trousers, thanked the approaching waiter and slipped out of the cafe onto the quayside, feeling almost as if she'd stepped into a new dimension.

Helen knew. Of course she did. (Years later, Kay had confirmed it.) Helen had always been aware of the candle Caro held for Lawrence during those university years. What she'd never known – and Caro would never tell – was the one-night stand they had shared. Just before graduation. One evening, that it seemed to Caro, had given Lawrence licence to stoke that pitiful flame wherever and whenever it had suited him. Never anything more than a hand held too long on her arm when Helen was out of the room, or a sideways look, but still…a hand, definitely held too long. Even through her happiest years with Mike, and only when he too wasn't in the room – and, of course, always with her implicit consent.

Her eyes glazed over. Shaking her head, she stood and hugged her arms and under the heat of the Cypriot sun felt cold. *Her implicit consent.* She'd never quite been able to withhold it. But it was, she realised with a rare kind of astonishment, over. Just like that. Finished. As easily and cleanly as deadheading a flower. God, she hadn't seen Lawrence in months, but if she were to bump into him tomorrow she wouldn't give him an inch, and somehow she knew this as surely as the sun that filled the Cypriot sky above. In fact, standing on the quayside of Kyrenia harbour, it was beginning to feel unbelievable to Caro that she ever had. The phone call Helen had described was stupendously selfish, but then so was Lawrence, and the only thing that surprised her was the fact that she hadn't seen it before! The City was stuffed full of Lawrences, and she'd never been in thrall to any of them. Then again, she hadn't been a painfully shy, and virginally young student

150

when she'd first started rubbing shoulders with them.

She shook her head, blindsided by insight. All those long years of feeling like she had missed out on something, when the only thing she'd missed was a bullet pinning her to the kitchen sink. She was fifty years old! She was free, healthy and really quite wealthy. And tomorrow she would be at the clinic. She had no reason to be envious of anyone!

Directly above, the sun was high and too hot for her to continue standing like this without shade, no matter how invincible she suddenly felt. She took her sun hat and pulled it low over her brow, making her way towards the castle, following a path that, thankfully, became cooler as it fell under the shadow of ancient stone.

The crowd was slow and the path narrow, and as Caro mooched along with the flow she felt an unmistakable relaxation of the steely-wired tension that had bound her recently. Tomorrow she really would be at the clinic, and for the first time all the twists and turns of life that had led her here made sense. If she had to take the same paths again, would she? Yes, she probably would. Unconsciously her hand slipped inside her bag and found her phone. She had an incredibly crazy idea that she might call her mother.

Immediately ahead, a large man and a woman in a sleeveless tent of a dress came to an abrupt halt as the woman read from the guidebook in her hands. '*The Ottoman influence,*' she said loudly, '*can be seen through the many architectural modifications in the interior.*'

Caro took a step aside and leaned back against the cool stone. The woman sounded exactly like she had this morning, back at the hotel. She looked down at her sandals.

It had been selfish of her to behave the way she had with Helen, and she felt ashamed about it now. Especially after seeing Helen on the boat. She hadn't asked Helen along as some sort of personal teddy bear to cling onto when needed. So she should stop acting as if she had. In a swift, clean move, she turned away and began walking back, brushing shoulders with everyone coming the other way. Whatever the castle held – Ottoman influences, Byzantine detail or just cool shade – she was no longer interested.

She walked back past the cafe where she'd taken coffee, smiling at the young man who'd served her. He smiled back (remembering the tip, probably). She passed the restaurant with the Chinese chef, which was now full. On she continued, resolute and cheerful, until she reached a stone bench shaded by the overhanging blooms of a eucalyptus tree. The phone was out and the number dialled before she could give herself time to think better of it.

Her mother answered on the third ring.

'What have I done to deserve this?' she said, puncturing Caro's resolve like a pin in a balloon.

'Nothing.' Caro stumbled. 'Nothing. I just thought I'd ring.'

Silence.

Caro turned the strap of her handbag over and pressed it between her fingers. 'So…how are you?'

'As well as can be expected, Caroline,' her mother sighed. 'And you?'

'I'm good.' She leaned forward, ten feet away from Kyrenia harbour, all blue and white light, salt breezes and the slap of waves. Where lions had once passed through. 'Actually I'm… I'm on holiday.'

152

There was a moment's heavy pause, and then, 'Are you now?'

'In Cyprus.'

'Very nice, I'm sure.'

Lions for the Romans.

Silence.

Lions and tiger and bears… Caro looked down at her hands. Her nails had carved five crescent moons into her palm. 'It's really quite lovely, Mum,' she said, and then, 'Perhaps I'll be able to persuade you to come one day?'

'Oh, I don't think so, Caroline.'

Caro pressed her lips together. 'So… Well, how's your hip?'

'My hip?'

'Are you moving okay now?'

'I've been moving okay for the last twelve months.'

'Right.' Despair covered her, head to toe, a sheet thrown over a corpse. What was the point? She twisted the strap around her palm. 'How's Sean?'

'Sean's fine.' Her mother paused. 'You could ask him yourself, you know.'

'I do, Mum.' Silence. 'We keep up on social media.' (Which meant that late on a Friday night she scrolled through his Facebook page.) 'I see what he's doing.'

'Social media?'

'You know, Facebook. I don't think he does Twitter—'

'His youngest, Amy?' her mother interrupted. 'You remember?'

Caro waited a beat, a moment of silence to express what she couldn't say in words: a lifetime of crushing disappointment at never being heard. Did her mother even notice that she'd interrupted? Cut her off mid-sentence? And if she did, how would Caro know? Her mother's silences were as incomprehensible to her as Caro's silences were to her mother. 'Of course,' she murmured, because that was what was required.

'She's off to start a nursing degree this autumn. Sheffield University.'

'Is she?' Caro managed. 'That's great.' And the very last part of the giant mosaic she'd been building in her head for weeks, the pattern of how she would tell her mother, fell away, splintering into a million estranged pieces. How could she say it? How could she possibly tell her mother what it was she was intending to do?

'Sean's so proud,' her mother continued. 'He was over just last week, mending the fence for me.'

Caro tipped her head back to the sky and put her hand over her mouth, her eyes stinging with tears. By doing everything wrong, her brother had done everything right. Caro, on the other hand, in doing everything right, had done it all wrong. Straight As, from primary upwards. University. A good job. And then somewhere, soon after, a turn that had taken her further and further away, until now she was so alien she might as well have lived in a different solar system. Whereas Sean was like their father. Resolutely average. Wrapped up in the sandwich of his days, bacon butties in the morning, pork chops at night, newspaper, armchair, football, coffin. And the irony was that her mother had despised her father. Which wasn't so unusual, because growing up it had seemed to Caro that her mother despised everyone. According to her therapist, this had been the source of her anxiety and fear, the driving force behind her ambition, her need to excel, to become the someone her mother could admire. The someone, that is, apart from her mother's own mother…the dead grandmother with whom Caro could never compete.

At the time, it was such an elaborate theory Caro had brushed it off, put it down to the therapist's need to justify eye-watering fees. But fourteen years later, when Mike had left, citing her 'ambition', and the long, lonely evenings of her fourth decade had provided plenty of time for introspection, she had re-examined the theory. Again and again.

God knew, she knew the story well enough. How, upon realising there wasn't going to be enough room for both of them in an already packed air-raid shelter, Caro's grandmother had pushed her mother in and closed the door.

She took my hand, Caroline. I can still feel her doing it. She took my hand and pushed me in.

Her mother had been seven years old. She spent the rest of the war waiting for her mother at the garden gate. Then she grew up and had a daughter of her own, naming her for the mother who had never come home: Caroline.

Imagine that, Caroline? Imagine having the courage to choose to die?

'So.' Her mother interrupted her thoughts. 'I've potatoes on the hob I need to get back to.'

Caro startled. 'Potatoes,' she murmured, and remembered a Sunday morning once, spent at the sink peeling potatoes with her mother. Such a long time ago.

'So…' Her mother's voice trailed off, and on a sunny waterfront, three thousand miles away, Caro heard the hesitation. Maybe her mother was remembering as well? That same Sunday morning?

'Have a nice time now,' her mother said.

'I will.' She swallowed. 'I—'

But the call had ended. Or rather, her mother had ended it. Almost instantly, her phone began buzzing again.

She looked at the name flashing across her screen. *Danny Abbott.* The last thing in the world she wanted to do was to talk to anyone else, because the only thing she wanted was to have found a way to talk to her mother.

She swiped her screen, held the phone against her ear and said cheerfully, 'Hello, Danny.'

At sea, everything looked different. Kyrenia shrank. It became a toy town, and all its storied houses and warehouses were nothing more than coloured blocks against the backdrop of northern Cyprus. The wind stayed calm, and as the boat moved along Kaveh pointed out the town's old defences, the castle on the east side, the three remaining towers that had once linked the town's protective wall. He knew so much and, listening to him, Helen allowed herself to drift off. She was a sailor, carrying a cargo full of tigers. Byzantines lined the castle ramparts… Or she was another Helen. Helen of Troy. Except Troy was in flames and she was sailing away with no husband on any horizon.

'The town,' Kaveh said, 'was built with sandstone that washed down from the mountains.'

Helen looked from Kaveh back to shore. Kyrenia did

look as if it had been carved from the landscape it stood upon, ancient and integrated. The polar opposite of how she felt right now, having stepped outside her skin so completely.

'Stones from the old walls,' he said, raising his hand to point. 'Used to build the houses. They all did that. Venetians, Ottomans, even the British.'

'Like a mosaic?'

Kaveh smiled.

'You're very knowledgeable,' she said.

Now he shrugged.

'I studied history at university,' Helen said, and turned back to the town. 'I think it's important to understand what went on before. We forget so easily.' Turning to him, squinting into the wind, she added, 'Don't you think?'

He didn't answer straight away. He was still looking at the town. After a long pause, he said, 'It wasn't important to me before. History.'

'Oh.' Helen looked at him. 'It is now, though? You know so much.'

'Yes,' he said. 'It is now.'

It is now. And there was something so openly sad in his voice; she would have asked him more, but he'd raised his arm again and was now pointing at something else.

'Up there,' he said. 'This is the castle of Saint Hilarion.'

The moment was gone. She turned to where he was pointing. 'It's beautiful.' It really was. Too beautiful for words, so she sat watching the shoreline, the mountains, the wise old town, the blue Mediterranean. 'I had,' she breathed, 'no idea Cyprus was so beautiful.'

Kaveh turned to her. 'How could it not be? Cyprus is where Aphrodite rose from the sea.'

'Aphrodite?'

'Goddess of beauty.'

'Oh yes.' Helen blushed.

Kaveh was still looking at her, so she blushed even more until, in a torrent of beetroot-coloured confusion, she finally looked away.

On they went, Kaveh steering the boat closer into shore now, back towards the harbour. The wind rose and fell, sometimes brushing her face, at other times dropping away completely, and Helen felt as if she could do this every day for the rest of her life. She had no idea of the time. Maybe 11? So what would she have been doing at home? Buying milk in Tesco? Why would she be doing that when she could be doing this? When she looked back to shore she was almost surprised to see how close to the harbour they were – nearly at the breakwall.

'Uh oh,' Kaveh said, and it wasn't anything more than a mumble.

Helen turned, saw the look on Kaveh's face, and felt a cold wash of fear. 'What?' she said. 'What's the matter?'

He nodded, his eyes fixed on the water twenty yards ahead.

As soon as she saw it she knew. The patch of water they were both looking at now was black. Instinctively she glanced up at the sky, where a small but bitterly dark cloud had moved to swallow the sun.

'Get ready, Helen. It's going to be bumpy.'

She looped the jib sheet around her hands, and as she did she heard a shout. Up ahead, another sailboat was already crossing the dark patch. She could hear the rattle of their sails, see how violently the two figures in neon orange life jackets had leaned to counterbalance. This was the wind they were heading towards.

'Pull!' Kaveh called.

She pulled. The wind hit. The jib rattled and she pulled again, tighter, harder, so hard her hands burned. Still the jib rattled.

'Get ready,' Kaveh yelled. 'We're going to tack. Like we did in the harbour. Otherwise we'll be pushed into the wall.'

Tack? For a moment she was confused. Then Kaveh called *Ready about!* and pushed the tiller downwind and the boat changed tack, the boom swung across and Helen ducked, scuttling across the bow like a beetle, tugging and yanking the jib as she sat up on the rail and flung herself back, counterbalancing, counterbalancing... Like a pip between thumbs, the boat shot forward. The rope slipped and twisted and gouged her hands. Her arms shook, her jaw clamped.

'*Pull, Helen!*' Kaveh shouted.

'I am. I am...'

And then she felt it. The massive shove from behind as the wind puffed its cheeks and blew. The rope spiralled out of her hands, the mainsail fell, the boat tipped and Helen hovered, teetering on the rail, ninety degrees, staring down at the water. Heart punching her throat, she turned to Kaveh. His face an inch from hers.

'*Jump,*' he shouted through the wind.

Did she say anything? She tried to.

'*Jump onto the sail. NOW!*'

Helen looked down. The sail was in the water, as flat as a bed sheet. How was she supposed to jump onto that? She opened her mouth; her teeth were chattering. The water was black. 'I—'

'*You can, Helen. You can do it! Jump onto the sail.*'

And that was all she needed. She jumped.

'*Now swim!*'

Crawling off the sail like a big, clumsy baby, she plunged through the water, a shocking cold engulfing her face and head. When she bobbed back up, there was Kaveh swimming to the stern, and the boat was lying sideways in the ocean like a fallen horse.

'*Helen, release the mainsail and climb back in.*'

The mainsail? She yanked at the first rope she found and it went slack.

'*Good. Now climb in.*'

Clambering over the fallen sail, shoes scrabbling and hands grabbing, she hauled herself back into the hull of the boat.

'*Now hold on to something. Move with the boat and hold on.*'

Kaveh had swung all his weight over the centreboard, rocking it backwards. Helen grabbed the rail and wrapped her foot underneath the seat. She could feel the momentum Kaveh was beginning to create, and she worked with him. Tipping and leaning, the two of them moving together. Then suddenly the sail popped up, free of the water. On the cusp the boat hovered, seemed to shake, then fell forward, scooping and flinging Helen back into the upright hull, where she lay, looking up at the dome of sky, relief shaking every cell.

Slipping free of the cloud that had caused the pocket of wind, the sun blazed a gazillion watts. Under her nails, the roughness of rope fibre lingered. Pushing back on her elbows, she lifted her head and looked out across the bay to the sandstone mountains, birthplace of Aphrodite. All of this she had time to process as seawater dripped down her nose and pure, unadulterated joy poured through her veins. The boat was upright; the world was beautiful. She had found her joy.

'Helen?'

She sat up. There was Kaveh, hanging onto the stern.

'Is there a chance you could help me up?' he said, but he too was laughing.

'To sailing!'

'Sailing!' Helen held her glass up to meet Kaveh's.

'Were you scared?'

Was she scared? The question lingered.

The lesson had lasted an hour. Sixty minutes out of a whole lifetime and, sitting in this restaurant with damp hair and the smell of the sea on her arms, she couldn't understand how that was possible. Because for Helen, those sixty technicoloured minutes had been as decisive as the centreboard had been for the boat. Slicing her life into sections. A *before sailing* and an *after sailing*, in which she now lived. As someone different. Someone who could capsize and survive. Helen of Troy who? She may have launched a thousand ships, but Helen Winters had uprighted one!

She was happier than she could ever remember being. Filled with a sense of achievement she wasn't sure she'd ever experienced. It made her think again of all those times she'd stayed on shore, packing thermos flasks and creating nutritionally balanced picnics so that everyone else could go off and experience what she just had.

Why? Why had she done that? She could kick herself. And everyone else. Why, for example, hadn't Lawrence ever spoken to her like Kaveh had? Why hadn't he encouraged her? Why hadn't he even asked her? Then again – and the thought soaked up any sea-salted giddiness that still lingered – why had she waited to be asked? She looked up at Kaveh. 'I was terrified,' she whispered. 'When can we do it again?'

Kaveh laughed, a loud and genuine sound. 'Can we have some lunch first?'

Smiling – which she couldn't stop doing – Helen picked up the menu.

'You don't need that,' Kaveh said. 'They do the best moussaka in town. I'll order for us.'

'Okay,' she said, and put the menu down. She had a feeling she'd let this man decide anything for her. And then she remembered. Caro, who should be here already. 'What about Caro?'

'I'll order for Caro as well.' Kaveh stood up. As he did, his phone bleeped. He paused to read the message, an inscrutable look on his face. Then he tucked the phone in his pocket and walked away to the back of the restaurant.

Helen picked up her glass. She could only guess what Caro would make of the fact that not only had the restaurant been chosen for her, now the menu had too. And where was she anyway? It was already ten minutes past the arranged meeting time. Reaching into her bag, she found her phone. She had two new messages. One from her son, one from her husband.

The lasagne you bought is two days out of date now. Do you think it's safe to eat? Jack.

Maybe able to get an earlier flight. Can't wait for some home comforts and snuggles. Love L

The phone slipped from her hands, her fingers too slack to hold it. The tendrils of damp hair at her neck were cool and the wine on her lips richly sweet. Three feet away, through a shimmering door shape of heat and dust, was Cyprus. *Lasagne? Home comforts?* She wished she hadn't picked it up.

In response – as if her phone were animate, primed to reprimand her – it buzzed a new message. Helen picked it up. What if, three thousand miles away, Lawrence had somehow been able to read her thoughts? Cautiously she swiped the app open. But the message wasn't from her husband, it was from Caro.

Took a taxi back. Sorry, really didn't feel like lunch, have a bit of a headache. Have fun x

Helen pushed the phone across the table, leaned back in her chair and scooped her hair off her neck. She wasn't surprised by Caro's message. In fact, she had almost been expecting it. What would have been surprising – astonishing, actually – was if Caro had turned up and eaten the food that Kaveh had presumed to order for her in the restaurant he had chosen.

'Is everything okay?' Kaveh was back at the table, holding two steaming plates of moussaka. He looked at her banished phone.

What could she tell him? That the thought of seeing her husband after all this time left her numb? That she was finding it hard to actually like the full-grown child her son refused to stop being? That Caro was sulking? She shook her head. 'Caro has gone back to the hotel.'

'Ah.' Kaveh nodded. He called something to the tiny kitchen at the back. Cancelling the third order, Helen presumed.

'She wasn't feeling well.'

He nodded again, leaned over his plate and, using his hands, wafted the scent up to his nostrils. As if he didn't care about Caro being unwell, or as if he recognised it for the lame excuse it was.

Helen picked up her fork. It *was* a lame excuse, but still she felt a vestige of loyalty. 'She has a headache,' she said. 'I expect it's the sun.'

Kaveh lifted his head. 'Perhaps,' he said. Like it was a question. *Perhaps?*

'Well,' she flustered. 'She said she enjoyed Kyrenia very much.' Caro hadn't said anything of the sort, and Helen wasn't at all sure why she was doing this. Defending someone who wasn't under attack.

'That's good.' Kaveh leaned forward and topped up her wine.

Only when he'd stopped pouring did she put her hand over the glass. She was thinking about that *perhaps?*

With the flask still in his hand, Kaveh looked first at her

hand and then at her, and shyly Helen withdrew her hand.

'You can sleep it off in the sun,' he said. 'It's what afternoons are made for.'

'Is it?'

'Of course.'

Relaxing, she took a mouthful of the blood-rich wine and held it in her mouth. The taste was as full as a cushion, alive with a fruity richness. Through the open doorway she could see how a scooter had come to a stop in front of the restaurant and a young boy was now hopping off, a net bag full of lemons in his arms. He wore flip-flops and shorts and his lean, dusty brown limbs were perfect, and the same great sweep of serenity that had cloaked her several times that morning came again. As though all the world were so very well, and if only Caro were here to enjoy it. What would she be doing now? Lying in the hotel room with the curtains drawn when she should be here, tasting this delicious wine, watching this wonderful world pass by. Another pang of guilt. This had been Caro's holiday. She put her glass down. 'She isn't normally like this, you know. Caro, I mean.'

Kaveh looked at her. 'Like what?'

'So…' Helen frowned, winking the tip of her nose. So…what? It was hard to find the right word. 'Well,' she started, 'she's usually a lot more fun.' This was true. Over the last decade or so, as both she and Kay had become increasingly bogged down by family, Caro had come into her own. She was always the one who arrived cool and collected, armed with champagne. It was something Helen admired and, if she was honest, had been envious of. If she was really honest, at times tremendously envious. 'Anyway.' She shrugged.

Opposite, Kaveh did the same, tucking into his moussaka.

Helen skewered a piece of aubergine and also began eating. What she had said was true. Caro was usually more fun; her life had seemed full of spontaneity and adventure. She was thinking now of the time she'd rung Caro, Saturday morning kids' TV blaring in the background, and Caro had answered from the airport, the siren call of a thousand destinations in the background. Where had she been heading for the weekend? Prague. Or Lisbon? Helen couldn't remember now. What she remembered was the desolation she'd felt as she'd put the phone down and contemplated the gridlines of her own weekend: the side of the football pitch, the aisles of Asda, the inside of the dishwasher. Those times had been hard…when the juxtaposition of their lifestyles had been thrust before her. But that was over now. And sitting there with her fork at her mouth, she began to understand what the morning had really meant. The seismic measure of it. How it had swept away emotions so entrenched they had almost rusted into place. All the envy and hopelessness, the sad regrets, the useless crockery of her life seemed to have melted away. Envy? Of whom? That felt as feasible as a dodo walking through the door. Why? Why would she ever want to be someone else other than the person who could capsize a boat in an ocean and put it right again?

Kaveh sat back, threading his fingers together. 'I expect she is a little nervous,' he said.

Helen nodded. She tipped her glass back, and was so caught up in the jubilation of what she was thinking that it was only as she swallowed that she actually heard what Kaveh had said. 'Nervous?' She frowned. 'Of what?'

Kaveh scooped up the sauce with his knife and licked it clean. 'It is a very big decision. Becoming a mother this way.'

A burst of wine exploded from Helen's lips. She grabbed a napkin, pressing it to her face. She hadn't heard right. 'A…what?'

Knife at his mouth, Kaveh looked at her.

'A *what?*' she asked again. Her mouth itched. She wanted to laugh. Mother? Caro?

But looking back at her, a shadow crossed Kaveh's face so deep it reached Helen, sending goosebumps all along her arms. He put his knife and fork together. Then he took his cigarette packet, turned it upside down and tapped one free.

'Kaveh?'

Keeping his eyes on the cigarette packet, Kaveh spoke quietly. 'Is this something you didn't know?'

The goosebumps melted. She felt…she didn't know what she felt. She leaned across the table. 'Is *what* something I didn't know?'

Kaveh shook his head. 'I'm sorry.'

Leaning back, Helen took hold of her glass. She could hear her heart thumping in her ears. Something very strange was happening and she felt a little scared, a little impatient. 'Whatever it is,' she said, 'that you thought I would know, I didn't. So…' She took a deep breath, and when she spoke her voice was iron. 'I think you should tell me.'

167

Kaveh lit the cigarette and filled his lungs, exhaling long and slow.

'*Tell me*, Kaveh.'

He nodded. 'It's not so unusual,' he said. 'I think a lot of women use our hotel.' He shrugged. 'Maybe it is recommended, I don't know, but we come to recognise them. When a woman of a certain age—'

'A certain age?' Helen breathed.

Raising his eyebrows at the cigarette packet, Kaveh continued, 'When they are…unaccompanied and past their youthful years… We know even before they arrange the transport.'

Arrange the transport? Now she had no idea what he was talking about. Except that one word. *Mother.* Which he hadn't repeated, but which she was sure now she had heard. Palms flat on the table, shoulders hunched, she leaned across. 'What are you trying to say?'

It was then he leaned in to meet her. 'Your friend is here to become a mother, Helen.'

Helen looked at him, their noses an inch apart.

'I'm sorry, I really thought you would know this.'

Frozen, she flicked her eyes right and then left and then back at Kaveh. What was he saying? What had she just heard? When the ice that had momentarily encased her cracked, she peeled her hands from the sticky cloth and eased herself back. Kaveh was still looking at her, and with such a look of genuine contrition on his face she was furious. 'Caro,' she snorted, 'is fifty! Like me!'

'Which is why she is here.'

This time she held his gaze. She had a funny feeling of

being outside herself. Of seeing herself looking at Kaveh, who was looking back at her. And he looked so weighted. The light in his eyes had changed; now they were dark with trouble. Whatever he was telling her, he really believed it.

He sighed. 'She is arranging transport for tomorrow morning. 7am. She needs to get to a clinic in Nicosia.' He turned his palms to the ceiling. 'This is a place where they make miracles happen. I don't know any more than that and… I don't want to.'

Helen shivered. Again she felt an urge to laugh. It was ridiculous! Caro wasn't here to get pregnant. She was nearly fifty-one years old, and as much as she liked this man, the whole idea was… 'I don't believe you,' she said, exasperated.

He didn't answer. Instead he gave her a small, sad smile, lifted his phone, swiped through and then held it up to her.

A text. Something in Turkish. But there was Caro's name – *Miss Hardcastle* – and the room number. And there was *7am*. She sat back in her chair and crossed her arms. 'It's in Turkish.'

'It came about fifteen minutes ago,' he said. 'It's from Marianne at the hotel. She's asking me if I want the job. If I want to take Miss Hardcastle into Nicosia tomorrow morning.' He looked up at Helen. 'I have done this before, Helen.'

'Well,' she said coldly. 'Do you? Want the job?'

'No.' He put the phone down. 'Tomorrow is a free day for me. I don't want the job.'

'Right.' And that was that. A silence descended, him on one side, her on the other. She picked up her glass.

Kaveh had the wrong end of the stick. Caro wasn't going to have a baby. She would never do anything so stupid. She was all sorts of things – a touch selfish, a touch neurotic, a woman who…a woman who carried around a handbag of medication and passed it off as hay fever tablets. Wasn't it just a few hours ago that they had sat opposite each other and she had asked Caro directly?

If I ask you something, will you be honest with me?

It was inconceivable that she hadn't been. That she could be keeping something like this from her. Thirty years they went back. Caro knew everything. Caro was the one who had mopped up blood clots from her kitchen floor, who'd persuaded Helen that she was ready to hold Daniel, when she'd been terrified that she never would be. How could she *not* have told her? She shook her head, her mouth stretched to a wire. 'You're wrong,' she said after what seemed an age. 'I've known Caro nearly all my life and you're wrong.'

10

Soon after, the lunch ended on a sadly subdued note, and by the time they got back to the hotel Helen felt far enough away from the morning's sailing that it could have been someone else's experience entirely.

Kaveh dropped her off at reception, full of apologies and concern about the repercussions his mistake might have caused, and Helen was not graceful. Not at all. She was curt and cold – so cold that by the time she reached the hotel room she was warm with shame.

Inside, the room was cool and dark. As Helen eased the door open, she could see the shape of Caro in bed. She paused, hand clasping the doorknob. A baby? How could she even say that out loud? For a few years now, between the three of them – Kay, herself, Caro – a tacit understanding had grown, under the terms of which nobody mentioned the subject of having children. Complaining about the ones that were already had was fine, but the possibility of more? Caro never brought it up, so they had learned not to talk about it, and the feeling Helen had (and she was sure Kay thought so too) was that that ship had sailed and Caro had come to terms with it. Which Helen admired. There was, after all, a lot more to life than having children – something she wished she'd learned a little earlier. So how could she break that now – this wall of quiet and mutual understanding that had worked so well?

Certainly not by waking Caro and blurting it out. Tiptoeing, she made her way across the marbled floor towards the balcony to sit and wait, to find a way of beginning. But she was only halfway across when Caro pushed up on her elbows. 'Did you have fun?' she said, her cheek creased with the folds of the sheet.

Helen looked down at her hands. 'Yes,' she managed. 'It was great.'

'Oh.' Caro yawned. 'And you're angry with me for leaving you with him?' Her voice was muffled and lazy with sleep.

'Him?'

'The sailing man.' She waved a hand. 'Karim—'

'Kaveh,' Helen said quietly.

'Right.' Caro looked at her.

And because she couldn't bear to meet Caro's eye – because it could be true – Helen turned to the chest of drawers and put her hat and bag down. 'I'm not angry,' she said.

'You are,' Caro laughed.

The hairs on the back of Helen's neck went stiff.

'It's written all over your face!' Caro eased the sheet back and swung her feet to the floor. 'I'm sorry, Helen, I just had this headache and I really didn't feel—'

'You can't even see my face!'

'Okay.' Caro nodded. She looked down at her feet. 'Well,' she said quietly. 'Even if you're not, you have a right to be. I was pretty selfish this morning…about everything. So…well, I'm sorry.'

Helen swallowed. The words she was going to need to say were gagging her, jumping around in her throat like fish in a net. They wanted out, but she just couldn't say them. And looking back at Caro through the mirror – her slim figure and expensive haircut – the whole idea became even more fantastical. Caro, embarking on motherhood? This was Caro, for heaven's sake! Strong, successful, sensible Caro, not some deluded—

'Helen.' Caro's voice was suddenly loud. 'You're swaying! Come and sit down.' She patted the bed next to her. 'Now.'

It was the simplest thing to do, so she went over and sat down.

Caro smiled. 'Reverse sea legs?'

Helen shrugged.

'Was it good?'

'It was…yes…' She closed her eyes. She had neither the energy nor the will to try to explain how extraordinary the morning had been. How beautiful. Not now, not in the face of this.

'This was never going to be straightforward, was it?'

Slowly Helen opened her eyes.

'You and I, going away together?' Caro sighed. 'I know I can be selfish.'

'Caro—'

'Please, Helen, let me say this.' Caro stretched her legs out and flexed her feet so her toes were looking back at them, all ten, glossed pink. Helen stared at them. She couldn't remember the last time she'd painted her toenails.

'I'm so glad you decided to come,' Caro said, her voice quietly serious. 'I *really* am, and I'm really looking forward to Kay coming, but…' She turned to Helen. 'Please don't get upset. I've lived on my own for so long, I just feel I need some time to myself. To get acclimatised, you know? To company again?'

Helen didn't speak.

'So.' Caro shook her head and laughed. 'I've decided that tomorrow the best thing would be if I take myself off. It will give us both some space. You might go sailing again?'

Slow as an owl, Helen turned to face her. 7am, Kaveh had said. 7am.

'I need to unwind,' Caro continued, running her fingers through her hair. 'Work has been worse than usual. Really hectic. I'm sure you've noticed how tense I've been?'

She didn't answer. She didn't nod and she didn't shake her head. She held Caro's gaze and she sat and waited.

'So…' Caro said lightly, colour spreading across her cheeks. 'Well, if you don't mind?'

'Why would I mind?' And by the time Caro looked away, Helen knew she was lying.

'Okay!' Caro stood up. She looked around the room as if something from the moment was missing. 'Okay,' she said again. 'I'm going to take a shower.'

The bathroom door closed, the toilet flushed and the thin clatter of water raining down started the sound

174

of the shower. Only when it had widened out, when the clatter became a broad hiss, did Helen unclench her fists and fall back on the bed. Outside, a bird swooped to sit on the railing of the balcony, its little chest pumping, its head twisting all sorts of unlikely angles. Helen watched it.

Caro was lying.

There was no forethought to what she did next, no stopping to contemplate the right or wrong of it. She simply got up and walked across to Caro's handbag. Tucked away in the back pocket were the white packets of medication she'd seen the day before. She took them out, fingers numb at the tips as she read through the labels: oestrogen patches, progesterone vaginal pessaries… Caro wasn't so much keeping her engine lubricated (as per Dr Ross's description) as rebuilding it from scratch. But…it wasn't proof of anything.

She turned, scanning the room, and through the partly open door of the wardrobe she caught sight of a corner of blue: Caro's suitcase. Three strides had her across the room, one fluid movement had her swinging the empty case onto the bed, and a quick, sharp pull had the zip open, the inside of the case displayed, the brochure tucked into the back pocket revealed.

She pulled it out. *Dilekler IVF Clinic.*

There it was. Her ears rang, her legs went to water, her stomach to lava. Hands shaking, she took the brochure out onto the terrace, sat down and opened it up. And as she read, Helen could think only one thing: how right Kaveh had been. *Dilekler* was surely a place where miracles were made.

Age.

Biology.

None of these things mattered. This was a place where babies were manufactured, and if you couldn't provide the right ingredients they were provided for you. Babies made. Not out of love or commitment or passion. Not out of duty or violence, revenge or even that dullest reason of all, sheer stupidity. Here babies were simply made to order, and somehow... She leaned forward, fist at her mouth. Wasn't that worse? A baby made to order, like curtains? She snapped the brochure shut. Her heart was racing and her brow was sweaty. And Caro? Caro had been lying to her!

A minute later, as she heard the bathroom door open, the first thing Helen thought was that she'd left the suitcase open on the bed. The second thing was that she didn't care.

'Hel—' Caro's voice cut off. There was a silence, then the swift and expected pad of bare feet across tiles, and another silence.

Caro was standing behind her. Helen could feel it. Neither of them turned, neither of them moved, like an odd middle-aged version of musical statues.

And because she could see it – how Caro's face would be shutting down, the thinness of her lips, the raised drawbridge of her jaw – something very heavy bloomed in Helen's chest. A great lead-petalled flower of dread.

Silently Caro moved into her line of vision, picked the brochure up and folded it back into its envelope.

'When,' Helen breathed, 'were you going to tell me?'

'When it was done.'

When it was done. The shock was physical, compressing

the air in her lungs so she had to sit upright, put her hand to her chest and forcibly inhale. 'When it was done?' she gasped.

Caro didn't answer.

'You lied, Caro,' Helen said, her voice shaking with the effort to contain a fury that fed on a myriad of emotions. Anger at being lied to, confusion at being lied to, frustration and disbelief, a deep sorrow and, somewhere, shame. Caro wanted to be a mother. She hadn't come to terms with anything, and she hadn't found a way of telling them that.

'And you went through my things, Helen,' Caro said, and her voice trembled too.

Helen's jaw set, as stiff as leather. 'Is that where you're going tomorrow?' she whispered. 'Is that the time you want to yourself?'

Caro nodded.

'And you've booked a taxi for seven?' Now they were facing each other. 'Kaveh told me. He thought I knew. He presumed that, as your friend, you would have told me.'

And without a word, Caro turned and went back inside.

How long Helen sat, numb with shock and disbelief, she had no idea. Eventually the sound of the hairdryer stirred her. Had her staring at the open balcony doors. So that really was it! Caro wasn't going to say another word. She wasn't going to come back out and explain herself. And she wasn't going to apologise for all the deceit – because deceit it was – that had brought Helen to Cyprus in the first place. Would she have come if she'd known? Of course not! Weak with confusion, she stood up. So – all their years of friendship were worth only this? Agitated and panicked almost, as shaken as a bottle of fizz, she went to the doorway and watched Caro finishing her hair.

The hairdryer switched off. Caro bent to unplug it, and in the new silence Helen's words were loud. 'You can't do this,' she said, because if Caro wasn't going to ease the door an inch, allow any kind of discussion, what choice did she have, other than dive in like this?

Caro returned the dryer to the drawer. Looking at Helen in the mirror she said, 'Why? Why can't I?'

Helen opened her mouth. Why couldn't Caro do this? 'Because it's not right!' she gasped. 'It's not natural. It's not normal. You can't just take another woman's egg… I mean, I presume that's what you're doing… You haven't…'

Caro had turned away.

'You can't!' Helen cried, and her voice rang around the room, so pained, so desperate to be heard it had Helen gripping the door frame, shrinking away.

'And this,' Caro sighed, 'is exactly why I didn't tell you.'

Helen looked at her.

'You sound like my mother. Judgemental.'

Like. My. Mother. It was a slap. Nasty. Swift. Stinging. She slumped down on the bed, burning with fury now. She wasn't like Caro's mother. She wasn't like *anyone's* mother, and it wasn't okay that Caro, of all people, should keep shoving her back into that mother box. As if that had been her only role in life, as if that was the only prism through which she could ever be seen. It wasn't anyone's mother who'd thrown herself off the boat just a few hours ago! Who'd jumped into an ocean. 'That's not fair, Caro,' she said, a ticking bomb in her voice. 'And what's more, it's

178

childish, which tells me exactly how little you actually know about kids. The compromises you're going to have to make. You're doing something I disagree with, and because you don't want to hear, that's how you react?'

For a moment Caro didn't speak, but Helen saw the way her shoulders dropped. Knew she had bought herself a moment. She watched as Caro came and sat down on the bed next to her.

'Well,' Caro said quietly, 'how much did you know? Before you had your kids?'

Helen kept her chin down, her voice tight. 'It's not the same, Caro.'

'Isn't it?' There was a lightness to Caro's voice now, a joking tone almost, that was nails on a blackboard to Helen. 'Tell me, is there some sort of exam I should be taking?'

'I can't,' Helen seethed, 'believe that you think this is funny.'

'I don't,' Caro said. And she stood up again. 'Quite the reverse, Helen. I know it's a shock for you, but actually I've thought long and hard about this. A lot longer and a lot harder than most people. I mean, you didn't exactly plan your first, did you?'

Helen snapped her head up; her jaw had dropped and her mouth was open. 'I can't…' But her breath failed her. 'Don't do that, Caro. Don't go there—' Daniel hadn't been planned, but Daniel hadn't lived either. And every reference to him was a precious bauble to be handled with exquisite care. Not a curve ball, thrown in like this to make a cheap point, to advance an argument. A selfish, blinkered argument.

179

'All right!' Caro pressed her hands to her temples. Her head was shaking. 'I'm sorry,' she said. 'I didn't… I'm sorry. Forget I said that.' She dropped her hands, clasped them together and held them under her chin. 'But *why?*' she pleaded. '*Why* shouldn't I? I have the money to support—'

'Kids,' Helen hissed, 'need a lot more than money, Caro.'

'I know that.'

'Do you?' Helen stared at her. 'Do you really?' She shook her head. What did Caro think she knew? What did anyone think they knew before they became a parent? Whatever it was, it was as worthless as a glass hammer. And wasn't that the problem with this whole baby-made-to-order service? Like trying to solve a maths problem when you've started with the wrong equation. Trying to get a square shape to fit into the big, blank, round hole of your life? 'A baby,' she sighed, 'doesn't stay a baby, Caro. It's not like a chihuahua that you can keep in your handbag and take out and cuddle when you want. It walks. And then it runs. And then you spend every spare moment of your life running after it. It talks and it shouts and you spend every minute shouting back at it. Picking up after it, cleaning up after it. Worrying yourself sick making sure it's eating right, not taking drugs, not getting run over, not getting abducted. Sometimes just trying to like it. Just making sure it's okay is a lifelong marathon and…' Her mouth fell open, all out of words, all out of energy, all out of everything. She sat and looked at her hands. Was that what she thought?

For a long while neither of them spoke. Then very calmly Caro said, 'With all respect, Helen, that is only your experience.'

She shook her head, feeling the dismissiveness of Caro's words like soft but persistent blows to the head. It was true. Motherhood for her was and always had been exhausting. When her children were younger she'd spend daylight hours yearning for space from them, only to crawl into their beds just to feel the warmth of their sleeping bodies. She couldn't wait for them to be off, and now they were she wasted hours checking Facebook to catch a glimpse of them. They were the sum of her and completely separate from her. Aliens, with Lawrence's nose, her eyes, arrogantly naive opinions and disgusting habits, whom she loved more than herself. Twenty-five years – half her life – desperately trying to anticipate their needs and wants. A high-stakes game whereby if she loved them well enough, her only reward was that they would be free and safe to leave her. No wonder she was exhausted. She fell back on the bed. She wanted to laugh. Yes, it was *only* her experience, but how naive Caro was! For all her wealth and success, how ridiculously naive. She closed her eyes. How could she tell her what it was like? How could she possibly begin…? The bed sagged as she felt the weight of Caro sitting down very close by her shoulder.

'Helen,' Caro whispered. 'I've worked so hard all my life. I have a beautiful home, money in the bank, a job I love. You know I tried. I *really* tried waiting for Mr Right to come along, and maybe he did. But he was too bloody early and I wasn't ready.'

Helen opened her eyes. 'You make it sound like a bus, Caro.'

Caro tipped her head as she looked at the ceiling.

'Michael wasn't a bus. He was a coach with reclining seats and a toilet and a big screen TV, and my tragedy was that I didn't know he was the only one coming. That it really was only buses after that. Damaged, useless buses with graffiti. Cranky, unreliable, with no bloody wheels. And you know what the funny thing is?'

Helen shook her head.

'Even with no wheels,' Caro sighed, 'I always thought I could make them work. Remember Lewis?'

She nodded. Lewis, the most boring man Caro had ever dated. Nice to look at, but only one topic of conversation: himself.

'I'd made everything else in my life work, hadn't I?' Caro said. 'So I really thought I could, and would, make it work, but…' She smiled. 'In the end it turned out that I was as much of a crappy bus to him as he was to me. Difference was…*is*…men don't have to compromise.' She shrugged. 'And then it was too late.'

They stayed like that, Caro sitting, Helen staring at the ceiling.

Lewis had been unbearably boring, that was true, and the idea that he'd chosen to leave Caro for a younger, even more boring version of himself was ludicrous; but lying back, hands behind her head, Helen knew that Caro had missed a chapter. And, as hard as it was going to be to mention it, the story wasn't complete without it. She let her gaze wander across to the open balcony doors, the rise of the mountains beyond. 'What about Singapore?' she asked quietly.

Caro nodded. 'Do you know how long it's taken me to come to terms with that? That I missed my only chance?'

182

No, no. That was wrong. Talk about rewriting the past. Helen sat up. Her hair had fallen across her face. 'You didn't *miss* your chance, Caro. Having an abortion isn't missing your chance.'

For a moment Caro looked at her. Then she half snorted. 'Helen. If I hadn't, I would have lost everything. My job, my career... There would have been no coming back. Every single thing I had ever worked for—'

'I get it!' Anger warming again, Helen lifted a hand. Caro hadn't rewritten anything. This was an original recording, learned by rote, recited word-perfect. 'It happened to me as well,' she said. 'When I fell pregnant with Daniel, it wasn't that convenient for me either. Remember?'

'Oh.' Caro looked at her. 'But that's not the same, Helen. You weren't—' Abruptly, she stopped talking and turned away. 'It wasn't quite the same situation,' she finished quietly.

'Maybe not.' Helen stared at the back of Caro's head. 'I mean, I was only a marketing assistant with an organisation I truly believed in. I wasn't earning six figures and flying business class. Not the same at all.'

'I didn't intend to sound—'

'You made your choice, Caro,' she said flatly. 'And I made mine. And for better or worse, we have to live with that.'

Caro nodded. She stood up and walked over to the open door. 'Maybe,' she said. 'And maybe not. The goalposts have been moved now, haven't they?'

Helen swung her legs to the floor. As surely as if they'd been darts, Caro's words still stung. *Not quite the same*

situation. No, it hadn't been the same. She had given up a
career dedicated to preserving old buildings. How could
that ever be compared to the hard and glittering reality of
Caro's bank balance? Chin lowered, hair falling forward,
she watched Caro move out to the terrace, and an idea
that she didn't want to shine light upon stepped forward
anyway – clearly formed, visible, complete: Caro nurtured
a superiority over both her and Kay. She was better than
Kay because of her income and she was better than Helen
because of her career. How else could that comment be
explained? *Not quite the same...* Now she tingled with rage.
'Moved!' she said, spitting the word like a glob of phlegm.
'Ha! Caro! That's the biggest understatement of all time.
The goalposts have been ripped out and thrown away! It's
a different game now. Women of seventy having babies?
That's obscene!'

Caro turned. 'I'm hardly seventy.'

'No!' Helen stood. 'But you will be when the child is still
a teenager! Who's thinking of that, Caro? Who's thinking
of the child? The doctors? You? You're fifty, for God's sake!
If you go ahead and have a baby, it won't have any family
other than you. No aunts, no uncles, no grandparents. And
what's more, it'll be lucky to still have you!' Her hands
came to her face, pressing her cheeks together. What she
was saying she truly believed in – had felt herself in those
pockets of grief she still fell into since losing her parents.
'God, Caro! The world is a lonely enough place as it is!'

Caro's response was as swift as it was simple. 'Don't you
think I know that?' she said.

Hands still pressing at her face, Helen stared. And

stared. A terrible realisation surfaced. 'So,' she said, and paused. 'You're having a baby for *company*? To make yourself less lonely?'

'Is that,' Caro said quietly, 'so terrible?'

'Yes,' she gasped, because the detachment in Caro's voice was obscene. 'At your age, yes it is! Can't you see that? Can't you—'

But Caro had turned away.

Arms flailing, Helen looked around the room. Caro at the school gates? At sixty? 'It's wrong and it makes me furious… That people can be stupid and selfish, and others who should know better are making a fortune from it!'

'Is that what you think, Helen?' Now Caro turned back to her. 'That I'm stupid? And selfish?'

Helen slumped onto the bed. Tears sprang up, warm on her cheeks as they rolled down. She'd often thought Caro was selfish, but selfish in ways that were forgivable and unimportant. They went back a long way. Caro was Caro, and their friendship easily trumped the last-minute cancellations she sprang upon them, or the utter lack of awareness she had regarding their familial responsibilities. But this? How could she forgive this? 'You made your choice, Caro,' she said sadly. 'Like I made mine. We have to take responsibility for the choices we make. We just have to!'

Leaning against the door frame, Caro looked up at the sky. 'I want someone to love, Helen,' she said, and her voice cracked.

'Don't we all,' Helen whispered.

'Helen.' Caro sighed. 'You don't know how lucky you are. You never have. You have Libby and Jack. You—'

'No.' Helen shook her head.

'You do!'

'No. I don't!' She dropped her head to one side, all the fight gone. 'You can't get beyond the baby, Caro, so you don't understand! I don't have Libby and Jack, any more than I have the stars and the moon. And that's exactly the way it should be. They go off and leave you, and what's left is...what's left is me and Lawrence, and half of that, the me bit, I don't even recognise any more.'

'Well.' Bending her head to look at her nails, Caro said quietly, 'I've had enough time to find me. I'm pretty sure who I am.'

'Are you?' Helen leaned back against the bedstead. She looked at Caro. 'Well, good luck with that, Caro, because I'm telling you now, a child will chew you up and spit you out when it's done. And afterwards, if you can still recognise any last bit of yourself, good luck.'

Caro raised her palm. 'Enough,' she said quietly. 'Enough.' And she went out to the balcony.

For a long moment Helen sat looking after her, the note of reproach in Caro's voice reverberating around the room, ringing in her ears. Had it been that bad, what she'd said? Was there something wrong with her? She loved her children, but wasn't it true? She wasn't the same person, for better or worse, good or bad. Her children had reshaped her. Stamped all over the mould and squeezed out something else altogether. The best and worst of her. And perhaps that's what would-be parents should face. Vows of parenthood, not marriage. Are you prepared, for better or worse, to face what you may find in each other afterwards?

She pushed back on her hands, stood up and walked across to the door.

Caro turned.

'Look,' Helen said. 'You're going through a wobble. I'm going through a pretty big one myself. It's scary and it's really fucking sad, actually…knowing so many things won't come round again.'

The smile Caro managed was enough for Helen to continue. 'It's the second half,' she said. 'We're beginning the second half of our lives and we all know how it ends…' Suddenly she stopped talking. 'Why are you shaking your head?'

Caro had crossed her arms and *was* shaking her head. 'We don't have to accept that ending, Helen.'

'Caro!' Helen felt her jaw fall open. 'You're not immortal.'

'You say I made a choice?' Caro answered. 'What you've never understood, Helen, was that I didn't. There was no choice to make. You honestly think I could have stepped aside from my career and taken the time out then to become a mother?'

'You never tried.'

'Because I saw what happened to those who did.'

'Right.' Helen blinked. 'Well,' she said, 'if it was so important you could—'

'Everything was important! It was *all* equally important. And it's not fair, Helen, because men don't and never have had to choose. So now things have changed. Now I do get a second chance. Now I've got the time, the money and the wisdom, and most of all it's my life. I get to choose.'

Helen blinked. Caro really couldn't see it. Then again, who could? Who could really understand the awesome responsibility of creation? 'It's not just your life, though, is it?' she said. 'You will be an old woman when—'

'SPF, Helen,' Caro said lightly. 'Yoga. Sixty is the new fifty.'

'Wow.' Helen's mouth tightened to a tiny ball. 'Wow,' she whispered. 'I never thought you'd be capable of something so selfish. For once, just once, Caro, can't you think of someone other than yourself?'

Her words were bullets, hitting their mark with silent and deadly precision. She was out of the door before Caro had even fallen.

It was the most hurtful thing she had ever said, and she had known in advance. Chosen her poison with precision, tipped the arrow perfectly. But wasn't it true? Wasn't it what she and Kay had discussed secretly for years? Caro lived as she pleased. Caro was number one in Caro's life. Whatever Caro wanted, Caro got.

Among the blue and white sunloungers and the yellow umbrellas, Helen stopped in the middle of the lawn. A waiter approached. He was carrying a tray of food – charred chicken kebabs, with slices of lemon at the side of the plate. As he passed, the sweet, rich smell that filled her nostrils was nauseating. How could anyone be eating at a time like this? When her best friend, a woman she had known for most of her life, had turned out to be…a stranger? Behind her, ice chinked against glass. Helen turned to the sound, then turned back and looked up at the room she had just left. The balcony was empty. Caro would be inside, wounded, and there wasn't a single part of Helen that wanted to go back and help. She felt tremendously sad and overwhelmingly weary.

She scooped her hair, still matted and rough with sea salt, up from her neck. Now she'd come to a halt she couldn't think where to go. In the shaded corner of the patio an elderly couple were sitting playing cards. On the other side of the pool a woman sunbathed. Helen narrowed her eyes. The sunbathing woman was also *of a certain age* and she didn't seem to be with anyone. Was she here for the same reason? She glanced back up at the room. She needed to get away, and there was only one person on this whole island who could help her do that.

Head down, she hurried across the lawn towards the hotel entrance. Standing behind the reception desk was the same woman who had greeted them on arrival yesterday. Was it only yesterday? So much seemed to have happened – compared to twenty-four hours back home anyway.

The woman looked up. So like Kay, same all-knowing eyes.

'Hello,' she said. 'I was wondering if Kaveh was here?'

'He has gone home.'

'Oh.' Helen hovered by the open door. Of course he'd gone home. She knew that, and that wasn't the question she'd wanted to ask. But how could she just come out and ask for his telephone number? She cleared her throat and tried again. 'It's just that I had a sailing lesson with him this morning and I think I may have left something on the boat.'

This time the woman raised her head. Black plates

of eyes that looked Helen up and then down and then up again and then went back to her papers.

Embarrassed, Helen didn't move. *Women of a certain age.* She was one of those as well, and heaven knew what this woman was thinking now. If they came and went, came and went, all these *women of a certain age.* Was she mistaking Helen for one of them? Or worse – the idea swept through her – was she thinking that Helen wanted Kaveh as some sort of sperm donor? She had an urgent desire to hold up her hand. Point out the ring. *I'm married! I already have kids.* Behind her a couple came in, brushing past her shoulder.

The woman behind the desk lifted her head to greet them.

Hopelessly undecided as to what to do next, Helen moved across to the sofa.

'Here.'

And she looked up to see the woman holding out a piece of paper with a number written on it.

Outside in the courtyard, hands trembling, she stood by the fountain and watched a dragonfly zip through the silver water. Its tiny, iridescent wings shimmered small oceans of colour, just like the kingfisher on her magnetic Wilko notepad stuck to the fridge back home. Helen's mouth turned down. She was a long way from home, a long way from fridges and reminder notepads and... Fuck it! She took out her phone and dialled the number.

'Helen,' Kaveh said, after she'd (unnecessarily) introduced herself. 'Another sailing lesson?'

'Umm, no. I owe you an apology.'

Kaveh stayed silent. (How wise he was.)

'You were right,' she said.

Again he didn't speak.

'I can't believe it!' Not trusting herself not to cry, she swung away from the hotel and began walking up to the entrance gates, gravel grinding through the thin soles of her sandals. Her free arm was across her mouth, her eyes blurry. 'She's going there tomorrow morning and we've just had the most terrible row.'

'Helen?'

'So...' Helen tipped her head to the sky. 'So I'm ringing to say I'm sorry, Kaveh. I'm sorry I was so angry. I... I didn't want to believe it.'

'Where are you?'

Where was she? She turned and looked back. She'd walked through the hotel gates, a hundred yards or more along the road. 'Outside the hotel.'

'And where is Caro?'

'In the room.' Helen looked back at the gates. 'I can't go back,' she whispered. 'I can't face her. And I know she doesn't want to face me.'

There was a long pause and then Kaveh said, 'Would you like me to come and get you?'

It didn't take him long. Ten minutes, maybe twelve. He came on a moped, stopped in front of the hotel, took out a spare helmet for her, and if the woman behind the desk saw or noticed, Helen didn't give a fig. She wrapped her arms around his waist and dropped her cheek against his back. And as they sped off she didn't think about Caro or Lawrence or her children. She didn't think about anything at all.

11

They travelled in a cloud of dust. Past white houses topped with flat roofs, guarded by grapefruit trees, mandarin and orange. Past carob bushes, where the ripening pods poked through like blackened fingers. Past shimmering silver olive trees, green almonds. Three children cradling one dog, a woman pulling a wagon filled with grey sacks. And as they travelled further, the dust subsided, the air became fresher and the land began to fall to the sea. Until finally the twinkling strip of azure light that was the Mediterranean came into view.

Muscle by muscle Helen began to relax. Shoulders unhunching, fingers unfurling, eyes drifting from one thing to another. Everything passed as if she were watching a film. A series of images, as harmless as a muted TV.

She recognised the turn into Kyrenia from the morning, but Kaveh didn't take it. He continued instead along the coast road, where rickety roadside stalls selling oranges were more frequent than houses. Eventually he took a left turn, continuing on until the road narrowed to a lane,

192

curved left and stopped. Up ahead stood a shack, outside it two plastic tables with two fat ashtrays. From beneath one table a dog eyed them without raising its chin. Next to the dog sat a man, so still he could have been painted in.

Kaveh brought the bike to a standstill. He nodded at the empty table and disappeared inside. Still clutching her helmet, Helen slipped into the tableau as quietly as possible. Across the track, beyond a strip of scrubby grass, lay the ocean. She stood and stared. The waves rolled in and rolled out. The breeze came from the west, where the sky was orange, and within moments she understood why Kaveh had brought her here. This was exactly the kind of place she needed to be. Soon enough the sun would set, the tide would turn, the moon would rise and the day would eventually leach away – lost, like every other day, among the sands.

And then she would be able to go back to Caro. Go back and pour them both a glass of wine and – what? Apologise? She laid the helmet on the table and the word slipped away. She could barely think it, let alone say it. She wished things had gone differently, but it was wrong. She believed that what Caro was doing was wrong. So how could she apologise for being honest? She took out her phone, then, without looking at it, put it away again. They'd had disagreements before. Rows even. *Show me two women who haven't come to blows over half a lifetime*, Helen had always said, *and I'll show you two acquaintances, not friends.* It wasn't possible to be so close to someone else without seeing all their warts. And that was the titanium thread of their friendship right there, Kay included. Their ability to forgive in each other everything that fell short. But this?

193

A salted breeze touched her face, and with it Helen felt the salt of her own tears. It was too much. Caro's selfishness, she felt, was too much.

Kaveh came back with wine. He didn't comment as he put the glasses down. He took out his cigarettes and she picked up her glass and together they sat, him smoking, her sipping, the sun waning.

Here I am, she thought. Sipping cold wine by the Mediterranean Sea, and I never want to leave. She lifted her chin and looked at Kaveh. Lucky Kaveh, who didn't ever have to leave. Who always had…this. 'Have you always lived here?' she asked quietly.

He shook his head. 'I was born here and then we had to move.'

Surprised, Helen turned to him.

He shrugged. 'I am Greek Cypriot. This part is Turkish. We were moved to the south when I was a child.'

'Your family?'

'The whole village.'

'Oh.' She didn't know what to say.

Kaveh smiled at her, leaning forward as he tipped ash.

'So…now you've come back?'

He nodded. 'Yes, I came back.'

For a long moment Helen looked at him, but his expression was inscrutable. She turned back to the safety of the ocean. 'Are you married?'

'Yes.'

One little word – *yes* – causing such a thump of disappointment.

'But' – his voice was soft – 'she is in the south.'

194

Slowly Helen turned to him. 'She didn't want to come back?'

'No.' And he didn't take his eyes off her.

Helen stayed silent. Then, because it was the only way she could say what she wanted to say, she turned back to the waves. 'Do you miss her?'

'No.'

The man at the other table got up, raised a hand to Kaveh and then lumbered away, the dog following. Helen watched, almost surprised that he could, and had, moved.

'Where is your husband?'

Yes, she knew that was coming. She placed her ringless hand on top of her ringed hand. 'Somewhere in Nepal,' she said, watching the dog.

'Nepal?'

She could hear the surprise in Kaveh's voice. 'He's just climbed Everest.'

Kaveh let out a low whistle. 'This is impressive.'

'Is it?' Helen turned to him.

'Isn't it?' As he stubbed his cigarette out, he looked at her in a way that she hadn't been looked at for at least twenty-five years, and it torched everything up to the last five seconds of her life. Her stomach liquefied. 'Do you miss him?' he asked.

And meeting his eyes, she said, 'No. No, I don't.'

Who looked away first? She didn't know. She just knew that now she was looking at the ocean and his hand was on hers. Warm and rough, their fingers entwined, pushing against each other like limbs.

'Let's take a ride,' he said.

*

They travelled back up the coast road and turned inland. Although nothing had been said, Helen had made her decision. Wherever he took her she would go. She had one life under the stars, and she would go. She laid her head on his shoulder and thought of her namesake, wondering if this was how it had been for her also. Had it been just one look from Paris that had started it all?

The engine slowed. Helen looked up. Kaveh was preparing to turn off the main road. Up ahead, nestled against the mountain, she could see a cluster of houses growing up the hillside like a blocky white vine. Instinctively she knew that this was where they were going. She laid her head back and pressed closer against him.

Within minutes they had reached the village, Kaveh threading the bike through narrow streets where moss grew in the shaded aqueducts, lilies and roses bloomed in tiny front gardens and scarlet geraniums waved from window boxes. In the square a group of old men, sitting under the shade of a pomegranate tree, played backgammon.

Kaveh stopped in front of a small, flat-roofed house. Without speaking, he took her hand and led her inside, where it was cool and dark, and straight up the stairs into a shuttered bedroom. Here he turned, put his hands either side of her face and pulled her into a kiss.

A kiss that she didn't feel the start or the end of. That swept them onto the bed and into an embrace that closed the world down and zoomed his copper-coloured skin up so very, very close. She put her lips to his arm and his shoulders, pressed her cheek against the brutal stubble of his chin, threw her arms around his back.

And the unbelievable joy, the tangle of limbs and the film of sweat. The wine on his breath, the soft lobe of his ear, his silver, silver hair, curling damp at his neck. She could have cried. She could have laughed.

Hours passed.

Making love, sticking to sheets, tracing freckles and scars and hairlines. The sun set and the moon rose and they still hadn't covered the life-maps of each other's bodies, and it was astonishing to Helen. The way his fingers traced her caesarean scar, the spread of his hand across her breast, his tongue in her mouth. Silver light flooded the room. Stars twinkled and, finally replete, Helen fell asleep to the dry whispers of a million cicadas.

Kay hadn't registered the full-sized Daniel Craig or the gun he pointed at her. She was lip-synching along to 'Murder on the Dancefloor' while reading the blurb on the back of a *Your Five Weeks to Sugar-Free* DVD. Giving up at *Week One*, she put it back and picked up *Butterflies*. And immediately there she was, back at the old dining table, mock GCSE papers spread out, Wendy Craig burning the dinner on the boxy TV set in the corner of the living room, her mother serving peas and salad cream, her father in his overalls, knees black with grease. Her mother serving peas and salad cream? These days her mother would be as likely to wear a pea as serve one.

Her hands trembled as she tried to stuff the DVD back into place. Just this morning, her mother had thrown another fit, and this time she'd hit her target. Craig had been characteristically good-natured but, listening to him on the phone, Kay could tell he was shaken. It was unforgivable what age did. *Unforgivable.* Her gently spoken, patient mother slapping faces like a madwoman? The thought of it had her shaking her head. No. *No. No. No.* When it was her turn she'd take a bottle of champagne, rent a Porsche and drive it off the cliffs up at Hunstanton. *Thelma and Louise* style. Except she wouldn't drag Helen and Caro along, obviously. Not unless they wanted to come… This thought made her smile, made her wonder how Cyprus was going. Okay, she presumed. Caro's appointment was tomorrow, and after the initial mix-up over the rooms she hadn't heard anything more. Tomorrow she'd be joining them. Mountains to her east, ocean to her west. No laundry. No cooking. No shopping. No cleaning. Another smile, much broader, which was still plastered all over her face as she turned and bumped into Daniel, who wobbled precariously and probably would have fallen if a gangly limbed member of staff hadn't rather resourcefully grabbed his revolver.

'Careful,' the boy grinned as he straightened up 007. 'Or he'll shoot.'

'Good,' Kay drawled. 'Get it over with.' And she wheeled her empty shopping trolley past him, revelling in the astonishment on his face. God, she loved being fifty!

She was here for groceries, basic provisions for Alex and her parents, a few frozen dinners and plenty of toilet roll. So where to start? She looked up, caught a glint of something sparkly and turned her trolley. Ladies' Fashion, of course. Where else?

The glint turned out to be a gold fringe on a scarlet sarong. Probably the most useless and inappropriate garment she'd ever seen, designed for the Shakiras or the Chers of this world, not the Kay Pattersons. Oh, but it was lovely. Her fingers trailed the tickly gold fringe. It was wavy and colourful and lovely and... *And* she had a pull-over towelling robe thingy that would work just as well. Reluctantly she let the fringe slide through her fingers and walked on to Household Items. Five minutes wasted, brushing her hand over the fake fur fleeces and sequinned cushions, stopping to smell the smelly candles, and she'd reached the end of the aisle. Tesco at night, she thought, as she found her trolley wheeling itself towards the magazines – *Climbing World, Carp Fishing, Scootering: What Flicks Your Switch?* – was a prairie of possibility. Everything within reach. Because what, for example, was to stop her from right now buying *Climbing World* and transforming herself into a human stick insect? Or buying that DVD? Quitting sugar and increasing her energy levels to a degree whereby she could actually cope with her life? Or buying that sarong?

This time she was in charge. Manoeuvring the trolley through 180 degrees, whizzing back and throwing the sarong in her trolley. No need to even check size. Perfect. Yes, everything was possible! And what was more, she was certain that everyone else who came here at this ridiculous time of night had come to the same secret conclusion. Why else would they be here? And where else, nowadays, would they find this feeling of solace and hope?

She'd even begun to recognise faces. A white-haired man with a nose of red veins who always lingered at the engine oils. A nurse, still in uniform, who sat in the magazine aisle flicking through *Hello*. These people didn't come here to shop. They came to escape from jobs or marriages or kids. From life. Just as she did.

Or had.

Before mobile phones.

Because now, as if answering a cue, her phone had started ringing. Approaching the end of the freezer aisle, Kay stopped short. It was late enough to panic. No one rang her at this time except her father. Scrambling through a handbag-sized snowstorm of receipts, trolley tokens and open tissue packets, she grabbed for the phone.

Caro's name flashed up.

'What's wrong?' she said, leaning over the trolley to wheel forward with her elbows.

'Can you talk?' Caro answered.

'Well…' The directness of Caro's response had stalled her. 'I'm in Tesco,' she started.

'Tesco!' As Caro digested this information, there was a rush of air, a barely disguised sigh of annoyance that Kay heard all the way across Europe. 'Why,' Caro breathed, 'are you in Tesco at this time of night? You've got a plane to catch in the morning.'

Kay smiled. Caro sounded just like Caro. So whatever was wrong wasn't that bad. She slid back the cover of the nearest freezer and, as she stood looking at its frozen contents, experienced a small rush of excitement. She *did* have a plane to catch tomorrow! Somewhere warm.

'Kay?' Caro's voice was patchy, crumbled. 'You are still coming, aren't you?'

'Of course I am. I just have a few last-minute things to sort.' Like breaded haddock or fisherman's pie? What would her father prefer? (Alex was easy. Lasagne, shepherd's pie, breaded chicken. Repeat ad infinitum.)

'Right. Well, I wanted to warn you, because obviously I won't be here when you arrive tomorrow...'

'Okay.' She picked up a carton of Captain Haddock's Individual Fish Pies.

'Helen knows.'

Kay turned the packet over. Captain Haddock had a ridiculous face. 'How?' she asked, unsurprised at how unsurprised she was. Caro and Helen had never been able to stay out of each other's business. Why would this time be any different?

'It's...' Caro paused. 'It's a long story.'

'Can you shorten it?'

'Okay.' Caro paused. 'Okay, well, someone told her.'

'Someone told her?' Fish pies in hand, Kay glanced around the aisle, as if the person who had told Helen were hiding behind the frozen peas. This she was surprised at. 'Who,' she breathed into the phone, 'does she possibly know out there that could have told her?'

'There's a guy,' Caro said, 'that works here—'

A guy? Kay nodded.

'—and this morning Helen had a sailing lesson with him.'

She pressed her lips together, the twitch of a smile beginning. A guy, who Helen had had a sailing lesson with? Helen had gone sailing? Kay looked again at the picture of Captain Haddock on her fish pies packet, and she wanted to laugh. Would have, if it hadn't been for the ominous silence at the other end of the line. 'Oh,' she managed.

'Well, anyway, that's the summary.'

She nodded. Caro's voice was neutrally efficient, but she wasn't fooled for a second. 'So,' she said carefully, 'how did she take it?'

'Exactly as I thought she would,' Caro answered tersely. 'Which is why I'm ringing.'

'Right.' Kay threw the fish pies into her trolley, reached across and added the haddock fillets.

'We had a row.'

'Okay.' Of course they did.

'Quite a bad one.'

'Right.'

'And the long and the short of it is that, as always, Helen claimed the moral high ground. She doesn't think I should be doing this. She thinks it's wrong, Kay. She said that for once in my life I should try to think of someone other than myself. She actually said that!'

'Oh.' Kay closed her eyes. The distances that remained, even between the closest of friends. Hadn't she said the same thing herself to Helen about Caro? And wasn't it impossible to tell Caro that?

'Anyway.' Caro's voice was very small. 'It's eleven here and she hasn't come back.'

Kay flicked her eyes back across to the large clock behind the rows of empty tills. Helen should be back. Then again, at university she could remember the many times when Helen *should* have been back and wasn't. The difference being they were young and free then. The difference being it was half expected then. 'Do you know where she is?'

'She sent a text saying she's all right.' Caro sniffed. 'I'm guessing she's probably with him.'

'The sailing guy?'

'She doesn't even know him, Kay!' Caro's voice fell low. 'You know you hear about women falling for men abroad?'

Kay looked down at her trolley, to the crinkly eyes and white beard of Captain Haddock. 'How old is he?' she said.

'I don't know!' Caro answered, surprised. 'About our age I suppose.'

She smiled. *Our age* was middle-aged, so now she didn't know if she was worried about Helen or jealous. What she did know was that, unlike Caro, she wasn't at all surprised. Out of the three of them it was Helen, it was always Helen, who was most likely to do *something like this*. 'So,' she said. 'It's not a toy boy thing?'

'No!' Caro didn't pause. 'But it could well be a passport thing. I mean, as far as I can tell, he's an odd-job man. He's seen Helen and he's latched onto her. And she's angry with me, so she's vulnerable. But she's also married, Kay. It's not right that...'

It's not right... She thinks it's wrong... Kay sighed. She'd always been the bubble in the spirit level of this friendship. Always in the middle, persuaded to lean this way or that. For as long as she had known them, Caro and Helen had been engaged in unspoken, passively aggressive combat. Each of them trying to outdo the other. It had started with Lawrence, but where it would end she didn't know. Only that she didn't want to be there. Suddenly weary of it all, she said, 'Helen's a grown woman, Caro. Like you are.'

Caro didn't respond immediately. Only after a

long pause did she say, 'Don't you have an opinion?'

Did she have an opinion? No, she wasn't sure she did. The news of Helen's possible tryst was reaching her like radio signals from a faraway star. A beep on the horizon of the frozen goods aisle. Interesting, certainly, but still galaxies away from school reports and frozen dinners and an email that may or may not spell the end of her teaching career. 'Helen,' she said, 'will be fine. It's her life, Caro. Her marriage. Just like it's your life.'

But Caro didn't answer.

Kay frowned. Poor Caro. Choosing the colour of her child's eyes from a computer screen. And now this. Exactly what she'd wanted to avoid. 'Are you okay?' she said. 'Are you having doubts?'

'No, not at all,' Caro answered quickly. 'Anyway,' she added, 'it's done now. All frozen and waiting, so to speak.'

Kay shivered. She looked across the freezer and a hundred black eyes from a packet of frozen prawns looked back at her. The note of false bravado in Caro's voice hadn't gone unnoticed. She could hear how much she was going to be needed. No one was an island, not even Caro, no matter how much she believed she was.

'I'll see you tomorrow,' she said. 'And—'

'Yes?' Caro's voice was like a rope, desperately lassoing itself onto what Kay was about to say.

'I hope it goes well,' she said.

Swifts and swallows woke Helen. Black flecks swooping circles against the cool morning sky. A dog woke her, sharp barks snipping at the edge of consciousness. The smell of

Kaveh's skin woke her, a remnant taste of salt on her lips. She turned over, pushed her nose deep into the flesh of his shoulder and breathed him in. Then she fell asleep again.

Minutes later her phone woke her, a low, insistent buzz thrumming in her brain. She sat up, groggy and damp, floating above herself. Using the sheet as cover, she stumbled across the room and found her phone. It was Jack, calling through WhatsApp.

She swiped *answer video call*, and the first thing she thought when his face filled the screen was how pale he looked. He was at the kitchen table, and she could see that behind him the sky was dull and cloudy. She glanced out of the window in front of her, and it seemed incredible that her sky should be so blue and his so grey.

'That lasagne,' he said before she could speak. 'I think it must have been off, Mum. I've been *really* sick.'

Helen frowned. She was still half asleep and for a moment she had no idea what he was talking about. 'What do you mean?' She was looking at her kitchen, thinking how foreign it appeared.

He leaned forward, all pinched white. 'The lasagne was out of date, Mum. I think I've got food poisoning.'

'Have you been sick?'

'Three times!' he sulked, as if she was responsible. 'Should I call the doctor's? Have you got the number?'

Helen blinked. Half a continent away, and her eighteen-year-old son was asking for the phone number of a building less than five miles' walk from where he was sitting. Was he really doing that? She put her hand over her mouth and stifled a huge yawn. 'Do you feel sick now?' she said.

'No,' he responded warily.

'Well, when was the last time you were sick?'

'About one… I think.'

She sighed. 'Why don't you go back to bed? Sleep it off. If it's food poisoning it sounds like it's out of your system.'

'Who's that?'

Helen yawned again. 'Go back to bed,' she managed. It was all she wanted to do herself.

But Jack had leaned right into his phone and his eyes, so listless before, lit up now. '*Who*,' he repeated and raised a finger to point just above her shoulder, 'is that man, Mum! In bed behind you! *Who is that?*'

12

'K ay. *Kay.*'
The whisper travelled across the canyons of Kay's mind like a breeze across centuries. It wasn't real. It was a shadow, barely a memory of a memory, and she was so warm and the cushion was so comfortable... She was floating... Or perhaps she wasn't. She was flying. Of course! She pressed her cheek further into the cushion. Still on the plane, woozy from cheap white wine and turbulence, with no intention of waking up until—

'Kay.'

This time the whisper came with a feather touch, a tickle across the back of her knee.

'*Kay.*'

She swatted her knee and reluctantly opened her eyes. How lovely and dark it all was.

'Open your eyes.'

'I have,' she murmured.

'*You haven't.*' The touch came again, this time a pencil prod. '*Open. Your. Eyes.*'

With enormous effort, she did what she thought she'd already done.

'There we go. Now they're open!'

As she lifted her head she saw a dark head shape looming above, but the light beyond was dazzling and the back of her hand had stuck to the inside of her thigh, and her chin was wet with dribble, and her mouth…her mouth was as dry as the polystyrene rice crackers the Weight Watchers leader was always trying to sell her. 'Are we landing?' she asked, and tried to ease herself up. Blinking, she looked past the shape to a…pool? A flying swimming pool?

'Kay?'

She turned back to the shape, the gears of her mind clunking into place. Was she here already? Cyprus, with Helen and Caro?

'Blimey, Kay, how much did you have on the plane?' the shape said. 'I thought you were in a coma!' It laughed, and she realised *it* was Helen.

Looking around, trying to take in the reality of what was in front of her, she said, 'What time is it?'

'Quarter to five. I didn't think I should let you sleep any longer. Not if you want to sleep tonight.'

Quarter to five! She'd been on holiday for nearly one whole day and done nothing but sleep! She rolled her tongue over her teeth, a dry acidic taste in her mouth. Quarter! To! Five!

'Are you hungry? You've missed lunch.'

'I could eat.' When couldn't she?

'Chips? I can get a portion from the restaurant.'

'Grand,' she said and fell back, watching Helen pad

across the large terrace and disappear into the dark of the hotel.

Quarter to five. It wasn't becoming any more believable. Nearly five already. Back home she'd have taught at least four classes, answered countless emails, marked sixty coursework papers and negotiated any number of detentions. Back home she'd be thinking about trying to get home to empty the washing machine she'd filled that morning, thinking about whether to serve shepherd's pie or lasagne for tea. Back home she'd be... Kay stopped thinking, lay back and threw her arms across her eyes to shield them from the sun. Where had the day gone? Very vaguely she remembered changing in the hotel room after she'd arrived, and Helen's text: *I'm by the pool.* But the rest of the day? Alex had woken her at six that morning with a cup of tea. Lovely, but he'd set his alarm half an hour before she'd set hers. He'd always been a stickler for punctuality. The journey? She'd accidentally sprayed perfume in someone's eye when she'd tried a tester in duty-free, but really, why did people stand so close anyway? On the plane she'd watched a young mother unload iPads and earphones for her children, and now, yes, she remembered... The man next to her had been travelling home to see his elderly mother. And hadn't they ended up discussing familial obligations and the stresses that arise from such obligations? Yes, they had. His mother, her mother, her father, Alex, his father's elderly aunt, who would be 103 next year and who wasn't really an aunt and had turned up in 1974 and never left. On and on and on...

She dropped her head and rubbed her eyes. So how many of those little bottles of wine had she had? She remembered buying two. She remembered the man next to her buying her two…plus that gin and tonic at the airport… *Ugh.* No wonder she'd slept so long. Frankly, it wasn't half long enough. She leaned back and stretched her arms above her head, then sat forward and stared across the pool.

Craig had texted; she was vaguely sure of that. Grabbing her phone from her bag, she scrolled through. Yes, he had. And Alex! She reread Craig's text first. Her mother was safely settled into the home. He'd even sent a photo of them all in the gardens. Alex's text was shorter and to the point.

Having Shepherd's Pie tonight Mum. Sarah from work is coming. Love you. Bye.

Sarah from work? Kay smiled. Alex was going to be fine – the crowd he worked with at the garden centre would make sure of that. She dropped her phone, let her hands rest on her stomach and turned her head to the mountains. *Here you are, Kay*, she murmured. *You're in Cyprus.* She was, and it was every bit as beautiful as she'd needed it to be. A world away from her street, with its black wheelie bins and befouled pavements. So beautiful, that an idea strolled into her mind and sat down between her eyes. She could come and live here! Yes, she'd live here, by the sea, with the bougainvillea, the mountains, the grapes, those teeny-tiny white houses. She closed her eyes, fingers threading the gold fringe of her scarlet sarong… Yes, she'd live right here.

'This will sort you out until dinner.' Helen was back, holding out a plate of golden fried chips.

And suddenly Kay was ravenous. She took the plate.

'I must have been asleep myself,' Helen said, flopping down on her lounger. 'I didn't hear you arrive.'

'You were.' Kay's mouth was full of chips, but right now hunger topped manners (and it was only Helen). 'Sleeping like a baby,' she managed. She remembered now. After showering, she'd come down to the pool and spotted Helen immediately. She'd been lying on her stomach, arms tucked under her head, snoring long, whistly snores, so contented and childlike. Kay had had neither the heart nor the will to wake her.

She propped the plate on her legs, tucked her feet underneath her bottom and turned to look properly at Helen. What she saw took her breath away, and actually paused the chip eating. Helen had always been attractive, but right now she was beautiful. Radiant. Her cheeks were flushed, her eyes sapphire-bright, and her hair, which she'd tied back, fell in honey-coloured tendrils around her neck. Two days in the sun had worked wonders. Two days and… that's right… Kay narrowed her eyes… *Some sort of odd-job man*, Caro had said. And thinking about it, when she'd arrived at the hotel hadn't a man appeared from nowhere to help her with her suitcase? Was that Helen's Captain Haddock? She took a chip and held it up. Helen had always gone for rugged, athletic types but this man had had more stomach than hair, was wider than he was taller. Not Helen's type at all. 'You didn't come home last night, did you?' she said, and stuffed the chip in her mouth.

'Oh boy.' Helen stretched her legs and pointed her toes. 'News travels fast. Well, I don't need to ask *who* told you.'

Kay shook her head. She raked her hair back from her

face, made a fist of her hand and thumped her chest. Too many chips in too short a time. Nodding at the water bottle by Helen's bed, she wheezed out a response. 'Caro rang last night.'

'To tell you that I hadn't come back?' Helen asked as she passed the bottle. 'Which we will get onto... Or to tell you something else?' Her eyebrows had raised in great expectation.

Kay looked at her, tipped her head back and drank a long, cool draught. Well, here it was. The confrontation she'd been expecting around every corner, at the beginning of every phone call for the last ten days. After Caro's visit, her bombshell news, she had thought carefully about telling Helen. Carefully and in the end, briefly. On the one hand, it hadn't seemed fair that she should know and Helen not. On the other, much more persuasive hand, it simply wasn't her news to tell. The days when they'd lived in each other's pockets were over. Used up. And if a knife were to be sliced through the rock of their friendship, only the base, those first years, would have offered up a clean layer. After that, the sediment of life – those darkly separating lines of children, men, jobs – would be there, visible and unbreachable. They weren't twenty any more, sharing the same roof, the same toothpaste and (in Caro and Helen's case) the same boyfriend. No, her wavering about telling Helen hadn't lasted long – which wasn't, of course, going to make this any easier. She put the bottle down and said, 'She didn't need to tell me, Helen. I already knew.'

Helen pushed her sunglasses up off her face. 'You knew?' she whispered. 'Wait a minute!' Swiping her glasses

212

clean off her head, she sat up and leaned across the space between them. '*You knew?*'

'I knew,' Kay repeated, hand at her mouth, fighting the urge to burp.

'*Oh boy!*' Helen flung her sunglasses across the ground. For a moment they both sat looking at them. 'I don't believe this,' she said. 'I don't believe it!'

Kay sighed. The congestion of chips in her gullet had finally eased.

'How long?'

'What?'

'*When* did she tell you?'

'Literally two days before you flew out.'

'And you didn't think to tell me?'

'Of course I did! But it wasn't my news to tell.'

'*How…*' Helen closed her mouth. Opened it again. '*Why…*' Closed it again and lurched forward to grab her fallen glasses. Then, pressing her lips together as if she couldn't trust herself *not* to speak, she folded her arms and stared across the pool.

Kay looked down at the remaining chips on her plate. They both, she knew, needed a moment of digestion. She balanced the plate on her thighs, took the ends of her sarong and reknotted them over her chest. Then she eased herself back on the sunbed, all the more ready to weather the onslaught that she knew was coming. And come it did.

'*You should have told me, Kay!*' Helen hissed furiously.

Kay flinched. The plate flipped and chips spilled forth into the space between their sunbeds like water from a fountain.

Neither of them moved, and then, before either of them could even think of moving, a line of ants appeared. In silence they watched as the ants surrounded a lone chip, hoisted it up and began carrying it away. Like pallbearers with a coffin.

Sighing, Kay looked down at the sole chip left on her plate. In a fit of resignation she threw it down to the ants. When she looked up, Helen was laughing. So hard she had tears in her eyes.

'We were talking about this on the way over,' she said. 'Caro and me. Do you remember that taxi?'

'During uni? Of course I do. That's the second time in my life you've spoiled a perfectly good plate of hot chips.'

Helen was still laughing. 'The first time wasn't my fault. I never tripped you. You've just come to believe that.'

'True.' Smiling, Kay put the plate down and lay back, stretching her legs. She could sense Helen doing the same. She lifted her face, and the warmth of the sun was like a bath – easy, instant and welcome. 'I couldn't tell you, Helen,' she said quietly. 'You know that.'

'I know,' Helen replied, and her voice was thick with tears. 'But it's the deception, Kay,' she choked. 'She lied to me. And we…we had a terrible row.'

'I heard.' Kay looked up at the sky. Of course Helen was hurt. Deception hurts. She knew all about that.

Calmer now, Helen looked down at her hands. 'She didn't tell me because she was afraid of how I'd react… That's what she said.'

'Yes.'

'Well, I guess she was right! Because I couldn't pretend,

Kay. I think what she's doing is wrong, and I told her.'

Kay nodded. She put her hands behind her head, feeling the dampness of her warm, sweaty neck.

'I thought she didn't want kids.'

'Me too.'

'She's never said anything before.'

'No.' Kay's voice wasn't more than a murmur. What Helen was saying was true. Caro had never spoken of her desire to be a mother, or her regrets at not being one. She hadn't said a word. Then again, there were thoughts Kay didn't share. Wasn't this true of everyone?

'Well…' Helen leaned forward, wrapping her arms around her knees. 'What did you say? When she told you, what did you say?'

'I don't think I said much.' She hadn't. What could she have said?

'*Why not?*' Helen lifted her head, her voice urgent. 'If we can't say what we think, Kay…or…' Her face darkened. 'Was I wrong? Was I wrong to have been honest? I thought—'

'No.' Kay shook her head. 'No…' And looking at Helen's worried face, she felt only sadness.

'Because if I can't be honest with Caro – or you, but, you know – when she's about to embark on probably the most important decision of her life. I couldn't just…'

As Helen talked, Kay stared across the pool, trying to listen – really trying. Nevertheless Helen's voice faded. What had she thought when Caro told her? Helen pushing for an answer was making her realise that she didn't have one. Certainly not the black and white definitive response that Helen seemed to need. It wasn't that easy. The choice Caro was making needed consideration, time to…and then she understood. She didn't know what she thought because she hadn't actually thought much about it. She hadn't had time. She *never* had time. Caro had left that day and Kay had hopped right back onto the hamster wheel of her life. These midlife years she was in the middle of felt like a march, and there was certainly no end in sight right now. It was looking like Alex would live with her forever. Her mother could go on for years, and then her father… Her job (if she still had one)? Even the sofa of retirement she'd been looking forward to kept getting picked up and shoved further out of reach. Sixty, sixty-five…now sixty-bloody-seven! If there was one thing she didn't have time for, it was the luxury of thinking.

'Do you know what she said?' Helen was still talking.

Kay turned.

'She said sixty is the new fifty. When I pointed out how old she would be when the kid was still at primary school! She hasn't got a clue!' Helen's voice rose. 'She has no idea…' And rose.

'*Helen.*'

'What?'

'It's her life.'

'But that's just the point, Kay. It's not! It's another life altogether. And I don't think she has a single clue as to the responsibilities.'

'Did we?' Kay blurted. 'Before we had our kids, did we know?'

'That,' Helen said, 'is not the point.'

'Maybe.' She shrugged. It was and it wasn't the point. Helen was right: Caro didn't have a clue what she was letting herself in for. Just as she hadn't had a clue, not an inkling.

'Don't you have an opinion?'

'I...'

'Really?' Helen pushed.

'I'm... I'm surprised,' she managed, and closed her eyes, tears leaking through. Alex. Her heart. Twenty-two, six feet, eighty-eight kilos. Heart of gold and mental capacity of sixteen at best. Raspberry tea, because she liked tea and raspberries. Where would she be without him? And then, what would she have done if she'd known? If she'd been aware of what she was letting herself in for?

'I mean, I know you like to sit on the fence and—'

'Stop it!' It was a whisper, but it was a very loud whisper. 'Just. Stop. It. Helen. *Please.*'

And for a long time neither of them spoke.

Finally Kay opened her eyes, blotted them dry and looked down at the sad, droopy knot of her sarong.

As if it were a cue, Helen lay her head sideways on her knees. 'What should we do?' she whispered.

'There's nothing we can do.' She turned to Helen, who looked utterly forlorn. 'You and I, Helen,' she said, 'we've learned the hard way that things don't always go right. But Caro? She's never had to compromise, has she? In a way she reminds me of the kids at school.'

Helen smiled weakly.

'I mean, you can tell her until you're blue in the face that having a baby, on your own, at fifty, is not a good idea, but she's not ready to listen.'

217

'You think so?'

'I do.' Kay leaned forward, cupped her chin in her hands. 'It's hard,' she said. 'When people you love make choices you don't like. You know how Caro is? If you push this, you'll lose her. Are you prepared for that?'

'No.' Helen shook her head. 'I don't want that.'

'So, then.'

'We have to support her?'

'Yes, we have to support her.' She smiled. Now that she had actually had a moment, the conclusion to what she thought about Caro's choice came easily. Was she comfortable? No. Was she ready to judge? No. Would she turn her back? No.

Helen didn't speak. She lay back on her lounger and flung her arm across her eyes.

'You know,' Kay said quietly, 'she had to choose the colour of the baby's eyes. On her own. From a computer.'

Eyes wide with shock, Helen pushed back on her elbows and turned to Kay.

'She's been very lonely, Helen. She needs us. And...' Kay looked across at the backdrop of dusty mountains, the blue-black grapes and the green-black cypress trees. 'I think that's why we're here,' she said. 'Why she invited us. Her subconscious prompted her to.'

Helen sighed, reached a hand across and took Kay's, swinging it like a skipping rope. 'You always were the smartest,' she said. 'You know that.'

'Was I?' Kay smiled. She lay back, slotted her hands together behind her head and murmured, 'Bloody shame about those chips, though.'

'Shall I get some more?'

'No. I'm past chips now. It must be nearly cocktail hour.' And suddenly she sat up, her mouth twitching with a smile. 'How about a little Sex on the Beach, Helen? Or have you had enough of that already?'

'Kay. *Kay.*'

Kay opened her eyes to Helen standing in front of her holding two glasses filled with a peachy orange liquid.

'You fell asleep.' Helen laughed. '*Again!*'

'Really?' Kay frowned. 'How long were you gone for?'

'About ten minutes,' she said and handed Kay a glass. 'Kaveh just rang,' she added sheepishly.

'Captain Haddock?'

'*Kaveh.* He's asked me to go sailing with him tomorrow.'

'And?' Kay slurped on her straw.

'I wanted to check with you first. This is supposed to be a holiday for the three of us, although after what happened yesterday I should think Caro's going to need her space more than ever. From me, at least.'

Kay smiled. 'Go. Go and enjoy yourself. Caro won't want to go far, and that's fine with me.'

'You sure?'

'I'm sure.' She put her head to one side and frowned. 'It'll be all right, Helen. You and Caro. You've had rows before.'

Helen sat down on her lounger. 'I hope so,' she murmured. 'I hope so.' She took a long sip of the sugary drink. 'He's a nice guy,' she said, and looked down at her glass.

'Your sailing man?'

She nodded. 'I don't know what's wrong with me, Kay. I should be feeling awful. I'm married. I've just committed adultery and my husband is sending me messages about how he can't wait to get home and here I am having—'

'Fantastic sex?'

'Yes.' She looked up at Kay. 'Yes! God, it was fantastic.'

'I was joking, Helen.'

'Oh.' Helen stretched her arms out and looked across the pool. What she'd said was true. She didn't feel guilty and she didn't feel awful. She felt alive! The night she'd spent with Kaveh could well have been the best sex of her life. Far better than those pre-marriage angst-ridden university fumblings. And more enjoyable than any post-marriage fumblings. Why was that? Because she'd loved her husband, certainly in the beginning. And he'd loved her. Which, according to the fairy tale she'd bought into lock, stock and barrel, should have been all that was needed. Except it wasn't, was it? What was needed (it was looking far more likely) was a great slab of confidence which she could never have possessed at eighteen. The things they'd done! The things she'd done!... Maybe it was easier with a stranger? Lawrence wouldn't have recognised her. She hardly recognised herself. She drew her shoulders up to her ears, blushing by proxy for the lover she'd been. 'I never knew it could be like that,' she whispered.

Kay laughed. 'I'm not sure I want to know.'

'I'm serious, Kay.' Helen shook her head. 'It's like a miracle. I thought it was all over. That the best of it was, anyway.'

'No comment,' Kay said and opened her palms. 'Honestly? For this I will stay on the fence. Don't even try and drag an opinion from me.' Her towel pinged. Reaching forward to rescue the phone underneath, she said, 'It's your marriage, Helen.'

'Everything okay?' She nodded at Kay's phone.

'It's Caro.' Kay looked at her. 'She's on her way back.'

'Oh,' Helen managed. She glanced up to the room she'd shared with Caro and was now sharing with Kay. Returning to the hotel that morning, she'd found that Caro had already moved rooms. And it had felt to Helen, as she'd looked at the space on the bathroom shelf where Caro's toilet bag had been, that it was her doing. As if she alone, not the mundane practicalities of the booking, was responsible for the absence.

'Shall we go up and wait for her?'

She swirled the half-dissolved ice in her glass. Of course they should go up and wait, but every nerve in her body had tensed with anxiety. What on earth was she going to say? And what would Caro say to her? Despite what Kay had said, she wasn't confident that it would be all right. Not at all.

'Shall we go up and wait?' Kay persisted.

She nodded, but she didn't move as she watched Kay gather up belongings. She was thinking of Caro choosing the colour of her baby's eyes from a computer screen, and of course she was thinking of Kaveh. She looked up at Kay. 'It wasn't just Martin's affair, was it?' she said suddenly. 'That ended your marriage?'

Kay turned to her. 'And you're asking because?'

Helen shrugged. 'I just wondered.' She lifted her glass and looked at the sugary inch left. 'Too much sex, I suppose. Loosens the tongue.'

'His affair?' Kay flapped her towel out and folded it in half. 'Yes, at the time that's what ended it. But it would have come to an end anyway. Martin could never deal with Alex.' Dipping her chin to roll the towel, she added, 'I think even he'd say that now.'

Helen smiled sadly. If there was ever a couple who loved each other and were perfectly suited it had been Martin and Kay. 'How is he?' she asked.

'He's good. Quite helpful. Picks Alex up from work a lot.' Kay stuffed the towel into her bag. Hands on hips, she looked at Helen. 'Which he absolutely loves. So, once again, thank you.'

'Kay!' Helen flushed. Helping get Alex a job at her uncle's garden centre had been one of the best things Helen thought she'd ever done. If she could, she would repeat it every day for the rest of her life. 'It was nothing,' she said. 'Uncle William says he's the best worker there.'

Kay laughed. 'I'm sure he is. You know Alex. Once he sets his mind to something.'

'Like that motorbike he's building?' And as soon as she'd said it, Helen wished she could unsay it.

A shadow passed across Kay's face. 'Exactly,' she said, and took the ends of her sarong, draping them over her shoulders and knotting them at her neck like a chiffon-wearing superhero. 'He thinks he can renovate a bike with no experience and no skills. And then he thinks he can race the damn thing!'

Helen shook her head. Why the hell did she have to mention the bike? Dragging the shadow of that black tarpaulin that she knew had been worrying Kay for weeks, into the Cypriot sunshine. She could have kicked herself. At the very least, stapled her mouth shut. In fact, she thought as she swallowed another mouthful of sugary alcohol, this holiday would go a lot better from now on if she did just that.

'Who,' Kay said quietly, 'is going to rescue him when it all goes wrong?'

Helen looked up to see Kay standing, arms folded, staring off across the pool.

'Alex will need me for the rest of his and my life,' Kay sighed. 'It's black and white. It always has been.' Turning back she said, 'They'll always be our kids, won't they? And one way or another, they're always going to need us. It's just that Alex is going to need me a whole lot more than Jack is going to need you.'

Jack. Slowly Helen leaned across and put her glass on the table between the loungers. She only just made it, the bones in her arm seemingly having dissolved with the force of remembrance. 'He rang me this morning,' she whispered. And there was, or there had been, something so shameful about the whole incident – her son seeing her in bed with another man – that almost as soon as it had happened, she realised now, she'd blanked it out.

Kay looked at her.

'He thought he had food poisoning.'

'Did he?'

'No. He just ate an out-of-date lasagne.' And despite

the shame, a bubble of laughter rose up her throat. 'Two days out of date, Kay, and he's ringing me in Cyprus for the doctor's number!'

'Oh.'

'That wasn't the problem, though.' Turning to face Kay, Helen flushed and her heart picked up speed, *clippity-clop, clippity-clop, clippity-clippity...* Because it *was* true. It *had* happened. Her son had really seen her in bed with another man. And, incredible as it seemed, she'd forgotten. The heat, the exhaustion (a night of sex was far more tiring than she remembered) and, of course, Caro and all the things that had been said had sunk this memory more surely than a stone in water. If anything at all had echoed through this long, hot, surreal day, it had been Kaveh. His legs against hers, his breath in her ear. Even when she'd showered, every soapy movement of her hands had been a re-enactment of his hands. He was a drug from which she was struggling to wake, and problems that belonged in the realm of her ordinary life had had no more permanence than ripples on water. But it was true.

'What *was* the problem?' Kay asked.

'It was a FaceTime call.' Helen swallowed hard. 'And I answered it in bed.'

It took a moment for the penny to roll all the way down, to drop Kay's jaw and make a huge round O of her mouth. A moment which, despite the enormity of the repercussions, Helen quite enjoyed. Kay looked so comical.

'In bed?'

Helen nodded.

'This being...not your own...bed?'

She nodded again.

'And Jack saw—'

'He saw.'

'Oh.' They looked at each other for a long moment, and then Kay said, 'What did you do?'

What had she done? She frowned. 'I told him to take a Rennie.'

Kay's mouth dropped even further. Her mouth twitched and Helen could see how much she wanted to laugh, as she did herself. Because wasn't it ridiculous? Twenty-five years of marriage and not so much as a look at another man!

Gaining control of her jaw, Kay said, 'Seriously, Helen. What are you going to do?'

'What can I do?'

'Have you messaged him?'

'No.' She shook her head. Why hadn't she? Well, mostly because up until this moment she hadn't actually remembered that it had happened. But there was something else. Her children had been bursting into the most private corners of her life since they could walk. A bath in peace? Inserting a tampon? Half an hour in the garden always ended with a screaming child, a pricked finger and the smell of Dettol. A book? When was the last time she'd even opened one? And even now, two thousand miles away, Jack had managed to find a way to barge his way in. Jack. The same boy who'd once spent a whole weekend painting an A3 *KEEP OUT* sign for his bedroom door. (That sign was still in place.) 'It's not,' she said, dipping a toe into these newly appended waters, 'really his business. Is it?'

Kay shrugged. 'No…'

'*And…*' She was up to her waist now, warming to the theme. 'I know for a fact that with me gone he'll have practically moved Ellie, his girlfriend, in. He's probably having sex 24/7, and I'm not FaceTiming him at 7am asking stupid questions, am I?'

Kay laughed.

'So,' Helen harrumphed, 'I'm not going to do anything. I'll deal with it all when I get back. And…' She picked up her glass and looked at Kay. 'To answer your question properly.'

'Which question?'

'Why I was asking about Martin's affair.'

'Well?'

'I think I want a divorce.'

13

The air-conditioned reception area was much cooler than the pool terrace had been. So much so that Helen felt underdressed. Goosebumps trickled along her arms. Caro was just a few minutes away now, and thinking about that sent the goosebumps into a flood.

'I think,' she said, 'I'll just pop up and put something on.' She looked down at her legs to emphasise the point.

'Caro's due any minute, Helen.'

'I know, but—'

'You should wait,' Kay said firmly.

'Okay.' And now she was freezing.

'Go and sit in the sun.' Kay nodded to the armchairs across the foyer.

Helen didn't move.

'It's not going to be easy, Helen, whatever you're dressed in.'

'That's not really—' she started, then stopped. Whatever she was going to say would be justifiably blasted away by Kay. Because she *was* stalling. More than that; she was on the verge of bolting. Huge butterflies were looping the loop in her stomach as the thought of facing Caro again overwhelmed her. She was scared. Scared of another scene, certainly, but also genuinely scared that she wouldn't be able to overcome her own feelings. That when Caro needed her to be a friend, she wouldn't be able to be one. 'I'll…' Her voice trailed away and she used her hand instead to point at the armchair.

Kay nodded.

Helen moved away to sit heavily in the warmth of the sand-coloured cushion. She watched as Kay took her phone out, seemed to move onto the next problem; and, watching, Helen felt she would never fully understand or be able to emulate Kay's level-headed pragmatism. She was like a glacier, silently inching through the valley of the life that had been handed to her. It was something to be admired, and it made Helen feel as reactive and screechy as a firework.

'*Alex*,' Kay mouthed, pointing at her phone.

Helen nodded; she turned her face to the window. It was considerably warmer in this sunlit corner, and her goosebumps were duly melting. Chin on her hand, she looked out to the courtyard, the fountain and the mountains beyond. The idea that she should be sitting here in this paradise, waiting for her friend to come back impregnated with another woman's baby, felt as unreal as touching the pale sliver of moon that was just appearing beyond the stratosphere. Then again, nothing in her life felt real right now. Lawrence at the top of Everest? Jack ringing from a place that looked like a place she once knew? The only thing that was tangible was the feel of Kaveh's hands on her body. The thought squeezed her forward into a ball, elbows on knees, head down. How flimsy it all was! How ridiculously fragile that one night with a stranger could have sent her spinning off like this, away from everything she'd been perfectly content to live with for so very long.

She unfurled herself and leaned back. On the coffee table in front of her was a pile of Kaveh's sailing flyers. *Ask for Kaveh.* Helen smiled. The shocking cold when she'd jumped into the ocean!

You liar, Helen Winters. You fraud.

As if it would silence the voice in her head, she turned away and stared back at the mountains…*content to live with for so very long…* Who was she kidding? She hadn't been content for years. She'd shelved the person she had once been, because the marriage she had made had required that of her. And now, sitting in a pool of Cypriot sunlight, this moment of truthful realisation had her closing her eyes and whispering, 'No one held a gun to your head. No one made you.'

The buzz of a trapped fly filtered past. Kaveh was real, Cyprus was real, her discontent was very real, and it was time to stop pretending. And Caro? She bit down on her lip. It couldn't be denied. Out of the two of them, it was Caro who had had the courage to face up to her own unhappy reality. And then attempt to solve it. Beyond that, it wasn't going to help either of them if Helen refused to step over her line in the sand. She would, and could, do what Caro needed her to do. She would be a friend.

*

229

Kay dumped her handbag on the reception desk and waved across to Helen, but Helen had her eyes closed. Turning back to the desk, she scooped a wallet, a sunglasses case, her passport, a folded prescription, half a KitKat and a flier for a newly opened car wash out of her bag. Holding her phone by her chin, she said, 'Honestly, Alex, we went over this a hundred times.'

'Excuse me.' The woman behind the desk reached across and moved a rather beautiful orchid away from the debris of Kay's bag.

'Sorry,' Kay mouthed. Something about the exquisite delicacy of the orchid, its butter-yellow petals, made her feel inordinately ashamed. Carefully she gathered everything together, swept it back into her bag and said, 'I don't have it. I told you I didn't... Okay, then... Yes. Go and look... I'll wait... Yes. *I'll wait.*' She looked up. 'My son,' she mouthed at the woman behind the desk, and added, 'He's twenty-two.' Headlines of eight-year-olds left home alone with a family pack of cornflakes flashing through her mind.

The woman nodded, inscrutable.

'It's...well...he just sometimes has a few difficulties. If his routine gets interrupted.'

Again the woman nodded.

'I mean, he has a job.' She pressed the phone against her ear. There was no need to explain herself or Alex to anyone. Old habits...

'This is more than my son has,' the woman said in a voice that matched the ribbed iron skillet of her face. 'And he is twenty-seven.'

'Oh.' Kay smiled sympathetically. 'Oh. Well, he loves it,

actually. My son, I mean. His job.' And her face brightened, as it did whenever she talked about Alex and his job. He did love it and it had been an absolute godsend. He would, she knew, spend the rest of his working life there. 'He works in a garden centre and, gosh…' She reached out to the orchid. 'He'd love this.'

'It's a cymbidium,' the woman said, her fingers curling protectively around the pot.

'It's beautiful… Alex?' Kay turned her attention back to her phone. 'Yes, I'm here!… Right… And was it there?… It was. Good. Okay… No, wait. *Wait, Alex!* I'm going to put you on FaceTime. I want you to see this.' And turning the camera of her phone around, Kay held it so the orchid filled the screen.

'That's a cymbidium.' Alex's voice, on speakerphone, was clear. 'It's lovely.'

The woman behind the desk beamed.

Her own face flushing with pride, Kay brought the phone back to her ear. 'Okay, then. No, that's all. Yes, see you next week.' She was smiling at the woman, who was smiling back, nodding.

'I don't think he will have too many difficulties,' the woman said as Kay slipped her phone away.

'Thank you,' Kay whispered, tears filling her eyes.

The woman handed her a tissue. 'My name is Marianne.'

'Kay.' Kay wiped her eyes. 'What a lovely name. It's quite French for—'

'Cyprus?' Marianne shrugged. 'My mother was a big fan of Leonard Cohen.'

Kay laughed. 'My ex-husband too.'

'He was too miserable for me,' Marianne said.

'Me too! And I mean both of them – my ex and Leonard.'

Marianne put her hands on the desk, leaned forward and laughed out loud. Taking a tissue, she wiped her own eyes and said, 'So you are enjoying your stay here?'

'It's just my first day, but yes.' She smiled. 'Yes I am.'

'You're here with your friends?' Marianne said and looked across to Helen.

Kay nodded. 'That's right,' she said. 'Just a girl's week away.' She left it at that. If Marianne knew where Caro had been today, and why she was here – well, that was something that could remain unsaid. 'I really needed it,' she gabbled, to fill any gaps in which unsaid things might somehow become said. 'My mum is not well at all. In fact, she's gone into a care home for a week.'

If Marianne noticed, she gave nothing away. Her face was impassive as she asked, 'Does she live with you? Your mother?'

'No. Well, not far. We live on the same street, so I'm there a lot.'

Marianne nodded grimly. 'Mine lives with me.'

'Oh.' Kay turned to her. 'That must be nice for you. I admire the culture you have here, where this is normal. It's not the same for us.'

'Nice?' Marianne's eyebrow flexed like a bodybuilder's bicep. 'She's not even my mother!' she hissed. 'She is my husband's mother. My *ex*-husband's. I got rid of him and still I have to look after her!'

Kay's lips twitched. 'And I thought it was bad enough that I still have to send mine Christmas cards.'

'You are right, though.' Marianne leaned forward. 'It *is* the culture. Women are donkeys! Men expect us to carry everything. They are big babies. I should have married my Swedish boyfriend when I had the chance. Then my life would have been different. Very different.'

'Really?' Kay wanted to smile. It wasn't the first time random strangers had told her intimate details. There was obviously something in her face.

'Or…' Marianne's voice was low. She leaned further across the desk, as close as a sinner in a confessional box. 'I would do what your friend is doing. Not this one,' she said and nodded at Helen, who was still sitting in a pool of sunshine with her eyes closed. 'The other one.'

Kay paled.

Marianne straightened up. 'Why not?' she said, and shrugged.

Speechless, Kay looked at her. She didn't have an answer. She did not have an answer.

'She's here!' At the sound of the car, Helen was on her feet, her voice wobblier than an amateur soprano.

Outside in the courtyard, a red Toyota taxi had pulled to a halt behind the fountain.

Marianne withdrew behind the desk, and in slow motion Kay and Helen moved towards the front door, watching as Caro stepped out of the taxi, paid the driver and turned to the hotel.

Helen was first. Opening the door, shaking her head.

Trying and failing to find a way of saying something, stretching her arm out to take Caro's bag.

'I have it,' Caro said, without raising her head to look at Helen.

'I'm sorry, Caro.' Out it came. She took a step back, hands under her chin like a prayer. 'I'm so sorry.'

'It's okay.'

'It's not. I—'

'I'm tired, Helen.' Caro stood still, her bag swinging. 'For now, it is.'

Kay stepped forward and took the bag. 'Did it all go—'

'It went fine,' Caro smiled. 'I'm just really tired. It's been a roller coaster.'

'Of course.' Helen and Kay glanced at each other as they both spoke at once. They were, Helen knew, thinking the same thing. Caro looked absolutely wrung out.

A phone started ringing. They all looked at the bag on Kay's shoulder.

'Let me just…' Caro reached to her bag and took out her phone. 'I have to take this,' she said. 'I just…' She turned away. 'Danny?'

'*What the fuck, Caro?*' Through the tiny speaker on Caro's phone, Danny Abbott's voice bounced around the marbled reception like a very loud TV.

Everyone, including Marianne, stared at Caro, who had gone as pale as paper.

'What the fuck was Matt doing releasing that report? He's not even selling anything! Eighteen per cent, Caro? You know how much that is? That's £200,000 in one fucking hour. Because the dick releases a report that manages to sound the complete opposite of what it's meant to say! Fuck, Caro! Why did you leave him alone? You know he can't wipe his arse if you're not handing him the paper!'

'Danny—'

'I'm trusting you on this, Caro. You told me to trust you and I did.'

'Danny,' Caro pleaded. 'I'm in Cyprus. I've been… I haven't seen the report.'

'Because I can promise you one thing – if this doesn't get sorted I'll be out of Greenway Tech faster than you can say *arrivederci. Comprendo*, Caro?'

'Danny.' Caro put her hand across her mouth. Her eyes had filled with tears.

'You need to get your ass in front of a fucking screen – pronto! And when I say pronto I mean like—'

As swift as a cat, Helen swiped the phone from Caro's hand. 'And you need to watch your language,' she barked.

'Helen.' Caro reached for her phone.

But Kay already had an arm around her waist, steering her away as expertly as a Tesco shopping trolley. '*You*,' she said, 'are coming with me.'

'Who is this? Who am I speaking to? Put Caro back on.'

'Caro,' Helen said flatly, 'is currently unavailable.'

Danny Abbott didn't speak.

'Helen,' Caro whispered over her shoulder. 'I *have* to speak to him.'

Helen put her hand over the phone. 'What you *have* to do is rest.'

Marianne was out from behind the desk. A moving steam iron, hissing and clicking in a grey shift dress that strained across her back like stretched cling film. Now she was opening the door through to the elevators, glaring at the phone in Helen's hands, at the unseen Danny Abbott.

'Helen...'

The glass door swung shut, cutting off Caro's voice.

'Right,' Helen said, sitting herself down.

'Just put Caro back on.'

'I will not,' Helen said. She looked down at her leg. She was beginning to tan.

'Listen, darlin', I don't think you understand—'

Darlin! Helen's lips pinched in amusement. 'I'm not your darling, Mr Abbott,' she said. 'It is Mr Abbott, isn't it?'

He didn't answer.

'My name is Helen. I'm Caro's friend and we're on holiday together. Right now she's—'

'I don't give a rat's arse where you are.'

Helen took Caro's phone and held it in front of her like a hand mirror. Her mouth curled up. She was fifty years old. Twenty years' experience of dealing with children, eight years on the frontline of a doctor's surgery. Danny Abbott had picked the wrong fight! She brought the phone back to her ear and lifted her chin. '*Please*,' she said, in full-on receptionist mode, 'don't talk over me, Mr Abbott. Hasn't anyone ever told you how rude that is?'

Silence.

She smiled. She could see him now, sulking in the corridor.

'And I'd appreciate it if we could leave out the swearing as well.'

More silence.

Then, because she was enjoying this so much, she went for it. 'Would you speak to your mother like that?'

'What the...' But Danny Abbott's words twirled themselves up in knots of astonishment before he could even begin to straighten them out.

At the other end of the line, Helen leaned back.

Eventually the spluttering dripped away into another silence and then a long drawn-in breath. Danny Abbott coughed. 'I need to speak to Caro,' he muttered.

'I understand,' Helen said. 'You're worried about your investments. But I'm worried about Caro's health. She's tired and she needs to rest.'

'This is fu...' A short, sharp splutter of breath flew down the line. 'Ridiculous,' Danny hissed. He sounded as if his jaw had been wired.

'Have you ever been to Cyprus, Mr Abbott?' The question came out of nowhere, and at the same time sounded practised and rehearsed.

'Are you going to put Caro back on?'

'It really is the most wonderful place,' she continued.

'If you're not, I'll hang up.'

But he didn't, and so Helen talked on, because it came so naturally to her and because this was what they did. Any time a distressed child or an anxious pensioner needed distracting, Helen or Tina or any of the girls from the surgery would spring into action with this verbal soothing. Of course it felt familiar. So on and on she went. Describing the mountains and the vineyards and, soon after, the sailing. And as she talked, Danny Abbott's silences lost their hum of hostility and deepened with a calm she could almost see.

Until she got to the part about how she had helped right a capsized boat, at which there was a guffaw of uninhibited laughter. And it didn't feel strange at all telling someone she had never met of this stupendous achievement. In fact, someone she had never met felt like exactly the right person to tell. 'I was,' she finished, 'very proud of myself.'

'I bet you were,' Danny Abbott laughed again. There was a long silence and then he said, 'I haven't been sailing in years.'

Helen leaned forward. 'Caro's had a difficult day, Danny. Really difficult, actually.'

Danny didn't speak.

'Plus she's far more use to you rested. I'm sure you'll agree.'

'Of course.' Danny paused. 'Of course she should rest.'

'Shall I tell her you'll call tomorrow?'

'Yes. Do that.' He paused. 'Helen? It is Helen, isn't it?'

'It is.'

'What's the name of the place you're staying at? Don't worry, I'm not coming out there. Just what's the name of the place?'

She told him the name of the hotel. The conversation finished with Danny wishing them all a pleasant stay and a shy suggestion that the next time she was down in London, perhaps they could meet and laugh about this over lunch?

'In your dreams,' Helen whispered as she ended the call. She leaned forward, held out her finger and watched as a ladybird climbed on, shook out its wings and flew away. Ships? She could obviously still launch them.

14

When Caro woke it was still dark, and deeply silent. No orange street lights outside the window, no sounds of cars pulling into the Esso garage opposite. (When it was first built, she'd been annoyed. Now she couldn't imagine living without those disconnected voices that filtered through her window which, on so many sleepless nights, had come to be welcome anonymous companions.) She stared out of the window. Outside was the black hulk of the mountains, above an ink-blue sky quilted with more stars than she thought she'd ever seen.

One hand shielding her stomach, she rolled onto her back, and the smiling, hopeful faces of every doctor and nurse she had met yesterday swam before her. The reception she had been met with had humbled her. Had, in fact, backed her into moments when she'd so nearly walked out. Hour after hour, everyone had treated her with only kindness and respect and acceptance. As if she'd come in to get gallstones removed, a hernia treated. As if the decisions and choices that had led her to this place and this time were decisions and choices over which she'd had no control whatsoever. But she had. One abortion. Two morning-after pills. Decades of contraception.

It wasn't an exaggeration to say that the day had shrunk her. Torched the ring of self- confidence she'd fenced, and exposed her for the fraud she was. It had wiped her out. Packed into a taxi, tears of gratitude and fatigue and fear streaming down her face, she'd been waved off to wait. And hope. Told not to test before two weeks. Ordered to relax. Switch off.

And all she could think now was: if she hadn't been ready for this, the very first stage of the emotional onslaught, what else was she wholly unprepared for? What else did she, as Helen had said, have *no idea what she was letting herself in for?*

Rolling back onto her side, she closed her eyes and, after long restless minutes, fell asleep again.

Instantly she was back at the clinic, and the face of the nurse who'd looked after her loomed so close that Caro could see the line of sweat along the woman's upper lip, her bosom straining the buttons of her tunic. Maternal hands. Cheery, wide, capable hands taking hold of her shoulders. Shaking her. Except now the nurse had transformed. Now the nurse was her mother, hissing.

Just for once, can't you think of someone else other than yourself?

And she was up, pushing back against the hands, trying to escape. She was past the nurse/mother, wrenching the door handle, which wouldn't move. They'd locked it! Locked her in! And now the nurse had Helen's face, hissing:

Why? Why can't you, just for once, think of someone else other than yourself?

240

Then her mother was tucking her in. She was back in the bed, arms pinned to her side, the sheet over her mouth. Hard to breathe, but her mother was stretching the sheets tighter and tighter and she was stuck, and when she opened her mouth to explain…to try to tell her mother… dry cotton gagged her…and she couldn't get a word out… couldn't move a finger.

Just once…just once…think of someone else other than yourself.

Then she woke, mouth moving, cheeks wet, deep hollow thuds reverberating. And as she stared at the ceiling it took Caro long moments to understand that the thudding was her heart, the wetness her tears, the terror unreal.

Cautiously she slid her eyes sideways. The stars had gone, replaced by a sun that was already high and pale. Across from the hotel, the grapevines were swaying in a breeze she couldn't feel. Slowly she unclenched her fists, pushed herself upright and reached for her phone.

It wasn't there. With a sickening feeling, Caro lay back on the pillow, stretched her arms above her and looked at the ceiling. Danny Abbott had rung yesterday and Helen had taken her phone. By now he'd have rung Matt, who would have been trying to get hold of her all night. She closed her eyes. She wasn't ready at all to face the Danny Abbotts of the world, or even Matt, perhaps the most amiable CEO she'd ever worked with…if she still had a CEO, that was.

Do everything that you would normally do, Dr Macar from the clinic had said. *Rest. Relax. Switch off.*

She ran her hands through her hair. How the hell was she going to do that?

At her left ear a phone started ringing. Caro stared at it. She hadn't answered a landline in years. She hadn't even noticed it was there.

'Ms Caroline?' the voice at the other end said. 'This is Marianne, from reception.'

Caro rubbed her eye.

'I have a message for you from your friend Kay.'

'Okay.'

'She says to tell you that breakfast closes at ten and she is by the pool.'

'Okay. Thank you.' She was about to put the receiver down when Marianne's voice stopped her.

'Did you sleep well?'

'Thank you, yes.' Caro frowned at the question.

'Good,' Marianne said. 'You need your rest.' And she put the phone down.

Ten! It couldn't possibly be nearly ten? Still frowning, Caro eased herself upright, swung her legs over the side of the bed, looked across the room at her reflection in the dressing table mirror and, as she had so many times in her life, made a decision. No one would ever know how close she had come to bottling it yesterday. No one would know about the guilt and the shame and the doubt. What was done now was done, and there was only one way to keep moving: forward.

A low, grumbling sound came from her stomach, and with a sense of astonishment she realised she was hungry. She stood up, and the standing made her famished.

She was dressed and on her way to breakfast within five minutes.

*

Neither Helen nor Kaveh had spoken of the fact that they were now lovers. They were sailing a port tack, with a northerly wind, on white-ruffled waves over black, billowing depths. The sun was directly above. Kyrenia had fallen behind, and sailing, Helen had come to understand, was not suited to conversation. Pitched against an ocean, words were feathers that shredded in the wind. Besides, sailing was *doing*. There were always ropes to handle, sails to watch, wind to scent. Talking was superfluous, just as it had been the night they had spent together. And this, she thought happily as she wound the jib sheet around her knuckles, might just be the way forward for all relationships.

The wind calmed, and all around their little boat the waves responded like a thousand stroked cats. Kaveh let the mainsheet go slack. Now she could hear the ocean lap-lapping against the sides. Her hair fell forward. She pushed it back and, shielding her eyes, looked to the shore.

Yes, she was further out than she had ever been in her life. Out where the boat rocked and swayed and she rocked and swayed with it. Out where she didn't have to think about Lawrence or Caro or even how to face Jack. Out where, within the curve of the bow, she and Kaveh had become as easily familiar with the weight of each other's movements as a long-married couple in the marital bed.

He smiled at her; she smiled back and tilted her head to the great dome of blue above.

'Do you want to swim?' Kaveh was nodding past her shoulder. He had one hand back on the tiller, already turning it.

She turned to where he was looking.

'There's a beach up here. It is good for swimming.'

Without turning back, she nodded and began to wind her rope in. The boat caught the wind and moved forward. No words needed.

As they came closer into the tiny natural harbour, she could see that a wooden jetty had been built upon sandstone boulders that tumbled into the sea like giant dice. Kaveh nosed the boat into the jetty, Helen stepped off, and together they secured the ropes.

Hands on hips, she stood and looked down at the water. It was as clear as a window. Turquoise, navy blue, emerald green.

'Race you to the beach.' Already Kaveh had stripped off his shorts and was standing now in his underwear, yanking his T-shirt over his head.

'You're on,' she smiled and looked down at her own T-shirt. Easy enough to take that off and keep dry, but her bra? She looked up, past Kaveh to the beach. It was empty and wholly private, the sea being the only way to access it. Her mouth curled upward. Laughing, she took off first her T-shirt, then her bra, then her leggings and then her pants. 'Ready!' she said, tanned and plump and as naked and glorious as Aphrodite herself rising from the foam.

Kaveh turned with hungry eyes that moved across her body and set her blood tingling. He took a step towards her, but she turned away. 'Catch me first!' she cried, and jumped in.

It was so cold! And so salty! And every part of her body

awakened. And when he jumped in too and grabbed her ankle, she turned and used her arms to splash. Giggling and swallowing seawater, coughing, swimming, flailing all the way to the shore.

She hauled herself out, staggered forward and collapsed back against the sand, pebbles in her spine, orange light filtering through her lids.

'Helen?'

When she opened her eyes, Kaveh was leaning over her. The next thing she knew, his lips were on hers, warm and soft, easing her mouth open, pushing in with his tongue. And then his mouth was on her breast and he was on top of her, inside her, and his hair was all rough and bitty with sand. Air blew cool on her body, waves tickled her spine. She put her arms around his neck, felt the ridge of his back and gave herself over to the throbs of pleasure rising up, unstoppable. This radiant moment. Tipping her chin back to the sky, she laughed. This radiant, unforgettable moment...

That bled into the next and the next, each of them trailing glory, until Kaveh stopped moving and lay with his head on her chest, and she too became still.

And she remembered what that doctor had said as she'd looked into the tiny face of her perfectly beautiful, perfectly dead newborn son.

You will always remember this and you will be glad of that.

So this, she thought, is living. Photographic moments like that one and this, tragedy and bliss carried through to the end. The thought did not make her sad. On the contrary, a massive warm bloom of happiness filled every cell of her body. She was still making moments. So she was still alive. Lying with pebbles in her back and Kaveh's clumpy hair in her hand, a tear fell from her eye and ran down her cheek, landing so cold in her ear it itched.

Kaveh lifted his head. 'You are crying?'

She nodded. 'It's okay. I'm not sad.'

He sat up, and Helen did too, and they stretched their legs out and like children let the waves lap over their feet.

'It would be hard to be sad right now,' he said.

She squeezed his hand. 'I agree.'

He leaned forward and took a pebble. 'Your son. Have you spoken to him?'

Helen shook her head.

'What will you do?'

'I don't know.' Helen picked up her own pebble. 'Nothing,' she murmured. 'Until I get home.' Twenty-four hours on from that phone call and it still wasn't feeling any more real. She hadn't tried to call Jack and that made her feel guilty and sad. He hadn't tried to call her, and that made her feel worried and sad. She hadn't a clue what she was going to do. Apart from try not to let it spoil what was left of the holiday. And so far, in Kaveh's company, that was proving very easy. 'You know,' she sighed. 'I've spent a large part of my life trying to be the perfect mother. The perfect wife. Living up to an idea it never even occurred to me to question. And even if I'd got it only halfway right, I've completely blown it now. So…' She raised her arm and threw the pebble as far into the waves as she could. 'There's no point in trying to talk to him. It would only spoil…all this.'

Kaveh smiled. 'And what,' he said, 'is…all this?'

Helen looked at him. 'Well…it's fun.' She smiled. 'And right now, that's enough for me.'

Nodding, he leaned in and kissed her shoulder. 'It's enough for me too,' he said and leaned back on his elbows. His face had lifted to the sun and his eyes were closed when he spoke again. 'Will you tell your husband?'

Looking straight ahead, Helen squinted, and miles away, where the Mediterranean met the sky, the world seemed to squint back. 'Yes,' she answered. She hadn't even asked herself this question, let alone prepared an answer for anyone else, but now that it was here it was obvious. Of course she would tell Lawrence. How could she even consider stepping back over that horizon and going back to what she had come from? She turned to Kaveh. 'Will you tell your wife?'

Eyes still closed, Kaveh shook his head. 'We live separate lives now.'

Helen watched him. 'Why didn't she come with you?' she asked. 'When you moved back here?'

He smiled, a slow and lazy lopsided movement. 'It's like you said, Helen. I too have spent a long time trying to live up to an idea. For my parents mostly. I was ten when we had to leave here, and it broke their hearts. I spent the rest of their lives trying to mend them.' Opening his eyes, he shrugged. 'I married the right woman. I was an accountant, so I had the right job—'

'An accountant!' Helen laughed. She stared at him. How could this man, this windswept, weather-beaten, silver-haired, copper-skinned man, ever have spent years at a desk, crunching numbers?

And Kaveh laughed with her. 'Yes, it was boring!' He sat up, drew his knees to his chest and rubbed his chin. 'But I'll tell you something, Helen,' he smiled. 'Accountants retire early.'

'Do they?' she smiled back.

'I was good with numbers,' he shrugged. 'I made good investments. Then my parents died and I thought to myself, if not now, when? I had the finances, my children were grown. When, I thought, will it be my time to live the way I choose? Do you understand this?'

Naked as the day she was born, sand and sea sticking to every secret part of her, Helen stared at him. *Did she understand?* He could have plucked the words from the top pocket of her heart. 'I understand,' she whispered. 'Completely.'

'So.' He nodded. 'We understand each other?'

'We do.'

'Are you hungry?'

She burst out laughing. No, there really wasn't much need for words at all. 'I'm starving!' she cried. She was!

'Good.' His face broke into a wide, gorgeous smile. 'You like seafood?'

'I love it,' Helen said. She did. Right here and right now, she loved everything and everyone.

15

Standing in front of the laden tables, Caro eyed the breakfast buffet like a hawk. She couldn't remember the last time she'd felt this hungry. She was so ravenous she barely knew where to start, walking up and down the length of the table clutching her empty plate like a lost child.

'Caro!'

The shout flipped her plate and sent her lurching to catch it. When she looked up there was Kay, trailing yards of scarlet chiffon, beaming.

'Did you sleep well?' Kay looked at the empty plate. 'You must have if you're only just down. I'm back for seconds!'

'Has Helen got my phone?'

'*I've* got your phone,' Kay frowned. 'Helen's gone sailing.'

'I need to…' Biting down on her lip, Caro stopped talking. She turned back to the table.

'You need to eat, Caro. And then you need to relax.'

Relax. Yes. She nodded. *Rest. Relax. Switch off.* That was what she was supposed to do. 'I don't know where to start,' she said, and a lump bloomed in her throat. She looked down to see the plate eased from her hands.

'Go and sit down,' Kay said. 'What do you want? Bacon? Eggs? Some fruit?'

Caro nodded. The room had blurred; her eyes burned with tears.

Kay's hand was on her back, steering her to the table. 'We'll start there,' she said. 'Now sit down.'

'Here?'

'Here.'

In the middle of the table Kay had steered her to stood a large display of flowers. The envelope attached to them had one word: *Caro.*

Astonished, Caro looked at Kay.

'Not from me,' Kay shrugged.

With unsteady hands, she opened the envelope.

Sorry about yesterday. Your friend says I was rude. I was. Call when you're up to it. Danny x

Caro's jaw dropped. Her hand went to the back of her chair. 'The man's a monster,' she whispered. 'What on earth did Helen say?'

Kay laughed. 'You know Helen.'

Keeping her chin low, Caro looked up at Kay.

'She is sorry. You know that?'

Caro didn't answer. Without meeting Kay's eye, she lowered herself into a chair. The brief meeting between herself and Helen yesterday, was enough for her to recognise the truth of what Kay was saying. Helen was sorry. She'd heard it herself, but *Sorry* didn't take away the hurt. Only time would do that. Time, and a recognition of her own part in the prickliness their friendship so easily descended into. All those times, for instance, that she'd let Lawrence rest his hand on her thigh... How could she have done that? She reached out and let her fingers trace the padded petal of a white rose. The truth was that a friction created by such opposite characters, had always existed between herself and Helen. Her inherent seriousness had provided a safe shore for Helen's recklessness. This was undeniable. So what had Helen given her? She sighed. It was simple really. Fun. With Helen in it, Caro's life was more fun, and that had been true from the day they'd met. She felt a hand on her shoulder and turned to see Kay.

'I'll fill you a plate.'

'Thank you,' Caro whispered, eyes hot with tears. 'Thank you.'

Later, over coffee, with Kay choosing to be fooled by her easy and cheery descriptions of how the clinic had gone, Caro found that that was exactly what she had been expecting. As round and as wise as an owl, Kay also possessed that rarest of gifts – she knew when not to ask any more.

'Two weeks, then?' she said now, as she took the last two mini pains au chocolat from her plate and wrapped them in a blue napkin. 'It'll fly by.'

Apart from staff, they were the only ones left in the restaurant. They sat close by the entrance to the pool terrace, where a grey-bonneted chaffinch hovered in the open doorway, twisting its head as if checking for traffic before it hopped closer.

Caro smiled. 'It won't,' she said, and took the crust of pastry left on her plate and broke it apart, sprinkling crumbs through her fingertips for the chaffinch.

'You're right,' Kay shrugged, 'it won't. I hope you've got a good book. Or two.'

'I have.' Caro looked down at her hands. 'Did you...' she said, and stopped to pick flakes of pastry from her palm.

'Did I what?'

'Nothing.'

'Caro.' Kay reached across the table. 'You can ask,' she said. 'I'm going to be here for you. And so is Helen.'

Squeezing her hands together, Caro looked up. 'Did you know,' she asked quickly, 'with Alex?'

'That I was pregnant?' Kay laughed. 'I had no idea!'

'Really?'

'Really. But Helen did. She always said she did.'

'Yes, she did, didn't she?' Caro picked her cup up.

'She'll be back about lunch, you know.'

'She's sailing again?'

Kay nodded. 'She – and I – thought it would be good for everyone to have a little space.'

Caro leaned forward. It all seemed so remote now. The thing that had preoccupied her for so long – Helen and her marriage. For all she knew, she could be pregnant – on her way to creating her own family. Still, they had seemed so happy, Helen and Lawrence. From where she had been standing they'd seemed happy. She held her cup to her mouth, but her lips were pressed so tightly together it was hard to tell whether any liquid passed through. After a moment she put it down and it rattled in the saucer. 'She's married, Kay.'

'I guess she knows that,' Kay said, and leaned her elbows on the table to let her chin rest in her folded hands.

'I'd just hate to see her throw it all away,' Caro said. 'She called it a wobble, you know? She said we were both wobbling, and that's why I was doing what I was doing.'

'Well? Is it?'

Caro shook her head. 'No. It's much more complicated than that.'

'And,' Kay sighed, 'I suspect Helen's wobbles are similarly complicated.'

Caro looked at her. 'It's her business?'

'It most certainly is,' Kay said. 'Her business.'

Caro's book wasn't good – it was awful. How it had ever made the shortlist of a prestigious literary prize was beyond her. She flipped it closed, dropped it on the ground, lifted her sunglasses and squinted across at the other sunbed. Was Kay asleep or awake? It was hard to tell.

They'd found a shaded spot by the outdoor jacuzzi where, yawning, Kay had pulled out her lounger and plonked herself down. That had been (Caro checked her phone) two hours ago. After which the morning (for Kay) had passed in an easy stream of magazines and snoozes, brief swims in the pool followed by longer sits in the jacuzzi, snoozes, coffees, pastries and more snoozes. Occasionally turning, frequently snoring, slowly tanning.

For Caro the current of time had been bumpier.

Do everything that you would normally do… Rest. Relax. Switch off.

Everything she normally did was the polar opposite of this. Even in the office she had a standing desk. What did people *do* all day if they weren't doing what she normally did? How did people relax so easily? She looked at Kay again. People like Kay.

Sighing, she opened the meditation app on her phone, slipped her earphones in and lay back. Breathed in deep to a count of five, breathed out to a count of five…

The next step, if she was pregnant, would be to tell her mother. Or perhaps she shouldn't tell her at all? Perhaps she should just present her mother with a grandchild? At fifty-one? The shock might kill her.

If you notice your thoughts straying, just count yourself back down from five. The voice on her app was supernaturally calm.

Caro nodded at it, breathed in and counted down. Five, four…

Of course it wouldn't kill her mother! Her mother was indestructible.

It's okay to think of other things…

And then she'd have to decide on what to say at work. She had three versions lined up. Number one: the truth. Number two: Richard, her most recent ex? Because she could, in the beginning at least, pretend that they had been in it together.

…notice that your mind is wandering…

Or number three: a one-night stand thing?

…but try to bring your thoughts back…

Which was out of the question! She was fifty. Who was going to believe a one-night stand thing?

Be kind to yourself, the tiny, calm voice said. *Meditation takes practice.*

She sat up, yanking her earbuds from her ears. Her knuckles had pooled white, gripping the screen. She twisted round, put her phone down and sat, knees hugged to chest.

What *would* she say? For so long she had prepared herself only up to this point, seduced by a soft, shimmering armada of possibility which, now that it had sailed into view, was something starker and altogether more rigid. Judgements would be made. Things would be said (as they already had been with Helen) and she would have to weather them. Correction: from now on, she and her child would have to weather them. She shivered, feeling goosebumps spill along her arms, remembering another time when she hadn't prepared herself – a memory that had her biting her lip with a humiliation that was two decades old.

In her late twenties she'd had her nose fixed. Made straighter, smaller, far less ugly. Helen and Kay had always said there was no need, and her mother (whom she'd told in a misguided attempt to forge a connection) had dismissed it as *wasteful vanity*. But how brave she'd been. (Helen and Kay had said that afterwards; she herself had come to look upon it as hopelessly naive.) Forging ahead! So wrapped up in the profound changes she *knew* it would make, she hadn't stopped to consider any other reaction. But that first week back, in the boardroom, standing to deliver her presentation with the CFO introducing her, she had heard Glen Seamore (like a playground bully; she would never forget the man's full name), Head of Development, whisper loudly, *That's not Caro. That's an impostor! Bring back Caroline*

Hooter-Castle. The dreadful hushed sniggers as she'd pushed on through her talk were something she would remember on her deathbed. Her drenching humiliation, spotlighted by the projector.

She pulled her knees in, feeling the smooth warm of the canvas sunbed against the soles of her feet. Not this time. This time she would be ready. She would not speak of it. She would work twice as hard all the way through to the fourth quarter and then she'd take the time she needed. Money talked, louder and longer than anyone in the City, and Matt knew that. She could do a lot from home, and beyond that he'd give her the time she needed.

And if it didn't work in London? Well, she'd move on. She had more than enough put aside to take a break. She had both funds and a reputation that preceded her. Plus Alison Machowski, with whom she had stayed in touch, had added her to a private Facebook group and forwarded a list of preschool nurseries in literally every major financial hub in the world. It had shocked Caro – the idea of other women out there, so many of them, just like her.

A loud, breathy rasp blew past. Kay. As smooth and round as a seal, chin slack, eyes closed, arms flung out. Asleep *again*.

Caro put her hands behind her head, closed her eyes... but it was no use. She sat up, flexed her feet, scrunched up her toes, flexed them again. How on earth was she going to get through the next two hours, let alone the next two weeks?

'I'm going to take a walk,' she said.

Kay didn't stir.

She slipped her flip-flops on and looked across the garden. Beyond the manicured lawns of the hotel, the landscape changed dramatically. And outside the hotel entrance, she knew, the road stretched across the foothills for miles without so much as meeting another building. 'Don't worry, I won't go far,' she said, and smiled at her own joke. Then she stood, tied the knot of her sundress and tucked her hair under her sun hat.

The pool wasn't large and it didn't take long to walk the perimeter but, going slowly and stopping frequently, Caro stretched it out as long as she could without arousing the attention of the other guests. The portly couple behind the jacuzzi were no problem. They were obviously serious sunbathers, both of them as deeply oiled as a mahogany sideboard, neither of them moving all day except to turn and brown the other side. Like sausages in swimsuits. And the younger couple situated by the shallow end didn't worry her either. These two, plugged into earphones and iPads, constantly reached out to stroke each other. They were obviously at the beginning stage of their relationship. In love – or lust. Either way, a state of being she couldn't imagine experiencing again.

No, it was the woman tucked away by the perimeter boundary that Caro had noticed and had, unconsciously, been trying to avoid for three days now. They were of a similar age, and she was obviously alone. Caro had first seen her at dinner the evening they'd arrived, watching over Helen's shoulder as the woman politely but firmly cut short a conversation with another guest. She'd noticed because she'd recognised the script the woman had used. *My job is very stressful. I'm just here to relax.*

Approaching the woman now, she put her head down, using her sunglasses as cover through which to take a closer look. The woman had her own cover: huge sunglasses, a magazine propped open against her bent knees, earphones and a hat with a large brim. She may as well have erected a boundary fence, a *Trespassers will be Executed* sign. Her chin was set, her mouth firm. She didn't look as if she was reading, and there was one thing Caro was sure of: if she was here for relaxation, it wasn't working. All the sunshine, the gloriously azure sky, all the twinkling refracted light from the swimming pool, the heady scent of a flower bed filled with lilies, wasn't working a jot. As she neared, she eyed the woman cautiously and sensed that through those dark glasses the woman was eyeing her back, like felines in a jungle, stalking an unseen prize.

The hotel had come recommended by the clinic. And if the recommendation had been made to her, it would of course have been made to others. Hadn't the driver yesterday known exactly where he was going? Depositing her at the clinic with a poker face and a rigidly confident estimate of pick-up time, which had been right. Of course she hadn't asked. *Have you been here before? Do you often find yourself driving women like me?* She'd swallowed her pride and worked on her own poker face.

As she passed now, the woman suddenly dropped her chin and, over the top of her Dolce & Gabbana glasses, looked up. Caro wasn't ready, didn't look away in time, and for a tiny fraction of a second they held each other's gaze.

Then the woman pushed her glasses back up her nose and withdrew behind her magazine. Not a flicker of recognition passed between them.

Shaken, she continued on, across the terrace to the doors of the restaurant. Of course, she couldn't be sure. But if...if that woman was here for the same reasons... She couldn't stop herself; she couldn't stop the thoughts that followed. Why? What had brought her here? A life lived thinking only of herself, as Helen had described it? Or just bad luck? *MMM*, Alison Machowski had nicknamed the Facebook group she'd joined. *Midlife Moms Managing*. It had over 7000 members. All those selfish women, thinking only of themselves. They might as well adopt a costume, like that other infamous acronym. White hoods for the KKK, pointy black hats and broomsticks for MMM? No, it wasn't that simple. No matter what Helen said, it just wasn't that simple.

She shook her head. It was no good winding herself up like this. It was done. Chin up, she thrust an arm out, pushed the restaurant door open and went inside, where the air was instantly cooler. She took an apple from the bowl on the sideboard and wandered back to the large windows. There on the far side of the pool was Kay, still sleeping. And there... Caro looked again at the woman she had just passed, and a wave of relief surged through her, so huge it reached her eyes, filling them with tears. How lucky she was by comparison. She had so much more than a copy of *Grazia* to get her through this. Kay was here with her. And Helen. She brought the back of her arm up and used it to blot her eyes. Danny Abbott buying her flowers? What had Helen said? Well, whatever it was, it didn't matter.

What mattered was that Helen had her back, and despite their differences she always would. Kay too. Caro stretched her arms above her head and looked again across to Kay. Poor Kay. No wonder she was exhausted, arriving in the middle of a raging storm like that. The conversations that must have gone on yesterday while she was at the clinic! Kay should have been a diplomat. They could send her to Korea; she'd have the country unified in five minutes and dinner made in ten. But she didn't deserve this – not on her first holiday in years. She turned the apple in her hand. Her teeth had left imprints in the yellow-white flesh. It wasn't what Helen had bargained for either.

She wandered back to the sideboard, threw the apple in the bin and picked up a spotted banana. It didn't appeal. Nothing did, and suddenly she remembered the restaurant she'd wanted to try in Kyrenia. That was it! She would book the restaurant for this evening and she would pay for it, and together they would start this holiday over.

She put the banana back and made her way upstairs to reception. She needed help booking both a taxi and a table.

But upstairs the woman at reception – Marianne, she had called herself – was busy talking to an American couple. Caro mooched over to the rack of brochures to wait. She pulled out one on a vineyard tour and another on the beautiful Bellapais Abbey – somewhere that, even if Helen was hell-bent on sailing all week, Kay might be interested in. If she could stay awake long enough.

She'd barely opened up the brochure when she heard the American woman say *Kaveh* and then *boat*. Glancing over to the front desk, she saw that the woman had a sailing flyer in her hand. *Such a sad story*, Caro heard. Her ears pricked, her breath stilled. She stared at the brochure, but her eyes had ceased to function.

'…took a lesson with him yesterday,' the American man was saying. 'Hard to process really.' His accent (Midwest?) was so strong Caro had to strain to understand. 'Live all your life in one place like that and then have them just go on and pull the rug out from under your feet.'

'Rug?' This was Marianne.

'I came back and told my wife all about it, didn't I, honey? I said, imagine that happening to us.'

'I couldn't imagine.' This was the American woman.

'Having to pack everything up, forced out. One week they had. It was a week, wasn't it, honey?'

'That's what you said.'

'Leaving everything behind. The place you've lived your whole life. It was the whole village, wasn't it? Starting again from nothing.'

'Awful,' his wife said.

'Just awful,' he repeated.

The phone started ringing, so loud and shrill that Caro jumped. She folded the brochure and put it back. Took out another. Her hands, she noticed, were shaking.

'Hotel Adagio.'

Taking cover behind the stream of Turkish that Marianne had launched into, Caro glanced across at the couple. The man stood, straight-leg jeans, thumbs stuck in belt loops, jaw moving side to side. His wife, next to him, stared across the room, a cardigan folded over her hands.

She shook her head. 'He must be so lonely,' she said, turning to her husband. 'Did you think that?'

'Hard to say.'

'But you said he had to leave his wife and family behind?'

'Something like that.'

'Sorry to keep you waiting!' Marianne's voice was clean and bright. 'Now, what time did you say you'd like the taxi for the airport?'

'Eight?' the man said.

'Eight,' his wife nodded. She was still staring across the foyer. For a moment she looked straight at Caro, blinked, then turned to her husband and said, 'Eight should be fine.'

'Kay. *Kay.*'

She was floating…or flying? Here we go again, she thought, rolled over, brought the palms of her hands together and laid them under her cheek. Sleep, sweet, sweet—

'*Kay! Wake up!*'

Now there was a hand on her shoulder shaking her, a lot more roughly than Helen's pencil prods of yesterday. Reluctantly she opened her eyes. There was Caro, perched on the edge of her sunbed like a hawk on a branch. Two spots of pink had bloomed in the centre of each cheek and her eyes fizzed with energy, any trace of the vulnerable, fragile Caro from breakfast vanquished. Something had happened. Kay narrowed her eyes. 'What?' she said cautiously.

Caro leaned forward. 'I've just come back from reception,' she whispered.

'And?' Kay pushed herself upright. Once again her mouth was as dry as a cracker, and her right boob had completely escaped her bikini top.

'I think,' Caro hissed, 'that Kaveh is a refugee.'

Kay blinked.

Caro pointed at her right boob.

She looked down, then back up. 'Refugee? What do you mean?'

'Put it back in!'

'I am. *I am.*' She was, but the cups of her bikini, wet from the jacuzzi and never well structured in the first place, were now spacious enough to hold a week's shopping each. 'What do you mean?' she said, stuffing herself back in.

Caro shuffled forward. 'I was just up at reception. I was going to book a table for dinner tonight when I overheard this couple talking.'

'About Kaveh?'

'Yes! They were sailing with him – or the man was – and he must have told him.'

'What?'

'What do you mean, *what?*'

'*What* did he tell them?'

'That he'd had to leave his village. And that he has a wife and children…somewhere.'

'Well…' Kay frowned. 'So does Helen. Not a wife, but you know what I mean.'

If Caro heard, she didn't respond. 'Don't you see?' she whispered. 'He's latched onto Helen for a passport.'

'Caro!' Kay leaned back and slapped her hands on her knees. 'That's ridiculous!'

'Is it?' Caro sat back. 'He has a wife and family, Kay. He's obviously stuck here. Helen could be the perfect ticket out for him. And you know how impulsive she can be. Well, at uni she was, but she's wobbling now. She said so herself. Before we know it she'll be divorcing Lawrence and...' Caro shook her head. 'What?' she said. 'You think I'm exaggerating?'

Kay sighed. Out of all of them Caro had always been the plotter, the planner. She could, Kay had no doubt, Excel her way out of any situation. She'd already plotted the graph of Helen's romance, motivation, conclusions, repercussions...

'What do you think we should do?'

'*Do?*' It was like living in an echo chamber. Twenty-four hours, and wasn't Helen sitting in Caro's place asking exactly the same question?

'Yes! We have to do something, Kay! I mean, Lawrence is...' Caro felt her cheeks warm. 'Well, he's not Mr Perfect, that's for sure, but to throw away her marriage like this—'

'Caro!' Kay ran her fingers through her hair, tugging at spikes as if she were testing to see they were fixed in place. 'If Helen's marriage comes to an end,' she said, 'it comes to an end.'

Caro swung back on her lounger and folded her arms. '*Who* is he?' she said, her voice low. 'And more importantly, what does he want from Helen?'

'Perhaps,' Kay shrugged, 'he doesn't want anything?' She bent down and set about stuffing books and glasses and gum into her bag.

Caro stared at her. 'So we're not going to at least tell her?'

Kay looked up. She was thinking about the way Helen had looked yesterday. Radiant – happier, certainly, than Kay had seen her for many years. What she wouldn't do for a few radiant moments of her own like that. And then how pissed she'd be if someone stomped in and turned the lights off on them. Wasn't it better just to leave things? For today, anyway, and tomorrow, and soon enough they would all be home and back to reality. 'No,' she said decisively. 'I don't think we should. I think you should concentrate on relaxing and we should, all of us, try and just enjoy the rest of the week. Helen's going to have to deal with it all anyway when she gets back home. That's for certain.'

Pushing upright, Caro narrowed her eyes. 'Kay?'

'Jack,' Kay shrugged, 'rang Helen yesterday morning.' She looked at Caro. 'And Helen answered him with FaceTime, when it would have been better answering him *without* FaceTime.'

Caro frowned. Her eyebrows made neat little downward arrows.

'This was *yesterday* morning,' Kay said. 'Before I arrived.'

Comprehension bloomed. 'Where was she?' Caro whispered.

'In bed,' Kay whispered back.

'With…?'

'Yes.'

Caro's jaw went slack and she sat, as still as a statue, on the edge of the lounger.

Kay watched. If she didn't love Caro so much, didn't know all the vulnerable undersides to this brittle, efficient exterior she wore for the world, she might have laughed.

Slapped her on the knee and said, *There, Caro! Import that into your spreadsheet and see what happens.* Perhaps, she thought – and the thought took her by surprise – having a baby might be the best thing that could ever happen to Caro. Might finally put an end to her untested faith that life could and should be anticipated and then planned. 'Right then!' she said, because Caro still hadn't moved, and rivulets of sweat were crawling down her back and her scalp was itchy. 'I need a shower.'

'I just think—'

Kay was on her feet. 'Don't think,' she sighed. 'Just try *not* to think. Okay?'

Stunned, Caro nodded.

'I'm going to take a shower. Are you coming?'

Inside the lift, they stood shoulder to shoulder in air-conditioned silence – Caro thinking and thinking and then trying not to think, Kay knowing that Caro was thinking and thinking and then trying (and failing) not to think…

As they approached the third floor, Caro's phone pinged. She reached inside her bag, fumbling and scrambling. The doors opened and, head down, Kay followed her out into the quiet of the corridor, where Caro stopped short, her head bent to the screen.

Kay stepped around her and went on. So much, she thought, for Caro actually relaxing.

'*Kay.*' From behind, the urgent whisper reached her like a snake curling up her neck.

She turned.

'Lawrence,' Caro whispered.

Kay closed her eyes. God, she'd had enough. 'Please,' she started.

'But—'

'Enough!' she cried. One day! One day she'd been here, and it had been nothing but drama and conflict. She might as well have stayed on her settee and watched *The Real Housewives of Atlanta, Beverly Hills, New York...* anywhere really. It would have been a lot less expensive, a lot less worrying, and Alex would have known better than to disturb her snoozing. Yesterday had been exhausting. But she'd patched the two of them together again, and all that was left should have been a week of sun...and sleep. If either of them could, for a moment, just stop with all the interference in each other's lives. She was fed up. Her first holiday in decades! Opening her eyes, she lifted her palm, like a sarong-wearing policewoman. 'It's Helen's problem. Can't you see that?'

Caro shook her head. She was holding her phone in her hand like a child holds a ladybird. 'Lawrence—'

'Is Helen's husband—'

'Is here—'

'Is *her* problem—'

'Is *here*, Kay.'

'Here?'

'Here.'

Kay's eyes were plates. Her mouth made a shape. *Here?*

And Caro kept nodding. She held her phone up. 'He just texted me. He's downstairs. In the foyer.'

Part Three

16

Front desks weren't what they used to be. Back in her heyday, front desks had had a purpose. They were there to keep guests at a distance. To remind them of who was in charge. They were polished and wide, adorned with objects chosen for defensive rather than aesthetic reasons. Like the black bat flower display in the Argos, Istanbul. Her old manager, Remy, had ordered it, instructing them on how to position the thing for best effect. True, it was the ugliest plant Marianne had ever come across – like a black-tendrilled Grim Reaper – but it did its job. She couldn't remember a single occasion when a guest's unclean hand had strayed too close. Those were the days. Marianne grimaced. What did she have now? In the name of minimalism and this newfangled idea that guests should feel at home, all she had was a plank of insipid wood and something called a 'tablet' to swipe. The bench (she would not grace it with the name of 'desk') was so narrow she could smell the garlic on a guest's breath, or the alcohol. Anyone could stick their nosy neck over and see how clumsy her swiping still was. Guests? Made to feel at home? This was a hotel the last time she looked. All she had between them and her was her prize-winning orchid. And even that she'd had to bring in herself, confident that Sofia, the bossy new manager, with a degree in *tourism* and an approach to make-up similar to that of a toddler with face paints, wouldn't be able to resist its beauty. *If you insist,* she'd muttered to Marianne, unpicking hair from her lips. (But to the District Manager had purred, *Isn't it gorgeous? We thought it could only add to the aesthetics.*)

Right now, Marianne wanted to stick Sofia's aesthetics where even the Cyprus sun didn't shine. All this "progression" had left her feeling woefully exposed. And never more so than now. The man in front of her was a bear in a cage! Wound up like a demented toy, striding back and forth incessantly. And although the floor was marble, she wasn't convinced he wouldn't wear a track through it. Up and down he went. Up and down, and up and down! A tall, dirty, stubbly streak of a man. And no, he wouldn't sit, even though she hadn't phrased the suggestion as an offer and this had *never*, in her whole career, been misunderstood before.

Because, minimalism aside, Marianne was very good at her job. Mostly, the Hotel Adagio was an oasis of calm and taste. But on those rare occasions when mis-bookings had occurred, when taxis were late and when tempers had run high and chaos threatened, she'd come into her own, proving herself to be an impassive mountain of dignified authority, able to quell the most outrageous of tantrums. She was fifty-two. Plus her mother had been Serbian.

But this man? He was difficult. Perhaps he had Balkan

ancestry too? She studied him with heavy, lizard eyes, dismissing the idea almost as swiftly as she'd formed it. This man was English. His trousers, for a start. Who needed pockets at their knees? And his boots reminded her of a cousin who as a child had worn orthopaedic shoes. Then there was the thing that he'd come in with. A rucksack? Strapped to his back like the filthy shell of a tortoise. He'd deposited it on the floor, although he'd been aiming for a chair. One look from her, thank goodness, had been enough for him to think better. Still, the thought of it, tattered and filthy on one of the pastel armchairs, actually made her shudder. She picked up a stack of papers and tapped them together, lining up their edges. She would have liked to have done the same with this man – taken him outside and tapped the dirt off him. Once, when she was very young, she'd spent three months in England, in Bath, and had been quite taken by an Englishman, but in the end it was his inability to dress with any sense of style that had finished the relationship. That and his teeth.

'Perhaps,' she tried again, 'if you would give me the name of the person you are waiting for? Then I could ring through.'

The man looked up, almost startled. He took out his phone, then seemed to dismiss whatever he'd been thinking and walked over to her bench. 'Okay,' he said, running his hand through his hair. 'Let's try that.'

Shrinking back, Marianne edged her orchid away and saw, horrified, how tiny flakes of something now lay scattered like confetti all over the bench.

'Helen Winters,' the man said, and he turned and

leaned back so his elbows were pointing at her like two ugly pink doorknobs.

Which was a good job.

Firstly, because she might have slapped him for his rudeness if he'd been facing her. Secondly, because she'd already picked up the phone, and it hung in her hand now like a forgotten fork as she processed what that meant: *Helen Winters*. Helen Winters was the Englishwoman, staying with the other Englishwoman who was here for the clinic. And the third one. Kay? Who was very nice but had a poolside wardrobe that defied belief. (Tissue-thin scarlet might look passable on the young field workers of South India, but on a middle-aged Englishwoman with – how could she say this – an over-fondness for pastries?)

Helen Winters was also the Englishwoman who, at that very moment, was out somewhere with Kaveh having lessons in (not least) sailing.

And Helen Winters wore a wedding ring. Marianne sniffed. So this must be her husband. You didn't get to work half a lifetime on the front desk without growing a nose for these things. 'I'll ring through,' she said, and the calmness in her voice astonished even her. Her confidence (which, truth be told, had taken a bit of a battering as her clumsy, stiff fingers had struggled to keep up with the speed-swipers of this new world) swelled. So she hadn't lost it! Because, although it had been a while, she'd been here before. Back in the '90s, at the Four Seasons in Athens, when that American actor's wife had arrived a day earlier than expected. Actors! (The spontaneous turn she'd had to perform, pretending to be room service, was nothing short of Oscar standard.)

274

As she listened to the sound of the telephone ringing out in Helen Winters' empty room, Marianne smiled. He'd gone on to become famous, that actor. (And she still had his T-shirt, secreted away in her top drawer.) She drummed her fingernails on the desk...not desk...bench! What an afternoon it was turning out to be. Because, oasis of civility that the Hotel Adagio was, it could also be desperately dull. After this call – which wasn't, she knew, going to be answered – she would need to let her son know she'd be late back. He'd *have* to make himself useful, because she wasn't going anywhere – not before Helen Winters was back.

'Don't answer it!' Kay grabbed Caro's arm just as her hand had reached the receiver of the phone on the bedside table. 'It might be Lawrence,' she whispered.

They both looked at the phone.

Caro's hand trembled. Ignoring a ringing phone was like asking her to fly backwards. 'I can't,' she said. 'I can't not answer it.'

'You bloody well can!' Kay hissed. She pushed the telephone out of reach. 'What else? What else did Lawrence's text say?'

'Nothing. Nothing else. Just that he's here at the hotel.' She looked at the still-ringing phone. 'I *have* to answer that.'

'You—'

And the phone rang off.

The room buzzed with a silence louder than a fire alarm.

'Do you think,' Kay whispered, 'that Helen knows?'

Caro shook her head. 'I don't know.'

'Okay.' Kay took the ends of her sarong and tied them in a knot to end all knots. So tight she could feel the chiffon cut into her flesh. 'Read it again.'

'The text?'

'No, Caro. The front page of the *Daily Mail!*'

Caro stared at her.

'Of course the text!'

'Right…right.' She dipped her head and swiped through, and while she did, Kay folded her arms and stared out of the window.

'What a mess,' she muttered. 'What a bloody mess.'

'Here it is.' Caro read:

Hi Caroline. Appreciate this may come as a surprise but having cut Nepal short, I'm here in Cyprus. At the hotel. Unforeseen circumstances you might say. Are you close by?

'Unforeseen circumstances?' Kay laughed. 'Sounds like a telegram.'

'Why is he here?'

'Take a wild guess,' Kay muttered, still watching the view. There could only be one reason why Lawrence had cut his trip short. She turned to Caro.

'You don't think?' Caro looked down at the text again. When she looked up, her face was pale. 'You don't think?' Her eyes widened as her hand crept up to cover her mouth. 'He knows, doesn't he? He's—'

'No shit, Sherlock!' She turned back to the window. 'For a smart woman, Caro, you can be very slow.'

'But how? How on earth could he?' Caro stopped talking. Her arms went slack. 'Kay?' she said quietly. 'You don't think it was me, do you? You don't think that I'd—'

276

'Of course not!' Kay turned back, waving an arm in Caro's direction. 'It's Jack. Jack must have told his father about that phone call. Helen said she wasn't going to do anything about it until she got back, but he must have contacted his dad.'

'Oh.' Caro's mouth made a small round shape. 'What are we going to do?'

'Haven't a clue,' she sighed, and filled her lungs, puffed out her cheeks and stretched her arms wide enough to hold the room. '*Not a bloody clue!*' And in two strides she was across the floor and flat on her back on the bed.

For a moment Caro sat watching, then she too slung her legs up on the bed and fell back, and the two of them lay looking at the ceiling.

A long minute passed. The room was so silent Caro's ears began to ring. She put her hand across her stomach. Theoretically this should be the last thing she needed, this excitement. But it felt more natural to her than the state of enforced relaxation of earlier. The low-lying threat that underlaid the moment like a bass note was familiar and welcome. She knew this habitat. Thrived on it and had developed many extra senses to deal with it. Plus, and she couldn't help herself, it was funny. Like a sitcom or a farce. Any minute now and a vicar would arrive on the back of a motorbike. She started giggling, her shoulders shaking and her stomach wobbling with the ridiculousness of it all. Helen. Out of the three of them it could only have been Helen who could get herself into this situation.

'You okay?' Kay had propped herself up on her elbow. 'You're not going hysterical on me now, are you?'

'No.' Caro put her arm across her forehead, but she could not stop laughing. Tears fell, trickling down her cheeks and into her ears. 'Only Helen,' she gasped.

Kay flopped back down. 'That is so true!'

'Oh, Kay!' Now Caro sat up. 'Does this remind you—'

'Of course it does. Spring term, second year.'

'You remember? We had to keep Helen's dad in the living room while that boy… What was his name?'

'Haven't a clue,' Kay sighed.

'Andy? No… Adrian?'

'There were a few.'

'Well, whoever it was shimmied down a drainpipe while we kept her dad supplied with Rich Teas and pretended she was showering.'

'I remember,' Kay nodded. 'She thought it was so funny when we told her.'

Caro lay back. 'She thought everything was funny. We could never get her to take it seriously. Exams…anything.' She threaded her fingers together and looked down at them. 'You know,' she whispered, 'it's what I always admired the most about Helen, and yet I never even noticed.'

'Noticed what?'

'That the fun had stopped.'

'It stops for all of us, doesn't it?' Kay sighed. 'At some point.'

'That,' Caro breathed, 'isn't something I want to believe, Kay.'

Kay smiled. 'No, me neither.'

And with a momentum that belied both her age and the confines of the room, Caro suddenly rolled onto her side and propped herself up with her elbow. 'So!' she said. 'What are we going to do? Should we call her?'

Kay sat up. 'Well, we have a bit of time, don't we? She said she wouldn't be back for lunch.'

'Lunch?' Caro frowned in disbelief. 'Kay, lunch was hours ago.'

'It can't be! What's the time?'

Caro reached for her phone. 'It's three o'clock.'

'It can't be!' Kay wailed. 'It just can't be!'

'She'll be back any minute.' Caro was on her feet.

Kay leaned forward and cradled her head. 'I can't have slept all day. Not *again*.'

And from outside the window came the low and unmistakable tinny rumble of a moped exhaust.

They looked first to each other, then to the window and then back to each other.

'She's back,' Caro whispered.

'She's back,' Kay answered.

As synchronised as swimmers, they moved across the room and out to the balcony, and leaned over the rail.

And there she was! Dangling off the pillion seat of Kaveh's moped, helmet stretched out at arm's length, thick blonde hair flying behind, bosom bursting forth from her low-cut T-shirt. Glancing up and seeing them, Helen waved the helmet, pure joy lighting every feature. She looked, they both thought, probably more beautiful and more alive than she ever had. She looked as if she was having fun.

'What a perfect day!' she called, then put her hand to her mouth and blew them both a kiss. 'What an absolutely perfect day!'

*

'Please.' Marianne had decided to try again. 'Take a seat,' she said, her voice thin steel.

The man turned. 'Rather not,' he blipped.

Very curt. Very much the tone of a man accustomed to giving orders rather than receiving them. Enough! She was slacking and he was still stalking the room like Attila the Hun, which he wasn't. He was a dirty-looking Englishman, and this was her domain. She walked out from behind the bench, a pencil twirling in her hands like a stiff miniature acrobat. 'Sir,' she said. 'It is uncomfortable for our guests to have you…pacing like this! They are here to relax.'

The man turned, raised a slow, sardonic eyebrow and glanced around the foyer, which was empty, but that wasn't the point! It hadn't been empty a moment ago. A moment ago she'd had to watch as a German couple made all sorts of faces at each other, trying to book a day trip to Soli. 'Would you *please* take a seat,' she said, all patience expended.

And he did! Right behind the olive tree.

Her spine straight, Marianne gave him a curt nod and returned to her bench, where she shuffled with papers and opened Facebook on the tablet and pretended to be extremely busy…because she couldn't quite believe he'd complied. And as she'd swiped, a warm certainty swept through, energising her like a battery recharged. One thing she knew for sure was that a *degree* – in *tourism* – was about as useful as a three-legged table when it came to handling situations like this. Oh yes, she had years left in her yet.

She glanced at the clock. She should have finished

twenty minutes ago, and she was dying for a wee. When was Helen Winters going to turn up?

Out in the corridor, Kay and Caro were waiting for the lift to arrive.

'So,' Caro whispered, 'I'll go and keep him talking.'

'And I'll go down to the restaurant,' Kay whispered back. 'Kaveh will be parking behind the pool. I can intercept them.'

'Then what?'

They looked at each other blankly.

Helen hadn't heard their desperate warning shouts, and moments later they had watched as the moped disappeared underneath the canopy of the hotel. So, with much giggling and many interruptions, they'd scrambled together a plan. The only flaw in which was that they hadn't got beyond this opening tactic of keeping Helen and Lawrence apart.

The lift arrived and the doors opened with a *swish-ping*. They stepped in, turning automatically to the large mirror opposite.

'It's not my best look,' Kay sighed. Two large, melon-shaped patches of wet from her swimming costume had soaked through her sarong.

'It's not mine either,' Caro muttered.

Kay shook her head and redid the knot of her sarong. Caro looked great. Lean and strong in a Stella McCartney one-piece and matching tunic, which had probably cost more than Kay's plane ticket.

When the doors *swish-pinged* open at the ground floor, Caro didn't move.

'Hurry,' Kay whispered, and looked at Caro's stomach. 'Carefully. Hurry *carefully*.'

'I will, I will.' She was halfway out. Turning back to Kay, who was continuing on down, she asked, 'What am I going to say?'

'Bullshit him, Caro!' Kay threw up her arms. 'It's what you do for a living, isn't it?'

Caro's mouth twitched. She felt her bladder loosen and a tremendous urge to giggle rush up her throat. Her eyes pricked. 'I can't do this,' she whispered, and then she *was* giggling, crossing her legs, clutching the door and giggling hopelessly.

Like a curtain call, the lift doors began their *swish-ping* to close.

Kay slapped a hand on the button. 'Don't,' she started, but her own mouth was twitching. 'Don…' And she doubled forward, gasping with laughter.

The door began *swish-pinging* again.

'Why are we even laughing?' Caro gasped.

'Stop it!' Kay's voice was a squeak, which set them both off even more. Crying and hooting, she slapped her hand blindly against the side of the lift, trying to find the button, and halfway in, halfway out, Caro was squeezing her legs together and holding her stomach and pushing the doors back when they came too close.

'This is serious,' Kay gasped.

'I know.'

'Right…right.' Kay straightened her back, then scooped her arms to her chest to carry air into her body. 'Right,' she said a third time. And then a fourth. 'Right. Ready?'

Caro nodded. She wasn't really ready. She wanted to stay here in the corridor and keep giggling. When was the last time she'd laughed like this? *Really* laughed, just like this?

'Good luck,' Kay whispered, and the doors made their last *swish-ping* closed.

She gathered herself together, took a deep breath and lifted her chin. *Boardroom, Caro*, she whispered, *it's just a boardroom*. Then, head erect, she made her way along the corridor into reception. She saw Marianne immediately and she knew, although the woman didn't so much as raise her head, that Marianne had also seen her.

Apart from that, the foyer seemed empty. She turned to look at the entrance. Propped up by the settee was a rucksack. It had to be Lawrence's, but there was no sign of him. Her heart started hammering. He was outside, he'd found Helen already… Then she looked across at Marianne, who tilted her head the tiniest inch towards the olive tree in the corner. And as soon as Caro looked, she saw him. Almost hidden. Thin, weary, handsome still, but utterly exhausted.

She was only halfway across when Lawrence looked up through the foliage, saw her and said, 'Caroline!' As cheerfully as if they'd bumped into each other on a sunny morning, on the high street.

Caro smiled back. Kay was right. It was bullshit time. 'Lawrence?' she feigned. 'What on earth…?' She opened her palms to emphasise the question.

'Long story, Caro. Long story.' Lawrence already had his hands on her shoulders and was kissing her cheek. His own cheek was as rough as sandpaper.

283

'Goodness!' She pulled back. 'This is a surprise.'

'For me as well.' He put his hands on his hips and shook his head at the floor.

'And Everest! Astounding, Lawrence! Congratulations!'

'Thanks, Caro.' He looked up, almost shy. 'It was tough.'

'I bet it was. What an incredible achievement, though. This man' – Caro swung around to Marianne – 'has just climbed Everest!'

Behind the desk, Marianne gave a wan smile. 'Everest?' she replied, and her eyes went to the large, bulky pockets at the knees of Lawrence's cargo pants.

'So?' Caro swung back, smiling.

'Where's Helen?' Lawrence asked bluntly.

'Where's Helen?' Caro stalled. 'She's…well, she's sailing.'

'Sailing!'

'Yes.' Caro clasped her hands together. 'She's really taken to it. Actually.'

Inches away from her own, the series of contortions that Lawrence's face went through – disbelief, then scorn, then what Caro could only have described as a dismissiveness – were so readable he didn't need to voice what he said next. And what he did say, she could have scripted for him. 'Helen doesn't *sail*.'

Caro's face was a mask. 'Well, she does now.'

'What in?' he guffawed. 'A dinghy?'

Two days – it had only been two days since she'd stood on the waterfront at Kyrenia harbour and watched her brave, beautiful friend bob off into an ocean. Helen *did* sail. Helen planted melons in a wet English summer and Helen knew how to have fun. 'I think,' she said, 'it's a little more than a dinghy.' Her words were as sharp as arrowheads. Expectantly, she waited for them to find their target.

They didn't. Instead they fell flat and useless at her feet, and as Caro looked at Lawrence, she understood with a dazzling clarity that this was because she was standing in front of a man who had the skin of a rhinoceros and the sensitivity of a mollusc. In fact, the only thing she didn't understand was how she hadn't seen all this before. This hero of a man she'd mindlessly kept on a pedestal for so long. She smiled. 'You must be parched!' She put her arm on his shoulder and, without any forward planning at all, began steering him towards the bar at the front of the hotel. 'How long have you been here?'

Five minutes later and they were sitting in front of floor-to-ceiling windows which overlooked the dark peaks of the Kyrenia mountains. Straight ahead, across the dusty road, were drills and drills of vineyards, and, directly below, the blue corner of the hotel swimming pool (behind which was the car park). Playing it safe, Caro had positioned Lawrence with his back to the view. He'd barely blinked. A man just back from the Himalayas, she'd conceded, might be a little tired of mountains.

'And you haven't told her you're coming?' she asked as she passed him his beer. 'What a lovely surprise.'

Lawrence cocked an eyebrow. 'You think so?'

'Of course.'

He nodded at her orange juice. 'Not drinking, Caro? That's not like you.'

Caro shrugged. 'Trying to be healthy,' she said. 'It is a spa hotel, after all.'

Lawrence sat forward, dropped his head and clasped his hands together. 'To be honest, Caro...' From under his brows, he looked up. 'Can I be honest?' And he didn't wait for an answer; he didn't wait for permission. He just reached out and grabbed her hand.

Caro froze. Her fingers felt like sticks against his palm.

'I haven't come all this way to surprise Helen. Well... I have. But not in the way you're thinking.'

'Really?'

'Caroline.' Lawrence cocked his head. 'You've always had such an innocent heart.'

Caro smiled thinly. God, he was bad at this. With her, of all people? Caroline Hardcastle, bullshitter supremo of London City. Caro, who could sweet-talk a potential client into tripling their original starting position (and they'd still walk away thinking they were the smart ones). What *was* Lawrence thinking? That she wouldn't smell it? Wouldn't see through the greasy spread? She slipped her hand free. But then, why would he think otherwise, when she'd always turned a blind eye to it before?

He didn't seem to notice. 'The fact is,' he was saying, 'Jack called me.'

Caro nodded. Helen's useless, spoiled son.

Lawrence shook his head. 'He was beside himself, Caro. I've never heard my boy so upset!'

My boy? Caro sucked on her orange juice, and the slurp was much louder than she'd intended. Lawrence had spent a good three months of every year of Jack's life climbing a mountain or cycling the length of a country. Now…it was *my boy*.

'Can I tell you?' His eyes were as shiny as a puppy's.

And from nowhere, she wanted to slap him. How had she ever gone along with this? Had she really been so desperate for the flattery? The attention?

'Well, maybe it's better if I just show you.' He sniffed. 'A picture paints a thousand words, as they say.'

Horrified but equally curious, Caro watched as Lawrence picked up his phone. What had Kay said? Jack had called Helen on FaceTime, and she'd answered…on FaceTime.

Palm at his forehead, as if he were showing her proof of the end of the world, Lawrence held his phone up.

Caro put her drink down and took the phone. There it was. A screenshot. (So Jack wasn't completely useless.) And it was all Caro could do not to laugh. She dug her nails into her palm, bit down on her lip. There was Helen, hair like a huge golden cloud, all naked shoulders, and behind her was Kaveh (looking very handsome, Caro had to admit), equally naked. 'Oh,' she said. It was all she trusted herself to say. What the hell could she say?

Thankfully she didn't have to say anything. Lawrence dropped forward, burying his head in his arms and weeping. Like a child. A baby. Like the baby she might soon have. She put the phone down on the table between them and sat very still. Babies were one thing; fully grown men who'd just climbed the world's tallest mountain, weeping like this in public… *Pull yourself together*, she wanted to say, and she had a very clear, very sudden image of the dead grandmother she never got to meet, pushing her own mother down the steps of the air-raid shelter.

Imagine that, Caroline? Imagine having the courage to choose to die?

She folded her hands in her lap and waited for him to sob it out. Thankfully, the bar was empty.

It took a while but eventually he sat up and grabbed her hand. Again!

'I'm sorry, Caro,' he gasped. 'I just can't believe she'd do something like this! Twenty-five years of marriage. Who is that man? Do you know?'

She glanced at the image again, then back to the crumpled heap of the man himself, and the very last vestige of affection she had ever felt for him evaporated. What was left was simple and unambiguous. She pitied him. Plus it was all out now. He knew. It was exactly as Kay had guessed – Jack had told him – so she might as well tell Lawrence all that she knew. If only for Helen's sake. Lawrence and Helen's marriage might not survive what was coming, but Caro could at least help to make sure that Helen did. Kaveh, it was true, seemed a nice enough man, but nice didn't make him harmless. Uncomfortably decided, she nodded at Lawrence's phone. 'He works here.'

Lawrence's face hardened. 'Here?'

'Yes. Like an odd-job man—'

'Odd-job man! My wife is messing about with an odd-job man?'

Caro paused. With every moment that passed, the admiration she had always held for Lawrence was hardening into distaste. But she wasn't thinking of Lawrence now, she was thinking of Helen. Who had always been so impetuous. Who never took things seriously, and who was very capable of jumping out of the frying pan of a marriage straight into the fire of a new relationship. Which could so easily leave her burned in more ways than one. So yes, it was Helen she was thinking of when she said, 'To be honest, Lawrence, I am a little concerned.'

Lawrence went red. He made a fist of his hand and leaned towards her. 'What do you mean, concerned?'

Caro breathed in. 'I'm afraid I overheard a conversation earlier today. About this man.'

Lawrence leaned back and folded his arms.

Playing with her straw, Caro spoke quietly. 'He's actually a refugee. And…well, as far as I could make out, wherever it is he's come from, he has a wife and family. So…as I said, I'm concerned.'

17

'**K**ay! Slow down.' Helen couldn't understand a word of what Kay was saying – she was out of breath and gabbling like a lunatic. Plus Kaveh, who stood between them on the stairs, was on a loud phone call, so a burble of Turkish or Greek kept threading its way through Kay's speech, like a many-headed snake. She'd heard Lawrence's name and Caro's, and she thought she'd heard Kay say Lawrence was here. But that couldn't be right. He was in Kathmandu, or he had been two days ago. It was hard to concentrate. Her pants were grainy with sand, which kept taking her back to that beach. And Kay's boobs were showing through her sarong as huge wet patches; and most of all, she had a low-lying queasiness in her stomach. One of the prawns at lunch hadn't tasted right, and she was beginning to wish more and more that she'd trusted her instincts and spat it out. If it had been anyone else other than Kaveh sitting opposite, she would have.

As much to quell the churning in her stomach as anything else, she stopped on the top step of the staircase leading into the foyer and turned back to Kay. 'What *is* the matter?'

'Lawrence,' Kay gasped, 'is here.'

'Where?'

'Here,' Kay hissed.

Helen spun around. 'Where?' The foyer, as far as she could see, was empty. Apart from Marianne, who looked uncharacteristically animated.

Kaveh, head down, fiddling with his phone, reached the final step and bumped straight into Helen. Putting his arm around her waist, he steered her to one side.

'*Take your hands off my wife right now!*'

The voice that boomed across the empty space was extraordinarily loud. Everyone looked to where it had come from. They didn't need to look far.

Striding in from the bar opposite was Lawrence, closely followed by Caro.

'Lawrence?' Helen stared. It was definitely her husband, but a slimmer, more haggard version of him. He looked awful. Famished and strung out – the polar opposite of the sun-kissed man she had just spent the last few hours with.

Lawrence didn't speak. Face white with fury, he was rolling towards them like a tank, arm stretched out, finger aimed at Kaveh. Caro's face bobbing behind like a balloon on a string.

Her stomach cramped. (God, she felt ill.) Partly to unknot her insides and partly because the sense of hot irritation she was beginning to feel demanded it, Helen pushed her shoulders back. Stony-faced, full-chested, with stomach waves bigger than the Atlantic, she faced him.

'Hello, Lawrence,' she said with a calm she didn't feel.

And that stopped him in his tracks.

'This is a surprise.'

'*What the hell is going on?*' Lawrence barked.

Caro stepped out from behind. She grimaced at Kay, who grimaced back.

'Kaveh.' Helen turned to Kaveh. 'This is my husband, Lawrence.'

Kaveh raised his palms, as if he were in the middle of a gunfight.

'And Lawrence, this is Kaveh.'

'I know who this is,' Lawrence sneered. 'This is the refugee you've been shagging.'

'The ref...' Helen didn't have enough air to finish the word. She closed her mouth, snapped her head to Kaveh then back to Lawrence, and prepared herself to try again. 'Th...' The second time, it was worse. She was literally speechless, and glancing again at Kaveh she saw that he was too, albeit in a much more bemused, less offended way. Irritation flipped to outrage. *What the hell was he doing here? Crashing her holiday? Spouting about refugees?*

'Helen.' Caro took a step towards her, but Lawrence was quicker.

'Caroline's told me all about it,' he said very loudly. 'God, Helen, I never thought you'd stoop to this! What is he? Some sort of odd-job man?' He turned to Kaveh. 'Nosing around for a passport, are we?' Then back to Helen. 'You know he has a wife and child? Wherever it is that he comes from?'

'Cyprus,' Kaveh said. 'I come from Cyprus.'

No one heard.

Helen had turned to Caro, who'd moved forward to stand next to her. 'What have you been saying?' she said in a voice so brittle it sparked.

Desperately Caro looked to Kay, who shook her head. She turned back to Helen. 'I'm sorry but it's true, Helen. I overheard it. Right here.' Now she turned to Marianne, who upon Lawrence's entrance had amalgamated herself with the desk/shelf and become wholly invisible (another very necessary part of front-desk skills that had nothing whatsoever to do with degrees). On now hearing her name, she conjured herself back into the scene.

'Marianne, isn't it?' Caro said. 'That American couple?'

Marianne smiled beatifically. 'I'm sorry. I really don't know what you're referring to.'

'Me,' Kaveh smiled. 'They're referring to me. And, I suppose, in a way it's true. I am a refugee in my own country.'

Helen frowned. She turned to Caro, a feeling of cold disbelief stirring. 'What *exactly* do you think you heard?' she said.

Unconsciously defensive, Caro tilted her chin upward. 'When I was here before,' she said. 'I heard an American couple. They were talking about the village Kaveh had to leave. I'm sorry, Helen. He has a family too. Children.'

Kaveh leaned his head to one side. 'Oh.' His mouth made a small shape. 'I see,' he nodded. 'I see.'

Helen put her hands on her hips. She needed to stabilise herself. Sweat was popping all along her hairline, her palms were clammy, her stomach was rolling and the flush she was experiencing had, she knew, nothing to do with hormones (not least because the Novofem was working a treat) and everything to do with prawns. But there was something else making her warm, something she was shaking like a knotted string, trying to unravel it, trying to understand. Okay, Caro had heard something, but to then go and call Lawrence? She shook her head. She'd hardly seen Caro since their row – just that brief moment when Caro had arrived back from the clinic. But hadn't it been clear then? And hadn't she apologised? Made it understood how sorry she was? Obviously not enough. 'So,' she whispered, 'you thought you'd tell Lawrence all about it?'

'I…' Caro paled, then blushed. 'I…' she started, 'I…'

Helen pushed her hair back from her face. 'I thought we were over what happened? I apologised, Caro. That's all I can do. If it's not enough for you, then…' And she turned to wave a hand at Kaveh. 'Kaveh is Greek Cypriot, Caro! Yes, the things that you overheard are all true. I know he's married. Like he knew I am.'

Caro's eyes fluttered in disbelief. She glanced first at Kaveh, then back to Helen.

And watching the confusion colour Caro's face, Helen was infuriated. Caro's problem was that she was so bloody good at them. Hadn't she solved every one that had ever come her way? Including this latest…this baby problem? She was at the invincible stage. Three PowerPoint slides ahead of everyone else. Except this time she'd added two and two and come up with five. She shook her head, the smallest involuntary tick of fury. It was true, she could not give Caro her blessing, but she'd made a genuine apology and promised to stand by her, and if that wasn't enough then there was nowhere for the two of them to go. 'Happy now?' she said coldly. 'Now you've dragged Lawrence halfway across Europe? Satisfied with the chaos you've caused?'

'I didn't tell—'

'Are you proud of yourself, Caro?'

'*Helen!*' Kay stepped forward.

Helen turned to look at her, paused, then twisted back to Caro. She understood; Kay was the peacemaker, and if the boot had been on the other foot she might have stepped in herself, because she was furious! And her fury was going to hurt! And what she was about to say had been a long, long time coming! 'What's the plan?' she hissed. 'Destroy my marriage so you can have him for yourself?'

'No!' Finally Caro woke up. 'No!' she repeated, and before she could stop herself, added, 'Why would I do that, Helen, when you're doing such a good job yourself?'

Helen exploded! '*It's my marriage to destroy!*' she shouted. 'And it always has been. But you've never been able to accept that, have you?'

Caro didn't answer. She put her palms together, let her chin rest on her fingertips and looked at the ceiling. 'I didn't tell Lawrence anything!' she said, her voice as hushed as swept silk.

'*Really? Well, who did?*'

'*Jack did!*' Kay cried. Cape-sarong flying, she flew across the foyer, not stopping until she was a nose-length from Helen. '*Jack told Lawrence,*' she said, steely-eyed, and turned to look at Caro, then back at Helen. 'When,' she said,

295

shaking her head sadly, 'are you two ever going to stop? *When?*'

No one spoke.

Now Lawrence stepped forward. He took out his phone and stretched his arm towards Helen. 'It's true. Jack sent me this. I've been on a bloody plane ever since.'

Everyone except Helen peered in to see.

'Mmm.' Kaveh stroked his chin and eased back from the evidence.

'Jack,' Helen hissed. Her palms were really clammy now, freezing.

'My boy.' Lawrence was still holding the phone out. 'My boy had to see *this*.'

'Put it away,' Helen snapped. 'He's eighteen, and if I had a pound for all the things he's forced me to see I'd be a very wealthy woman.'

'You *are* a very wealthy woman,' Lawrence snapped back. 'And a very foolish one. Why do you think you've got this fella running after you?'

'Fella?' Kaveh said.

'Whatever suits,' Lawrence snarled. 'Passport hunter work better?'

'Passport hunter?' Helen looked at her husband. It didn't suit him. Lawrence did mountains, not nastiness. 'Have you actually heard a single thing that's been said, Lawrence?' she said wearily. But of course he hadn't. Because when, in twenty-five years of marriage, had her husband ever learned to listen?

Kaveh smiled. 'First, allow me to clear one thing up? I already have a passport. A Greek Cypriot passport, which, as a member of the European Union, permits me to travel wider and further than your own, I believe?'

Lawrence blinked; his jaw moved from side to side, as if his mouth was itchy.

'And secondly,' Kaveh continued, 'I'm too old to run anywhere. But if I had, it would have been for one reason only. I would have run after your wife because of her wonderful *joie de vivre*. It is infectious. And very rare. And if you can keep it close...' He shrugged. 'Well then, you are a lucky man.' He turned to Helen and smiled and, swept up in his words and his beautiful smile, she forgot in an unforgiving instant about the ball of nausea every nerve and sinew had been holding down.

So up it came! Engulfing her. The opening shots spitting from her clenched mouth like a geyser in Yellowstone. In a vain, last-ditch attempt to stay in control, stay standing, she stretched a hand out to the reception desk, but the wood under her palm wasn't enough. She was a rolling, moving ball of nausea.

'Helen?' Kay said. 'Are you okay?'

Helen swayed. She thrust her arm across her mouth and looked desperately for something, *anything* into which to empty the contents of her stomach. The only thing to hand was the orchid. She grabbed the pot, tipped its contents onto the marble floor, bent double and threw up, missing the flowerpot completely but drenching the orchid.

Under the mauve moonlight Lawrence's silhouette was sapphire-black, bent like a twig in the wind. He was a tall man and the table was low. 'Still two?' he said as he stooped to ladle a teaspoon of sugar into her cup.

'Yes please,' Helen whispered. Her throat was raw from retching and she was wrapped in Caro's cashmere shawl, lying on a sunlounger by the side of the deserted pool.

'There.' He handed her the cup.

Two sugars in black tea. It had always worked in the past.

She cupped her hands around it and let the steam warm her chin. She had spent the rest of the afternoon, and the early part of the evening, alternating between throwing up and falling asleep. She had a vague recollection of Kaveh on one side, Lawrence on the other, half carrying her up to her room. Beyond that, nothing. Caro and Kay, she supposed, would be asleep. She'd woken up wrapped in Caro's shawl and, remembering the terrible things that had once again been said, burst into tears. Then later, wandering downstairs for some fresh air, she'd found Lawrence doing the same. And now, with her stomach completely emptied, she was experiencing the feeling of renewed optimism that always presents itself after violent sickness. The opium of having survived. Yes, she was weak, but she was also cleansed and curiously hopeful. It was a strange, heady mix.

From over the rim of her cup, she watched Lawrence take his tumbler of whisky and ease back onto his own lounger. Across the terrace she could see the window of the room she shared with Kay. (The room she would still be sharing, despite Lawrence's request that she join him in the room he had taken.) She had no idea of the time – only that it must be late.

'Ten past eleven,' Lawrence said.

In surprise, Helen turned to him. She hadn't realised she'd spoken out loud. 'Aren't you tired?' she said. But she didn't need to ask. The moonlight that fell on his face only served to highlight the cavernous hollows under his eyes and the dips his cheeks had once filled. 'Lawrence,' she said with an affection that ran twenty-five years deep, 'you look exhausted.'

He nodded.

'You should go to bed.'

'I will.' But he didn't move.

Helen sighed. She drew her knees in, balancing her cup. Of course he should go to bed. And of course they needed to talk. She opened her mouth, not sure where she would begin. Before she could say a word, he said, 'I suppose I haven't been much of a husband, have I?'

Helen felt her shoulders drop. 'You've been the only kind of husband you knew how to be,' she smiled. 'And I suppose I've been the only kind of wife I knew how to be.'

Lawrence leaned forward, his shoulders a great rolling hulk. 'You know,' he said, 'it's like a sickness, Helen. This black dog inside me, and the only way I can keep it at bay is to climb…'

As his voice drifted off, Helen stared at his knuckles. They had pooled white, disconnecting completely the upper joint from the lower joint.

'So when I'm up there – I don't know how else to explain it – I don't have time to think about anything else. But I know it's not fair, Helly. Really, if I think about it, I don't know how you've put up with it for so long. And now all this…' He dipped his head, snapped it up again. 'What a wake-up call, though. Well, that's it! And that's a promise, Helly. We'll draw a line under everything. This will be the last time, I promise.'

Slowly Helen turned to look at him. She hadn't a clue what he was saying. 'The last time what?'

'The last expedition. For me.' He gave a sad chuckle. 'I really think I may have got it out of my system. I mean, Everest? Who can top that?'

Helen looked at him. How had her adultery turned into his victory? She turned away. 'What are you saying, Lawrence?'

'I'm saying come home.' Like an auctioneer slams a hammer, Lawrence slapped his tumbler down, reached across and took her hand. 'I'm saying come home with me tomorrow. We'll forget all this!' He waved his hand at the pool and the terrace and the mountains and the stars. 'We'll forget all this and start again.'

Forget all this? Now Helen looked at the pool and the terrace and the mountains and the stars, and she could have cried at the sheer depth of his misunderstanding. 'I don't want to come home,' she whispered.

'That cruise you were talking about? Norway, wasn't it? We'll do that first. We'll start with that.'

She brought the cup to her lips. Cruise? Her birthday morning, lying in the bath with the brochure. The grey-haired couple and their clunky, fake passion, compared to what she had experienced for real? What had she been planning to do with her life before he called from the highest mountain in the world? Buy more milk? Trim the forsythia? She tipped her head to the stars. There, possibly, was the Big Dipper. Was that it? Even if it was, there were still millions upon millions of stars still unnamed, still to learn. '*I don't*,' she said, this time loud enough so he'd have no choice but to hear, 'want to come home.'

'No?' Lawrence straightened his spine, opened his mouth to speak.

But Helen got there first. She pulled her hand free, slipped it under the warmth of the cashmere wrap and said, 'I'm sorry, Lawrence. I'm really sorry that you found out the way you did. And Jack. But I'm not sorry it happened.'

The only thing that moved was his mouth, in little sideways tugs, as the rest of his tall, wiry frame seized up in disbelief.

'I'm going to be staying here for the rest of the week, as planned. I'll come home then and…then I suppose we will go from there.'

'You're going to stay here? With him?'

'Lawrence,' Helen laughed gently. 'He lives here. This is his home.'

'Will you sleep with him?'

She breathed in, and her shoulders rose to her ears. Should she answer? Was it any of his business? He was her husband, so she supposed it was, and yet already it felt as if it was nothing at all to do with him.

'Is that it, then?' His voice was loud and hard. 'Twenty-five years and you're going to throw it all away for this… this person?'

'Kaveh?' She was so surprised, she said the name out loud.

'Whatever his bloody name is,' Lawrence hissed.

'Can't you see?' She shook her head. Of course he couldn't. 'I'm not throwing anything away for anyone, Lawrence. Not Kaveh. Not you. It's no one, Lawrence. It's *me*. This is about me. I don't... I don't think I want to be married...to anyone.'

Lawrence stared at her.

She held his look, and neither of them spoke.

'I don't...' he started, and his eyes were shattered glass. 'I don't understand what's changed.'

'I have,' Helen whispered. 'I have.' And it was true. She was fifty and she had changed. Not in the way she had expected. Nor in the whimsical way she had joked. There was no time curve going on, no bending backward. It wasn't possible to go back to the Helen of her twenties, nor would she want to. For that would mean no Daniel, and she wouldn't have missed his brief role in her life for every last star in the heavens above. Or Jack. Or Libby. She smiled. She wouldn't even have missed Lawrence. No. The Helen she was now was a composite of every Helen that had ever gone before. And it made her feel more complete than she thought she ever had.

'Helen—'

'Go home, Lawrence.' She took his hand and squeezed it hard. 'Please go home. Get some rest and look after our son. The freezer is full.'

18

'One, two...' Helen traced the list with her fingertip. 'Five...nine, ten. *Ten* Pringles snack packs!' She turned to Kay. 'Ten, Kay? Really?'

'All right, Chief Inspector.' Kay leaned forward and splurged her own thumbprint onto the page. 'Now count the G & Ts.' She glanced up at the clock on the wall. 'Caro needs to hurry up.'

'I had one a day,' Helen said. 'On average.'

'Which adds up to eleven.'

'Exactly.' Helen waved her hand. 'Well, how do you want to do this?' She held up the room service bill. It was longer than her weekly Asda receipt.

Kay lifted her handbag, ready to dump it onto the reception desk, looked up, saw Marianne's face and held onto it instead. 'Let's just split it.'

'Are you sure?' Helen smiled. 'They don't take Tesco vouchers here.'

'I'm sure,' Kay said. 'I had my fair share of Pilsners.' Wedging her bag against her stomach, she opened it and stuck her hand in for her purse.

'It's okay.' Marianne patted the desk, which was completely clear. 'Put it here.'

'I am so, so sorry,' Helen said to Marianne. 'I do mean that, you know.'

Marianne nodded.

'Where is it?' Kay said.

'At home,' Marianne shrugged.

'Is it okay?'

'The orchid has more blooms than ever,' she said, and turned to Helen. 'Whatever you ate, it likes. So…' She took the bill Helen handed her. 'Have you both enjoyed Cyprus?'

'Yes.' Helen and Kay spoke together.

'Not that I've seen much of it,' Kay said. 'Honestly? I don't think I've slept as much since I was seventeen.'

Helen smiled. It was true. Kay had barely left the hotel. One morning out at Kyrenia and another trip up to see Bellapais Abbey. The rest of the time she had spent flat out beside the pool, eating, then sleeping, then eating, and Helen couldn't have been happier for her. She was as plump and pink as a raspberry. Her chestnut eyes were flecked with gold again, her hair had lightened, softening the cut, and the lines across her forehead had receded under a covering of red-brown freckles. She looked better than Helen had seen her looking for years. 'Obviously you needed it. And Alex coped okay?'

Kay nodded. 'He was fine. Everyone said he would be, and he was.' Her eyes bloomed tears.

Helen took her hand and squeezed it.

From behind her inadequate desk, Marianne looked up

and blotted her own eyes. 'Compared to how you looked when you arrived, it is a transformation!' She turned to Helen. 'For both of you.'

And although Helen shrugged it off, she knew it was true. She was transformed. Of course, if she looked in the mirror she'd see the change Marianne was talking about. Her skin had deepened to honey (she always did tan more easily than Kay) and her highlights had lightened. But the transformation she felt most deeply was within.

Lawrence had left on Monday evening, having taken the chance to shave in the morning. The razor had scraped away weeks of Himalayan dirt, leaving the ravaged landscape of a face in deep shock. But what could she do? She was not his nurse. Nor his counsellor or his mother, housekeeper or nutritionist. She was still – just about – his wife, so she'd sat alongside him as such, over breakfast and lunch, listening to his pleas and his explanations and his plans, which continued to include her. Then, as they had agreed to reconvene back at home, she'd scuffed gravel with her sandal and watched the taxi leave, feeling...nothing much. Bewilderment, maybe? That he had not seen this coming? Because for Helen it was astonishing now to even contemplate the idea (let alone live it) that their life together could continue on the way it always had, him racing off ahead blinkered and deaf, her meandering behind.

We made vows, he'd said.

They had. And she had broken them. And she did not feel guilty. She only felt free.

After that, the week had passed much as she'd supposed it would. Over lunch she'd made sincere apologies to Caro –

again. And although it had been fine, she couldn't help but sense that, with her accusations of jealousy, she'd stirred up sediment that would have been far better left undisturbed. Not that she had any doubt it would settle again. It had been swirled up like this before, more than once, but left alone it always eventually settled. Until then, she would have to tread lightly. Which she had, fussing over Caro like a mother hen, making sure that she too rested.

Conversation about the clinic itself had remained off limits; this they all understood with a maturity that comes only from experience. It was too difficult and probably would always remain so. It was a dark body of water they would from now on navigate along separate shorelines, coming together only on the far side. Life, they had learned, was long enough for that.

Instead, the three of them had eaten breakfast together on a terrace dappled with sunshine as orange as a split fruit. They'd chatted over early dinners to the backdrop of birdsong. And easily enough, after the drama had receded, they had found a rhythm that wasn't altogether dissimilar to the flow of their university days. This, above all else, was what Helen felt most grateful for.

And, of course, she had been sailing. Every morning. Who now could stop her? And there had been a couple of sleepovers, and emails exchanged. Cyprus, birthplace of Aphrodite. How could she not feel that she would come back to this glorious island? But there were so many islands to travel to. And although Kaveh was a character dropped into this chapter of her life for whom she would always feel grateful, a snapshot that would take its place when the final roll-through came, he was not the hero of her story. That, she knew, was her role to step into.

She reached into her own bag ready to pay her share, and her fingertips found the smooth surface of the pebble she'd carried back from the beach that day. The stone that had pressed against her spine. Yes, this was a glorious technicoloured snapshot of her life, and if there was one thing she was going home with it was the certainty that there was more to come. *What's to stop you?* Kaveh had said on their last night together, when she'd told him of that lost gap year. Nothing. She knew this now. Not when there was even a name for it: *midlife road trip*. (She'd googled it.)

'Sorry.' Caro appeared in the doorway, pulling her wheelie suitcase. 'You know,' she said, standing very still, 'I felt odd when I woke up.' She looked first at Kay, then at Helen. 'And I couldn't face breakfast.'

Helen felt her legs go woolly. That was true; Caro had had half a banana. She took her credit card out and put the thought as far to the back of her mind as she could. If Caro was pregnant, if it looked like she really was going to have a baby at fifty-one...there would have to be adjustments, and most of them would have to come from her. She could do that. She wasn't too sure about babysitting – those days were over – but the rest she was increasingly sure she could manage.

'Here.' Marianne, who had disappeared into the back office, now bustled out, her arms full of Pringles snack packs. She pushed them over the desk towards Kay. 'Take these for the journey,' she said. 'They are out of date. I can't stand the sound of my mother-in-law sucking the salt off her lips. If you take them, I can say that there are none left.' Then she turned and marched over to Caro. 'I will take this,' she said, unpeeling Caro's fingers from her suitcase. 'Go and sit while I do your bill.'

'I can manage—' Caro started.

But the suitcase had been commandeered.

Helen's mouth twitched. Marianne was bossier than Caro.

With Marianne swiping for Cyprus, the three of them wandered over to the pastel armchairs and sat down to wait for the taxi. Or just about sat down. Kay was up before her bottom had made contact.

'Did you check the wardrobe?' she gasped at Helen.

'What wardrobe?' Helen said. Then, 'I didn't hang anything up.' And her face broke out into a huge smile. 'I've spent a whole week without hanging anything up!'

'My jacket.'

They both turned to Kay.

'My Vegas jacket,' Kay said. 'It's still in the wardrobe.'

'You have been to Las Vegas?' Marianne said, as she was holding up the key card to their room. 'All my life I've dreamed of going there.'

Taking the card, Kay shook her head. 'No,' she said wistfully. 'I haven't been.'

And sitting across the foyer, both Helen and Caro looked at one another.

Were they thinking the same thing? Helen didn't know. Dreamily she watched as Kay disappeared into the lift, on her way back to the room to rescue her jacket.

Las Vegas? It wasn't exactly an island, but it was full of myths and she'd never been either and... She looked to Caro. 'Have you been?' she said.

Caro shook her head. 'No.'

Helen smiled. Yes, they were both thinking the same thing. Inadvertently she glanced down at Caro's stomach, and Caro did the same.

Of course...that would depend.

To continue reading, buy *A Midlife Baby* now,
the second book in Cary J Hansson's
Midlife Trilogy women's fiction series.

https://geni.us/AMidlifeBaby

A Midlife Baby

Through the lives of three middle age women, Hansson continues this thought provoking and contemporary story on the complexities of female friendship.

Helen, Caro and Kay are back home, after their Mediterranean holiday.

While Helen remains intent on forging a new future for herself, life conspires to thwart her plans. Caro too is facing a monumental change and stuck in-between them, an exhausted Kay struggles to deal with her aging parents and an unforeseen threat to her professional future.

As events take an unexpected and dramatic turn, Helen is once again forced to confront a challenge to the friendship that has sustained her throughout her adult life, and accept that this time it may not survive.

For print and audio versions please visit:
www.caryjhansson.com

Acknowledgements

This is not the Oscars, so I'll keep it short. After all, as my mother liked to remind us, no one ever presented her with a medal for showing up, Every. Single. Day.

And anyway, if I were to include everyone whose path I have crossed on this long and difficult journey to publication, I'd be looking at more pages than is feasible in a standard work of fiction.

So, thanks to my team, Emily, Claire and Mary. Berenice, Amy, Andrew, Ben and Debbie.

Which leaves one more name. Well, not quite a name. A title: my husband.

Because without his endless faith, this book simply wouldn't exist. Thank you, L. x

Made in the USA
Middletown, DE
27 September 2023

39479226R10189